WITHDRAWN
FROM COLLECTION
VANCOUVER PUBLIC LIBRARY

VANCOUVER
PUBLIC LIBRARY
JUL 2 6 1991
CONTINUATIONS

TANGANYIKA

TANGANYIKA

Brian Brett

THISTLEDOWN PRESS LTD.

© Brian Brett, 1991
All Rights Reserved.

Canadian Cataloguing in Publication Data

Brett, Brian, 1947-

   Tanganyika

    ISBN 0-920633-81-1

I. Title.

PS8553.R48T3 1991   C813'.54   C91-097100-5
PR9199.3.B72T3 1991

Book design by A.M. Forrie
Cover art by Leonard Brett
Typeset by Thistledown Press Ltd.

Printed and bound in Canada by
Kromar Printing Ltd.
725 Portage Ave
Winnipeg, MB   R3G 0M8

Thistledown Press Ltd.
668 East Place
Saskatoon, Saskatchewan   S7J 2Z5

Acknowledgements

An earlier version of "The Thing That Grows In the Gasoline Tank" appeared in
The New Quarterly, and an earlier version of "Tanganyika" was a finalist in the
Cross Canada's Writer's Quarterly annual short story contest.

Cover painting: "Moon of the Red-Eyed Rhinoceros (White Rock, 1974)" by
Leonard Brett, from the collection of Jim Ziegler

This book is for Sean Virgo, and the arguments that make us wonder about lost
countries.

This book has been published with the assistance of The Canada Council
and the Saskatchewan Arts Board.

CONTENTS

SEP 3 0 1991

THE THING THAT GROWS
IN THE GASOLINE TANK

The tacked-together buildings were made of old, dirty pine, and he wondered what man had the stamina to live amongst such remarkable decay. There was nobody in sight; three crows walked the first roof. It was a grocery store: closed, deserted. His heart sank into his stomach as he peered through the dirt-caked windows at a home for spiders, its walls cobwebbed, an enormous nest.

A man ambled from behind the structure, an Indian — old and wrinkled like last year's apples. His long white hair covered his shoulders. "Fine day for a stroll," the Indian said.

Levy was taken aback. He'd already encountered more than enough Indians with their slow-talking ways. "My car broke down." He pointed to the dead vehicle on the crest of the hill.

"It sure picked a good place. This is the only garage for thirty miles in either direction."

"Garage?" Levy examined the ancient buildings cobbled together with dust and Drink 7-Up signs. Around the corner he noticed a rusted gas pump. "This is a garage?" He scratched his head, and managed to resemble what he was — a puzzled bureaucrat. The Indian smiled.

"What's the problem?"

"It just died."

"Let's check it out then."

They climbed the hill. The unbearable heat sapped the salt from Levy's skin. The old man didn't perspire at all, and once again Levy thought of apples — dried, wizened, forgotten, yet lurking in the basement. A pathetic cloud scurried for the horizon while the sun sat like a big, red egg in the middle of the sky.

"You're not from these parts," the old man said, halfway up the hill.

"No, I came up to negotiate with the tribe in Windridge — settle the complaints over that new housing project."

"How'd it go?"

"Awful."

"The houses were no good?"

Levy stopped climbing, and caught his breath. He thought about it for a minute. "No, the houses weren't any good."

"Then those people back there, they should get their homes fixed."

Levy hurried to catch up. "Unfortunately, it's not as simple as that. The contractor knows how to use the law."

"Your law says they're stuck with those houses?"

"Our law says they're stuck with them."

The old man nodded slowly as he continued up the hill.

When they reached the car the old man pushed and pulled a few wires and tried the ignition. It wouldn't come alive. "We'll roll it to the garage. I got tools there."

At the garage, that ramshackle monstrosity of a building, the man leaned into the machinery again. Levy rested his back against what resembled a rusted boiler tank, supervising. If the old man got the car fixed, he might yet make it to Vancouver tonight.

Levy watched the Indian take the carburettor off and set it on the fender. "No, it's not the carb.," he said, diving under the hood again. Then he removed the battery after carefully inspecting the terminals. "It might be the battery, but if it's the battery it's caused by something else." Soon the condenser, the voltage regulator, and the distributor were lying in the dust at the side of the car.

"Are you sure you know what you're doing?" Levy asked as the pile of parts grew beside the car.

"If you don't like my work, go to another garage," the Indian replied, yarding out the starter. "It ain't the starter." The starter was joined by the fuel pump and the alternator. "It's not the alternator either. I think this is serious."

"Serious?" Levy smiled, contemplating the machinery spread around the man's feet. "I did nothing to you."

"I never said you did."

"Then why take my car apart?"

"Broken things, they must be fixed. That's my job."

"What's wrong with my car?"

"It's serious."

"What's wrong with my car," Levy repeated calmly, "besides all the parts taken out?" Years of government experience had taught him to appear placid, no matter what the crisis, and he wasn't going to let this stupid Indian have any satisfaction.

"It's the thing that grows in the gasoline tank."

Levy felt helpless. The sun beat at his eyes, and he leaned against the building again, knowing that dirt coated the shoulders of his shirt. "The thing that grows in the gasoline tank?" He wanted to laugh. He'd been taken apart by a crazy man. How long would it be before he greeted the welcome lights of Vancouver now? It was a long walk out.

The Indian disappeared around the side of the building, and Levy thought he wouldn't see him anymore. He was wrong. In a few minutes the man returned with a fishing rod and a disgusting, sour piece of meat. He stuck the meat on a large hook. "You're not going to fish in my gas tank?" The Indian did. He popped the cap off and stuck the meat in. Then he stared at Levy. He fed out some line. After a few seconds he sat in the dust, legs crossed, rod straddling his knees.

Levy could have hit him, could have done many things, but they would do little good at this point. Besides, there might be others around. Unmoving, he tried to appear as contemptuous as possible. There was no sense giving the old goat satisfaction. If he could find a phone . . .

A cloud of dust puffed into sight on the horizon. It grew until it turned into a car — a ride? They were driving towards Bella Coola. At least there he could catch a plane and send the police after this crazy. The car roared ahead of its funnel of dust, gradually assuming noise and size. He was about to step onto the road when he noticed it slowing down. They were going to stop anyway. He didn't move. It was full of Indians.

A big, heavy-faced man leaned out the window. "How's the fishing, Chief?"

"Slow."

Everyone in the car laughed. An open broken-toothed mouth faced Levy as if it were going to swallow him. One of the women pointed at the pile of parts. They laughed again until the car shook.

The nearest woman stuck her head out the rear window. "What are you fishing for, Chief?"

"This government man, he's got the thing that grows in the gasoline tank."

Silence. Levy felt nauseous. "That's bad," a voice said inside the car.

"Very bad," nodded the old man.

"Well, good fishing." Everybody waved. The driver threw the car into gear, and they sped down the road, enveloping the old man and Levy in their dust cloud. Levy remained leaning against the old boiler with his arms folded as the dust settled like dry snow. The Indian also remained motionless. "I'll wait him out," Levy thought, "maybe he'll give me a break and put it back together once the joke's finished."

They didn't move for half an hour under the blistering sun. The Indian drew out his makings and rolled himself a cigarette. He was licking the paper when he got a strike. Tobacco, paper, and arms went flying into the air. The thing inside jerked at the rod, reminding Levy of a big ling cod fighting to return to the deep. The old man reeled in line. Levy didn't move. He watched, fascinated, as the Indian fought the bending rod. Suddenly, the line snapped, and the fisherman flipped backwards, landing on his shoulders. With his arms still crossed, Levy walked to the side of the car while the Indian rolled to his feet — looking even older now.

"He got away," the Indian said.

Levy gawked at the strand of line hanging from the gas tank. Everything was placid. Then something splashed inside, and the line disappeared like a snake being sucked into a hole.

"It's a big one, alright." The Indian brushed himself off, walking around the side of the building. Levy was afraid the man would leave him alone. It was true; there was something in his gas tank.

The old man returned with a narrow gaff hook and a second piece of meat. He pulled another fishing hook out of his vest pocket, tied it to the line, jabbed the meat onto the steel barb, and dumped it in.

"This time when he bites, you take the rod and I'll gaff him," he said to Levy who nodded mindlessly in agreement.

Time passed. They waited almost an hour until the rod suddenly curved again, and the Indian fought the thing, not reeling in quite hard enough to break the line. The fight lulled for a second, and he adroitly handed the rod to Levy: then grabbed the gaff. Levy pulled as hard as he could, his head back, the sun gouging his eyes. He felt the line separate, and he collapsed into the dust. Jumping up, he saw the man had jammed the gaff into the tank, was heaving, trying to jerk it out. There was a loud pop, and the gaff leapt towards them, seemed to stand on end in front of the sun. Levy gaped at the shadow as the sunspots seared his eyes.

It was a dismembered hand, slowly opening and closing, two hooks and the gaff embedded in the flesh. A piece of meat dangled between the gesturing fingers.

Levy sat down in the dust and began to vomit. Everything went grey . . . black . . . grey again . . . and he was conscious once more. There was wet stuff on his shirt front. The Indian stood beside him, holding the gaff with the unceasing hand.

"It's a man's hand!" Levy said.

"That's what grows in the gasoline tank."

Levy splashed dust onto his soggy shirt, drying it. "Do you get much of this sort of thing around here?" This was a dream. He knew it was a dream. Besides, nothing as big as that hand could get through the narrow neck of the tank, unless it was elastic. He was going to play along with it. He'd wake up soon.

"Once in a while," the old man said. "On your feet, and I'll show you what I've got. This business can add up."

"How does it eat meat if there's no mouth?"

The Indian shrugged. "Maybe the way a plant eats the sunlight, or the way your people eats my people."

They walked around to the back of the building. The old man asked with an air of concern: "How's your stomach now?"

"Better."

"Good. I want you to have a look at this."

There were two big doors, one of them frozen half-open. They slipped through the crack between. Inside, it was dark, windowless and smelled of oil and gas. The old man set the gaff on the cement floor, and the hand slithered away, dragging the wooden handle across the floor with a slow, frightening scrape. There was a flashlight on the table near the door, and the man turned it on. The faint light illuminated the hand which seemed to take forever crawling across the floor. At last, the thing came to the edge of a tank and went over the side, landing with a splash.

Levy and the old man approached the edge, and peered down. Within the dim light of the gasoline liquid Levy saw hands scuttling around the bottom, swimming and crawling in every direction. He stepped back, raising his chin towards the dark rafters of the building, attempting to hold onto whatever dignity he had left. "What kind of dream is this? How come it doesn't stop?"

The Indian smiled. "Look closer," he said, "these are the hands of my dead people." Then he gave a soft, sad laugh. "But you can never cling to what is already lost."

Levy peeked over the edge at the hideous hands in the gasoline almost ten feet below the cement rim. The old man pushed hard, and he fell. He came to the surface, gasping, choking, above him the faint silhouette of the Indian's head. The batteries were growing weaker in the flashlight.

Something touched Levy's side, and he brushed it off. The hands surged with a new kind of life. Another grabbed his leg. He saw them bouncing from the walls, speeding through the gasoline towards him. Five thick fingers tightened around his throat. They were trying to pull him down.

The head of the old man disappeared from the edge.

As if from a great distance, he heard the Indian walk away. And distantly, he heard him say: "Goodbye, government man."

THE HELL CIRCLE

"The moon jumped." He pressed his cheek against the window separating him from the night. "I'm sure of it. First it was there; now it's here." His fingernail traced its passage across the pane.

The glass was warm. His cheek began to sweat as he merged with the surface, melting. "I'm drunk again."

"I've heard this conversation before," Troll said.

"What's that light?"

Troll, luxuriating on the chesterfield, abandoned his contemplation of the ceiling. Across the lake an unnaturally bright lamp disturbed the darkness.

A fat green moth collided with the window and ricocheted into the dark. Thousands of insects fluttered outside, desperate to enter the room. "It's an invasion," Jim said as one flickered past his eye, "an invasion of moths dying to burn themselves."

The men fell silent. There was nothing left to say. The night gained strength, became a gelatinous black animal swelling outside the cabin until the stars approached the room. "When will you do it?" Troll asked, concentrating on his reflection in the window, his mongoloid face too big for his tiny body.

"When will I do what?" The words had an irritated twist.

Troll returned his attention to the ceiling.

A trickle of sweat oozed from Jim's skin onto the glass; then ran down the window. "I'll die old and bitter in my bed."

"No, you've come here because I'm your friend, and what are friends for but to mop up the blood?"

"You don't have to get involved. It's not your problem."

"It will be if I have to phone your wife and tell her your little vacation ended up with you dangling from a local pine tree."

"I didn't come here for that."

"Good."

"I'll die old and bitter in my bed."

Troll laughed as he sipped his drink; he was stubborn, refusing to lift his head from the pillow. The liquor flowed over his chin. "Speaking of bed, it's far too late and I'm finished." He got up, reeling goofily, so small beside Jim. "I'll see you in the morning."

"I'm sleeping in the study?" Jim refused to separate his face from the window.

"The sheets are fresh and there's an extra quilt in the closet if you get cold."

Jim lay on the bed beneath the casement, waiting. It wouldn't take long. The light began in a corner of the horizon, a hole opening inside another hole. As soon as he was sure he could see the road he slipped out of bed and into his clothes.

The front door shut too loudly. He cringed as he pulled it tight, and the creak of the ill-fitting door reverberated through the cabin.

The route was dim, but discernible. One. Two. He began to run. It was hard going, but the road levelled as it circled the lake.

The world was silent. He thought of snow, although it was the wrong season. Nothing was moving yet. His feet crunched on the gravel, making him an intruder. The sun wouldn't appear for a while, despite the expanding greyness; he loved the sound of his running.

He had gone a mile before the pain crept into his legs; his abused lungs began to hiss. A voice within his body spoke through his veins. *Stop!* it said. *You're killing us. The freeway of your blood can't feed the cells. You're killing us.*

The pain grew sharper. The voice cried out louder. He couldn't stop; he had to struggle beyond the agony. Once there, he could travel for miles, become mechanical, and worry about repaying any debts tomorrow.

A crow dived out of the sky as he rounded the corner. It screamed; then rolled behind him. He was conscious of the bird flying above his shoulder, cawing, before it disappeared. The lake was blue and glassy; he wanted to press his face against it, as if it were the cabin window.

Go on, mechanical man, your body has to go on. If you stop now, you will never start again.

The meadow was a ghostly planet of grey dead trees. Three deer: a buck, a doe, a fawn, foraging in the waist-deep fog — a variety of life that had no meaning. Startled by the noise he made, they fled, their strong legs driving them above the mist with each bound until they seemed to float across the low fog in the meadow.

He passed a few houses, forlorn among the trees beside the lake, and he thought of animal bones in a picked-over field.

His legs were dead.

His lungs were dead. All that remained alive was the running, his body refusing to let him down no matter how he mistreated it.

He stopped. He was across the lake from Troll's cabin. When he ceased running, the silence grew. He felt naked and alone. And happy. The letter-box appeared beside the road, a fantasy apparition abutting the forest. Jackson. That was her.

The sun overtook the bluff, a tired climber struggling through the pines.

There was a crease of textured rock alongside the path, pocketed with earth and peonies.

The path flowed to the lake shore, and he followed it, conscious that he was drunk with running. The peonies were shedding their petals, the path lined with brilliant scarlet fading to brown.

Through a clearing he saw her neighbour's house, or part of it — the building was massive and surrounded by trees — turrets and bay windows and crazy-angled additions — like the mansion in a horror film he'd once seen.

He snapped off a blossom where the path forked near her cabin. The bedroom window was open, and he pushed the curtains aside. "Jay," he whispered, "open the door."

She was a ghost in the bed, a body curled around a pillow. Lifeless.

"Open the door."

She jerked upright, lost, a bird captured in the hand. "Who's there?"

"I love you. Open the door." He tossed the flower, and it disintegrated in the air, showering the bed with petals.

"Jim, you frightened me. You frightened me. I knew you were at his place and I waited for you, but you didn't call."

She looked so bewildered that he became scared as well. "It's all right. Open the door."

When he woke up the sun had crossed the cabin, slashing the bed. She was tucked into him like a doll, her backside fitting the curve of his belly. He kissed her neck. He could see that her eyes were open, but she didn't move until his lips grew persistent.

"Why did you come? Why do you want me?"

He let his head rest on the pillow. The blade of sunlight was hot on his belly. It cut them apart at midsection. On the wall facing the bed was a framed photograph of her — she was standing in front of a waterfall, nude, her slight body disjointed by deep shadows. The pose was odd; she resembled an Egyptian tomb-painting or a puppet, her hands going in both directions.

He had trouble replying. "There's a danger in your mouth."

She started to giggle. For a moment he was silent; then he also began to laugh.

He didn't arrive at Troll's until four o'clock. The sky was clear and burning, and the crickets vibrated in the trees that surrounded the clearing as he walked through the door. Troll was seated at the table with a razor blade, concentrating on four lines of cocaine. He seemed disoriented for a second. "I thought I'd lost you."

"I went for a walk."

Troll returned his attention to the cocaine, his pudgy hands lining it up. "I couldn't sleep either. The night was too hot. I went up to your room after dawn, but you were gone."

"Yeah, the night was hot."

"You're in bad shape," Troll smiled, beckoning with a finger for him to take the first hit. "Let me ruin you some more."

Later, they walked to the beach, and swam and lay on the sand by the wharf.

"I phoned Jay," Troll said, "and told her you're here."

"Jay?"

"The lady at the art gallery last month in Vancouver. She lives across the lake."

Jim nodded. He saw her limbs unfolding in the morning, the sweaty sheet, their flight inside their bodies as something like a bird was born. "She's lovely."

"I thought you'd want to meet her again."

At the gallery, when they first met, they couldn't stop talking. The space was too confined. They fled for the rainy night. She pulled him into a doorway, and sideways they kissed, mouths melting them into one animal with a double-backed head. Then Troll appeared and they fell apart, pretending to admire the posters in the window, as if their desire needed privacy in order to survive.

She arrived an hour after dinner, and greeted Jim with open affection. "It's been a long time," she said, hugging him briefly. She turned to Troll, who handed her a drink. "It was nice of you to call."

"I thought you might like to see each other again."

In the front room they watched the night dissolve the sky. Their conversation was happy and confused.

" . . . and he still holds the country's unofficial free-style record . . . with that crazy head-up crawl he does."

"You do?"

"Unofficially," Jim said. "I never did anything right officially."

"When did you quit swimming?" she asked.

"Then. Six years ago."

"What have you been doing since?"

"He's been teaching physical education at a high school, and drinking himself into an early grave."

Jim smiled. "And not succeeding at either."

"I'll bet he can still swim like an angel. I saw him once, years ago, a national tournament, and it was awesome."

She put her glass down. "I want to see you swim."

Everyone glanced outside. The lake glittered with starlight. "I'm not in shape any more."

"By the time he finishes the Southern Comfort he will be." They laughed, but Jim noticed the sadness in Troll's eyes as he studied him by the window. The moths were returning.

Jim's legs separated him from the floor; they were dead meat. He had ruined them this morning, and he wasn't drunk yet. "When the bottle's empty . . . when the money's gone . . . ."

An awkwardness slipped into the room. "What's that light?" Jim asked, noticing the beam again. It had to be near the point where her cabin stood.

"The carpenter," she said.

"The carpenter?"

"The night carpenter. He mostly works in the dark. Charlie. He's been building that house for years. He's crazy. The light is on the other side of his place so I can't see it from my cabin, but you can everywhere else. It's powerful, whatever it is."

Troll opened the door that led to the deck. "On calm nights I can hear him." At first there was nothing; then distant, the sound of hammering echoed across the water, quiet as a heartbeat.

"I want to see you swim," Jay said.

He listened to the heartbeat. "Later."

The northern night grew larger. It was enough to make him dizzy, watching the night increase, encompassing patterns of stars until everything was above and nothing below, except reflected light. The night opened its eye, and the eye climbed above the ridge until it sat above them, pale and round; it made Jim think of a blister that festers and needs lancing.

They walked to the dock at the foot of Troll's driveway. She turned on the headlights of her car so they could see. The car's grill shone in the darkness, the dock swathed with light.

Troll walked out on the tipsy jetty and fell in. He was more drunk than he appeared. Jay giggled as he thrashed back onto the wharf, his jeans oozing. He stripped, and his knobbly frame shone pale at the end of the wharf. The organ between the dwarf's legs was enormous. "It's not the size of the body that tells the tale," Jim said. "Big nose, big hands, big trouble."

Jay laughed. She ran across the planks, throwing off her clothes. She stopped, awkwardly, and there was a curious silence as she and Troll hung at the brink with nothing ahead but water and the moon.

They remained motionless, trapped in a moment of sadness. There. Then. If they could have flown apart, disintegrated into individual atoms, it would have been perfect, a good shutdown, but they were human and could only go into the lake. As if they realized this simultaneously, they leapt out of sight. There was a loud splash. Jim strolled down the dock.

"It's good. It's good," she called out. "I didn't think it would be so warm."

Troll surfaced beside her. "Aren't you coming in?"

"Yes." He watched them roll and dive and splash in the lake, their skin reflecting the moon. They were devil swimmers.

"Here, I'll show you the breast stroke."

"Get off me, you fiend."

Jim began to undress, dropping his clothes onto the rotten decking.

He stepped to the edge. He loved edges, standing between one thing and another. He bent at the knees and heaved into the air, twisting sideways and head over heels.

Tendrils of weeds rose from the bottom and stroked his thighs; they were soon behind him. He surfaced twenty feet from the dock, and his arms took control.

It's all over, mechanical man. Your limbs are pulling you away. The fleshy liquid slid past him. He left the shore behind . . . and their laughter . . . . His body worked the water, accelerating. The night was so quiet, saturated with the muteness of the lake, their receding voices, the splash of his wrists against the surface.

He glided to a halt, far, far away.

There was nothing but serenity. He flipped over on his back and examined the eye. It was so bright, the stars around its perimeter knocked back and invisible. His murdered limbs no longer hurt, and the resilience of his body fascinated him.

Between three distant lights; the carpenter's lamp, the headlights of the car, and the moon-washed stars, he circled ... and circled ... and circled .... The others called him, their voices growing more worried.

"Jim, you can come back now. We're impressed."

He let his head rest underwater so he couldn't hear them, and like a moonchild soaked up the illumination from the sky.

Mechanical man, you are so smooth, so perfect a machine. You are a wheel that goes around and around in the water with nowhere to go.

The stillness made him think of the moment when the sudden beast of horror films rises and devours the unsuspecting swimmer. *Now! Strike quick, tear the limbs away, a pool of blood and bubbles leading to ...* But the beast didn't come, and he lifted his head; the shore voices grew insistent, luring him back.

He swam towards the dock. The water was gentle, caressing him as he glided across its surface. Once again, he gathered speed, a torpedo formed of moonlight and skin.

Something touched his hand; there was a moment of fright. His palm slid over her breasts and the surface of her belly, departed for a moment; then grazed her thigh. They thrashed amorously as they failed to cling together.

"It's beautiful," she said. "I didn't know it would be so beautiful. Why didn't you come back when we shouted?"

"I never heard you."

Troll was on the wharf, naked, rocking on his haunches, haloed by the lamps of the car.

Jim grabbed the dock and hauled himself out, flopping beside his friend while Jay paddled around them on her back, barely disturbing the surface. Her small breasts swelled out of the water.

"She's got ghost breasts." Troll laughed.

Affection surged through Jim, and his finger touched the man's thigh. Troll glanced at him.

She became inert, floating near the head of the wharf. Jim noticed a thin gold chain around her lower belly. Her blonde hair spread out like seaweed.

Troll leaned over the edge. "Ophelia, come back. Ophelia, dear sweet Ophelia, you're not dead. Come back."

She sculled away in the moonlight. "Now what got into her?" He watched her disappear, swallowed by the darkness. "Jay?" There was no answer. "Don't go too far."

"Let her go. There's no monster out there."

"Don't play with her. She's tight like a wire."

"I'm not playing — she's got the same disease."

"Let her go crazy on her own, then. Don't push her."

Jim began dressing while his friend studied the cracks between the decking and the lake underneath.

"I didn't mean to hurt your feelings," Troll said.

"You didn't."

"I don't know why I like you — you're such a pompous ass."

Soon they were both dressed, standing in the darkness, illuminated by the headlamps of the car.

Jim lit a cigarette. "Have you ever slept with a woman?"

"A few. Sure, but it's not my trick."

"You want to sleep with me?"

Troll shuffled away, and sat down, his soggy jeans squeaking against his thighs. "Sure. I always have."

"I couldn't."

"Now you're going to tell me you never made love to a man."

"Gay dwarves don't turn me on." Jim flicked his cigarette into the lake. It hit the water with a hiss, and died. "You're right, I'm a monster."

Troll's eyes widened, grew moist around the rims.

A carp surfaced and swallowed the cigarette butt; then disappeared beneath the wharf; neither of the men noticed. Jim rested his hand on his friend's shoulder. "I love you. I always have."

"You make as much sense as tits on a bull."

The soggy cigarette butt surfaced from the deep, spat out by a fish that will eat almost anything.

A flurry of splashes signalled her return. Troll stood up, separating himself from Jim. "I don't like it," Troll said, "her going out there, because I don't know where the limit is. If she failed in the water, I'd feel bad."

"And me, if I failed?"

Troll didn't say anything.

"You're lucky. You haven't got the disease. Most people are safe — it misses them."

"A drink to the disease! Where's my brandy?" Troll skipped away and picked up the bottle resting beside the car.

They took a sip. Jay reached the wharf, her hands rising like white flowers unfolding, and she grasped the wood. "It's so beautiful I want to stay forever."

The men faced each other sadly. Troll knelt beside her and held out the bottle of brandy. She sucked at its lip until her head receded beneath the water as he neatly tucked the bottle back, not spilling any. She burst to the surface laughing, and he pulled her onto the dock, where she sat, looking down. "Hey, there's a great big fish under the wharf," she squealed as Troll rubbed her shoulders with his sweater. "Sure," he said, "and there's a monster in the middle of the lake." They were close, and the sensuality poured from their limbs as he massaged her with the wool. It was a new way of making love.

She didn't dress. Instead, she picked up her clothes and carried them to the car, tossing them in a jumble onto the hood. Jim reached through the window and doused the lights so the battery wouldn't die; the sudden darkness made the moon seem huge. Troll fell back onto the hood and admired the sky.

She moved over to Jim's side and leaned her shoulder against him.

As if it had a life of its own, his hand slid over her buttocks until it cupped her vagina.

"When there's an eclipse," Troll said, "people call it blood on the moon, because the moon goes red like blood."

"I've never seen a total eclipse," she said wistfully.

The hand followed its own thoughts. It separated the wet hair and lips, pushing against the entrance. She moved closer.

"Do you still ride your luck?" Jim asked.

Jim could tell by Troll's attention to the lake that he was aware, but the uncontrollable hand advanced. She quivered, and pressed against it.

"Sure, I go south every winter and play with the amateurs. Small time."

"You quit early."

"I don't think so. I had a run of great luck, riding on the black. The thing about luck is knowing when it's over. I wish I had more money, but I'd be throwing away what I won on the wheel if I gambled hard again."

She opened her legs, allowing the finger to penetrate deeper. "Once you win, there's not much point in winning again, is there?" It was a statement as much as a question.

"I like to win. Other people need to lose. I need to win, maybe because I was short-changed when I was born." For a moment the three were close, like flies in a web.

"Does he only work at night?" Jim asked. The night carpenter. The light — neither incandescent nor fluorescent. It was commanding, unearthly.

"Until midnight," she said, "but he leaves the light on."

She shuddered as Jim discovered the core, and her buttocks began to rotate on his hand. Troll discreetly contemplated the distant beam; a strange, alienated segment of this lively darkness.

Jim held his breath; so much lay under the surface, so much power struggling to escape, centered at this moment on his hand and her shifting thighs.

Then she began to vibrate, having found her own answer. She pushed hard once, and then froze.

When they returned to the cabin, everyone was drained. Jim took up his station by the window while Jay, now dressed, lay on the floor. Troll made coffee, but she wouldn't have any. She had grown distant, lost. She watched the men with an emotion close to fear, and Jim worried there would be trouble. Then she announced she was tired, and left before they could gather themselves to stop her.

"I wonder about her driving. She's drunk a lot," Troll said, sipping at his coffee.

"Is she a good artist?"

"I don't know. I suspect not."

"I want to see what she paints."

"I haven't heard much about it, haven't seen her stuff either, but they say she's a romantic. Untrained. Never even studied at the two-bit schools."

"Sometimes losers are more beautiful than winners."

"It depends on your point of view."

Jim drew a finger across the glass, following the trail of a moth as it skittered along the barrier. "Sorry, I forgot. You're a winner." Tonight seemed to be the night for cruelty.

Troll finished his coffee deliberately. "You know, I can't remember when people started calling me Troll; if it was because of my gigantic stature, or my sunny disposition."

Jim smiled and kissed the window. "You don't wear it well. The self-punishment is my department."

"Why?"

Jim shrugged. "I don't know. I like pain."

As soon as he was sure Troll was asleep in his room, he dressed and left the study. His legs were dead under him and he couldn't run again. He picked up the phone with some stealth and dialled her number. It rang for a long time. Then the line clicked alive.

"Hello?" A remote and frightened voice floated across the wire.

"Do you want me?"

"Yes."

"Can you meet me? I'll start walking down the road."

"I love you," she said. Then the line died. He walked into the night, disturbed again by the creaking door. The road was silent, foreboding.

Jim didn't know why he had to be secretive; this business was plain enough to Troll. There was just a need for privacy.

He felt surrounded. The dead should be out, the shadowy lives that failed and were gone, and he was among them. Several times he stumbled, the gloom intense now that the moon was gone.

There was a mistake somewhere, a few disordered genes, a few crushing childhood incidents he couldn't recall any more, and he had come out crooked – the beast was in his head, the disease. Jim kicked a stone, and it knocked against an invisible tree.

His footsteps unnerved him. He was at the point of turning back, not from fear of imagined bears or the horrors handed down to him by centuries of imagination, but because he was out of place, because he assaulted this wonderful darkness which did not see him, did not want him.

If the beast exploded out of the shadows he'd be grateful. That would be easy. He could accept the claws raking over his skin – his belly slit open, his intestines slithering out, mixing with the dirt and the gravel.

There was no sign of her. Had she fallen asleep again?

At last, a distant motor. In a few minutes he saw the lights cutting the night like scissors; the car stopped beside him.

The crickets were going off like firecrackers when he woke. She was asleep, buried in his side, her hair floating over his groin. He moved away.

Outside, the grass was dry, and the sun overhead. He wandered around to the front of the cabin where the metallic surface of the lake glinted under the sun.

The bizarre, octagonal house next door was quiet, and he couldn't resist investigating. A skinny dog under a pine tree gazed sleepily at him; then it rolled over, as if it had just died.

Junk lay everywhere: old, rusted, and rotten. The yard was a wealth of machinery which grew in volume as he approached the house.

He found himself in a miniature cemetery. Even the graves were tiny. He studied the first small, wooden cross. It said: "Ajax Chainsaw,

June 23, 1976 - September 3, 1977." Below that was an epitaph.
"Cheap Junk." Jim snorted with laughter. Then he noticed a clothesline
stretched from the house to one of the taller pines. Hanging from it
was an impressive assortment of tools: a circular saw, a bent and rusty
square, a broken pruning saw.

"Those ones I keep closer to heaven. They were good tools," a
hoarse voice said from behind.

The old man had a sly, lopsided grin. He was wearing a ragged,
wide-brimmed straw hat, an undershirt, and a greasy pair of coveralls.
His skin was lobstered by the sun.

"And you bury the junk?"

"Just the bad tools." He nodded to himself, inspecting his yard. He
sat on a ship's propeller, took out his makings, and rolled a cigarette.

Jim realized there was an order to it all. One pile, a mass of rusted
and ancient bicycles, a symphony of circles. Another mound, saw
blades and pipes. Several of the blades were four feet wide. Across
another monstrous heap in front of the house lay a pitchfork with a
twenty-foot handle.

"That's quite the house you're building."

"It's coming along. It's coming along. But I've got a problem on
the other side. Maybe you can give me some advice. Done any
construction work?"

"Not much. I'm a wrecker myself."

"It's the same." When they reached the east corner Jim saw the
problem. Charlie was attempting to build a gazebo; so far, the roof was
completed. It rested on the ground like a toadstool that had erupted
in the night.

"Now everybody, they always build a house the same way, but I
make things differently. I started with the roof." He lit his cigarette,
and it exploded with a whoosh; far too much paper and not enough
tobacco. The cigarette died, and Charlie studied it, cross-eyed,
disgusted, but didn't spit out the stub clinging to his lower lip. "Now
I've got to get the rest of the gazebo under it."

The two men scrutinized the well-carpentered and shingled roof perched on the grass. "It's a beautiful roof," Jim said. "Why don't you dig out the dirt and build the gazebo underground?"

Charlie gazed at him with astonishment, the frazzled cigarette hanging from his lip. "I never thought of that."

"Let the ground hold up the eaves of the roof until you get the rest built."

"I knew it would work. What's your name?"

"Jim."

"I'm Charlie."

"Glad to meet you, Charlie."

"An underground gazebo; why didn't I think of that? It'd be great on hot summer days."

They sat on the corner of the roof, and Charlie rolled himself another cigarette. He offered the makings to Jim who rolled himself one. This time both cigarettes worked. The men were quiet, watching the smoke drift in the windless junkyard.

"Most people don't understand," Charlie said. "I can see you're different. They look at this house and this junk, and they say I'm making problems for myself, and I guess they're right, but everybody's got their problems; everybody needs a problem, otherwise they'd have nothing to suffer over, nothing to live for. And this house, this junk, it's my problem."

Jim nodded, sucking on his cigarette.

"You should move in with me, Jim. We could build great things. I can see you've got the mind for it."

"That's a generous invitation," Jim said, smiling at Charlie — the loneliness poured out from beneath the raggy hat, making Jim feel close to him. "But I'm afraid I've got my own problems."

"Everybody always does," Charlie shrugged, depressed. "What did you say your work was?"

"I'm a wrecker."

"What do you wreck?"

"Myself . . . my friends . . . my wife . . . ."

Charlie took off his hat and fanned himself with it. He was quiet for a while. "That's a problem, alright."

She was still asleep. She looked hot and uncomfortable, curled against the pillow, a circle of cloth and flesh, her hair webbing her to the bed.

He crouched and kissed her on the back, below the neck. She didn't move. He kissed her again, moving up her neck as she began to stir. There was a smile beginning on her lips, and he bit the corner of her ear. Then he whispered, "Open your legs." She squirmed against the pillow.

"Wake up and open your legs."

The sun was reaching for the other side of the day when she pulled the car off the road. He touched her thigh with his fingers; then climbed out. Hidden around the corner was Troll's cabin.

Troll was slicing carrots under the kitchen window when Jim entered. "You've turned into quite the walker. That's two days in a row."

"I need the exercise. My body's going to hell."

"You must be exhausted." There was a sardonic tone in his voice.

"I think I'll lie in the sun."

"What there is left of it. Dinner will be in an hour."

Shortly after dinner, Troll announced he had business in Vancouver in the morning and would drive down tonight so he could return late tomorrow.

Jim doubted there was real business in Vancouver. His friend was daring him to make his move. "This is sick," Jim thought. By the time Troll had to leave they were both depressed.

Jim waited for the car to disappear behind the pines; then he picked up the phone. "Troll's gone for the rest of the night. Come on over and let's party."

Jay arrived within the hour and they explored a bottle of Southern Comfort; the hard, sweet liquor ignited them. Once it was finished they staggered down to the lake.

They were so drunk they leapt in without removing their clothes. The image of her purple dress floating around her waist was going to haunt him one day. He pushed her onto the sandy waterline, running his hands up her buttocks, onto her belly, pushing the blouse above her breasts and their tiny nipples. Then he slithered out of his pants, and entered her. They embraced like two dragonflies locked in a corner of the lake while the last rays of the sun poured over them.

But she was nervous that Troll would return unexpectedly, and asked if he wanted to go back to her place. He realized they were both so afraid of the relationship that they had to keep it private. Yet once out of the lake, they took off the rest of their clothing, threw everything into the back seat, and still crazy drunk, drove naked to her cabin, swerving around a carload of startled tourists.

At the cabin she went mute for several minutes. The liquor was eating at her system. "Why do you drink so much?" she asked. "You only lose your ability to think."

"Exactly."

She dressed in leotards while he sat naked on the couch. Then she put on a reggae tape. "I have to dance. I have to clear my head."

It was a combination exercise-and-dance routine, and she executed it well, with a marvellous pathos. Her face was empty, lovely, and she reminded him of something. "You're dancing without strings."

"I'm a puppet." She opened her legs and slapped the inside of her thighs against the floor as she did the splits.

It was a graceful dance, and she must have practised it many times. "A wind-up doll," she said. Her face was rigid, emotionless.

When she finished she sat beside him, coiled against his belly. They lay there for an hour, not speaking, listening to their own thoughts.

At last he made the connection. The delicacy of her face. When he was twelve he discovered a shell on a beach; fleshy pink and scribed. Almost tropical. Rescued from the waves and rocks, it found a place on his night table — a precious object stolen from the elements. At least one thing could remain beautiful, timeless. Every night he contemplated it before he went to sleep. A small piece of the universe was safe. He kept it for years, his private path to good dreams.

One morning, he got out of bed and it crackled under his foot. Now, it seemed inevitable, but that delicate and final crunch haunted him for years.

He stood up. "I want to see your paintings."

She was lost, gorged with the sadness of the last hour. "I don't show my work to anyone these days."

"Why not?"

"They don't understand it."

He watched, curious, as she lifted a key off a shelf and unlocked the door to her studio, and he wondered if he could ever know her. The studio was windowless except for a skylight. There were no stars yet; twilight seemed to last forever on these northern summer days.

There was a single painting, a circular panel which almost filled the room. About a tenth of it was finished, but not in any one section. It had a reddish hue.

"It's a mandala. It's called 'The Hell Circle'."

He moved closer. Tortured bodies flew through the air, were severed by big mouths, sat at plastic-looking tables drinking blood-coloured liquids. They leapt from chariots. They fell from skyships. There were locked in painful and passionate embraces. "Incredible."

"I think it will work when it's finished."

"It works now."

It sat on nothing, seemed to float in the air. He realized the panel was mounted on an axle that came out of the wall. He touched the edge and gave a push. The painting began a slow spin.

"Charlie made the panel and mounting for me."

"The night carpenter?"

She nodded. "He can do excellent work when he takes direction."

"Doesn't his hammering and sawing bother you? His house is so close."

"No, I find it reassuring. There's a bolt on the mount so I can keep the panel in one place when I'm working, but this way I can turn it to paint any part I want."

He draped his arm around her shoulder. "What about your other paintings, where are they?"

"That's all there is. I destroyed everything else."

"Why?"

"They were finished, dead, and no one desired them. I've never sold anything." She laughed awkwardly. "Thank God my father died and left me his money, enough to live on."

"That's bitter." At the same time he was thinking, why does everyone have money except me?

"He was a beast. He deserted my mother and me when I was ten."

She locked up the studio, and they sat in the front room overlooking the lake. She played the same tape again, and they listened, while outside an osprey prowled the water as the first star — Mars — punched through the sky.

She was searching for something to say, but didn't know how to put the words together. He waited, aware of what was coming.

"Why don't you move in with me?"

"I couldn't."

"I've got a little money. We can live here. There'd be enough to keep you in Southern Comfort."

He wondered what ungodly thing it was that made anyone want him. There were so many offers. Perhaps they desired the wound. "You might find this difficult, but I love Gail. She's my wife; everything that the word means. Besides, I'm too hard. I'd break you."

As soon as he said this, he realized it sounded as if he didn't care about Gail. "She's different. I hurt her all the time, and she hurts me too, but that's not what it's about. She's strong, somehow. She's from another world, a better one, not ours." He grew thoughtful. "I think I'm jealous of her. She doesn't have the disease, and she'll survive anything I throw at her. Don't you see? You'd go down."

"Yes, but that might be beautiful too."

"I wonder why I only meet crazy people."

"Every animal finds its kind."

"How long have you been working on that painting?"

"Two years."

"At that rate, you've got a good twenty more years to completion."

"On a good day, I can do two or three square inches. Yes, about twenty years."

The mandala. It was larger than the door. She would have to take the house apart to remove the painting if she ever finished it. He sat in silence for several minutes. "Charlie made the panel in your studio?"

She gazed at him, not understanding what he was thinking. "Of course, it's too big."

"He's your father, isn't he?"

Jay was taken aback. "No." She picked at some lint on her leotard. "No. Oh shit. Yes, but nobody knows because he never married my mother, and we have different names." She glanced over her shoulder at him, frightened. "Don't worry, I do have the money."

"I'm not going to live with you."

"It was a nice thought." She took his glass from his hand and sipped the drink. Outside, the osprey was gone. "I'm very happy on my own."

"That doesn't mean I don't want to make love to you." He took the glass from her, set it on the mahogany table, and pushed her back. She smiled, crossed her arms over her chest, caught the corners of her leotard and pulled it down.

When Troll returned, he found Jim in the living room by the window, waiting for the night lamp to appear across the lake. "My God, you look ruined."

"I am." Between the alcohol and her love he was wrung out.

"I can see I've got some catching up to do. Troll poured himself a strong one. "I'm surprised you're here. I half-expected you'd be across the lake."

Jim sighed.

"You're about as discreet as a pig at the trough."

Jim's drink was empty. He needed more. "Get drunk."

"I'm trying. But I think you need some sleep."

"I've murdered sleep. I'm too wired to sleep."

"When you get back to Vancouver you'll have to take a rest from your vacation."

Jim shook his head.

Hours later the night spider had spun a web of leaden strands in his brain, and the heaviness bore his skull down so far that he lurched forward as he walked across the dried grass to the wharf.

Take off your clothes, his mind said to his arms, and he undressed. Naked at the end of the wharf he felt clean. He wanted to be a bird that could fly into the stars.

But his skull was stuffed with the spun lead sticking to the neurons. "I need electricity." He preferred talking low in the dark, especially when he was alone. Words desecrated everything.

"Now jump."

His body surfaced, carving the water; he aligned himself with the light. The alcoholic stupor dissipated, and he swam.

When he reached the centre he was exhausted, but he knew he could make it. *I'm on my way.* He circled, treading water. *Take me into your body.* Again, he thought of the horror films and the unexpected monster that rips off legs and exposes the guts to a lonely night. Nothing came. He was alone.

Since there was no beast to take him down, he wished his body into a bird shape that could attack the sky, fly into the white hole — the moon that was a circular, open doorway.

The carpenter's menacing light glowed far away.

His limbs became heavier with each stroke; the spider had taken to spinning its web through his blood.

The web was pulling tighter, shrinking the elastics of his arms and legs. There was a moment as he approached the shoreline when he doubted his abilities, but that doubt gave him strength, and he swam faster. Then his hand embraced a slimy stone underwater. The broken shore was above him. He began to climb, becoming the spider himself, scaling the rocks until he fell onto the dried grass fronting her cabin, where he remained.

In the pine forest that sheltered the two houses, a deer browsed on the bitter grass.

When Jim heard it, he sat up and clapped his hands. The noise startled the deer; it screamed, crashing through the low branches of the trees by the cabin.

The sudden, sharp sound took him beyond himself. He was the walls inside the cabin. He was everywhere. He was her.

Jay awoke, frightened. There'd been a noise. The deer rushed past her window. As she listened to the fading echo of its hooves, she realized she was shaking. The alarm clock showed it was near morning, and she hadn't slept well, her head full of odd dreams. If he didn't arrive soon it meant he wouldn't come at all. Drowsy and lonely, she pulled the pillow close, and drifted into sleep once more.

He was back in his own body again. There were no muscles left. They were dead meat. As he sat in the grass, waves of dizziness rolled over him. The nearby cabin was miles away; he found himself dreaming of her under the sheets, under him, watching her come forward out of the distance behind her eyes, convincing herself, for a short while, that everything will be good.

He was on his feet, lurching as if he were a tree deciding whether to stand or fall; he got his equilibrium, and stepped forward, first one foot and then the other. *Body, beautiful body, you mustn't fail.*

He stopped. There was a noise. A match flared at the other point, in front of the crazy house. The flame reflected the old man's face and hat before it went out. The glow at the end of the cigarette remained. Charlie had been there all the time.

Jim oozed into the lake. He knew he wouldn't make it back.

He swam parallel to the small bay, crossing in front of the point. The shaggy, straw hat was motionless, silhouetted by the beam of light that showed around the corner of the house. Jim stopped swimming. He treaded water in front of the silent figure. "I'm not a loser; I'm throwing it away."

"Why?" Charlie's voice had a sly edge.

He wanted to reply, *Why not?* but that wasn't the answer. There were many answers, yet none of them fit. He turned on his belly and began the journey home.

It's a dream. There's a swimmer, drowsy, and full of over-extended blood, moving away from a light towards a shoreline of darkness. His body shines as the moon searches for the horizon. Every stroke is mechanical, pointless, leading to the centre of the lake where the world is empty.

As he swam he became aware of something to his left. With each stroke he lifted his head a little more out of the dream. Then he became frightened, his strokes more urgent, the remaining strength focused on more speed, but the thing continued at his side. He couldn't leave it behind.

It was an animal, a fox. It swam parallel to him; its ruptured breathing signalled exertion, yet it was tireless. He slowed to let it pass, but the fox also slowed and they eyed each other, ten feet apart.

Then the fox released a sudden, painful bark, and sank out of sight. It surfaced, this time without fur — the foetus of a fox. It sank again, and surfaced again, bloated and bigger. The fox-thing grew before his eyes like a butterfly emerging from its cocoon. With a loud bellow it dived once more, and returned huge, its head and shoulders rising five feet above the water, a dinosaur made out of skinless flesh. Tentacles whipped across the surface of the water, erupting from the hidden trunk.

Jim stopped swimming, and the creature circled, barking. Its tongue stretched out, mingling with the tentacles. Then its shoulder split open and a flood of gurgling fluid surged out, followed by an egg which fell into the water and floated away.

Another hairless head discharged from the opposite shoulder, but remained attached by a tendril. Both heads began barking discordantly at the moon. Several rolling humps surfaced behind the creature, encircling Jim. He treaded water, breathless, unable to comprehend, yet fascinated.

The creature's tongue jerked into the sky, and stood perpendicular. The end of the tongue bulged, expanded into a fluorescent green flower head, unfurling petals that dropped to the water until just the seed-pod remained. That exploded and phosphorous seeds scattered in the air like fireworks. The seeds showered Jim and sank, glittering, into the deep.

As he watched the seeds going down, he realized the head was also disappearing. The creature sighed before it receded beneath the surface, leaving a few bubbles.

But when it was gone he noticed there was something beyond, dim in the midnight light of the stars, a skinny bird pointing at the constellations.

Exhausted, almost unconscious, he hovered in the water as the bird drifted closer. It stood on a piece of wood. Motionless, the erect head was silhouetted by the last rays of the moon near the horizon.

He tried to swim towards it, but couldn't lift his arms. He couldn't swim any more. The strength was gone. Gone. Gone. All gone. *Body, beautiful body . . . .*

The moon went out like an electric light; the stars grew brighter.

And the bird was not a bird. It floated closer, dispelling the dream, becoming real, in focus at last — a hammer, standing upright on a board. He reached out and grasped the board, and lovingly ran his fingers around the handle, knowing he was in slow motion, that perhaps ten, twenty minutes, an hour, had passed since the creature sank and the bird-hammer came into view. The dream was not a dream any more, it was his life.

He couldn't remove the hammer from the board. It took a while to comprehend that the handle was bolted to the plank so that the hammer would remain standing, its metal claw upright.

This was the work of the night carpenter, a crazy burial at sea for a still-living hammer. "The hammer will not fall," he giggled, clutching the board, his link with survival. A long black shape emerged on the lake's surface, near the fallen moon, and he wondered if it was the fox, returning.

"Now I've seen everything." He couldn't stop giggling, even as his amazing hand refused its hold on the board, even as the board slipped away and his other thrashing arm pushed it further. Water entered his lungs, and he coughed, but when he coughed he sucked in more water. A violent splashing erupted as he spun around, above and below the surface. The pain stung his lungs, hurt too much, and sparks filled his eyes.

The pain stopped. There was a moment of distant tranquillity, and he opened his eyes, conscious that his chest was moving, breathing, though water filled him now. *Where is the surface?*

The moon clicked on.

He recalled his face pressed against the window, the words: *The moon jumped.* And the words were lovely, echoed through his blood as it began to slow. He thought he was watching the moon, but he was looking down, at an expanding point of light, another kind of circular door.

The moon was on the bottom of the lake. From a far off place he heard himself whispering, *Avalanche, will you take me with you when you fall . . . ?* and his sluggish brain repeated the words. The light grew more intense as the moon rose to greet him.

It shot out a tentacle that waved in front of his eyes for a moment, straightened, and tapped against his leg before it hooked under his arm and dragged him through the water. He stopped with a thump against the side of an object that echoed dully.

He flopped around, banging against hard edges that wouldn't stabilize. A voice, deep, far away, seemed to say "What a big fish we caught tonight." And he wondered if that was God's voice. A jolting pain in his back. It hit him again. A flood of water gushed out of his mouth.

But he didn't want to return. He was happy. *Leave me alone,* percolated through his brain as his lungs caught fire, and he choked again, mixing air with water. "Leave me alone . . . it's alright . . . I'm happy." Another slap against his spine and he fell forward in the boat, more water dribbling from his mouth. The moon was at the front of the skiff, ringed with metal, mounted on the prow, blinding. Hordes of green spots danced before him.

He tried to concentrate. It was a hook, a rusty hook on a pole. A gaff. He realized he was lying in a pool of slime from his lungs, blood from his arm. He'd been gaffed. *Blood and rust . . . blood and rust. What a strange combination,* he thought, trying to understand why they fit so well together.

He wanted to say, *Get that hook away from my eye*, but the words came out as another dribble of slime.

There was a vulture seated in front of him, at its feet, a fox. The fox wagged its head enthusiastically, tongue lolling. With horror, he realized the tongue was growing longer and longer on the floor of the boat, wrapping around his ankle. He tried to jerk away, but his body shuddered, and went limp. The fire in his lungs wouldn't die.

Then the vulture spread its wings, pushed against the water on both sides of the boat, and they began to move, dragging the moon across the lake.

The vulture was wearing a straw hat. A tiny point of light glowed orange under the hat. "Yessir, Jim," it said, "I can see we're going to build some great things together."

FEVER

Here comes a stick walking down the road. At one end of the stick is a wrinkled hand attached to a woman who begs for whatever anyone will give. No one gives her anything.

The skin is pulled tight over her socketless eyes, and she wears a dirty grey robe full of holes. There's a monkey on her shoulder, chattering at the afternoon.

Behind the old woman a child sings in Arabic the many attributes of the monkey. The boy's face is scarred with round sores which resemble eyes. Five eyes. The group comes to a shambling stop, and the monkey flips backwards onto the cement sidewalk in front of a café where it goes through its limited routine.

The only healthy one is the monkey, Joel thought as he pressed a *dirham* into the woman's groping hand.

He hurried down the boulevard, past the sidewalk cafés, the crowds of Moroccans, and the obvious tourists. He'd been away from the hotel for an hour.

Entering the room without knocking, he dumped a bag of prescriptions and potions onto the dresser table, suspecting most of it was useless. "Hello, I'm back."

The two Americans nodded solemnly.

When a man is ill, dying, those nearby hold up their masks of comfort and compassion, wear a sick face, as if attempting to draw the disease into themselves. The American couple were masters of the art, and he wondered how many cancerous uncles there were back in the States.

Kenny lay on the bed, swaddled in a thermal blanket, and Joel almost laughed. The man resembled an apparition from deep space in a golden wrapper, a candy bar from the stars. But at least the tinsel-like blanket preserved an illusion of warmth when the chills struck.

As he sat on the edge of the bed, he wondered how anyone could feel cold in this heat. A drop of sweat trickled to the end of his nose and he shook it off. The American couple left quickly. They hadn't eaten today.

Joel wiped the man's head with a wet towel, and Kenny groaned when it touched his fever-sensitive skin. Joel didn't know what was wrong with the Englishman, let alone how to care for him.

The hospital hadn't been any help. This morning, they'd waited three hours for the doctor to finish his lunch break. There were no beds available, and Kenny flopped about on the floor while the nurses giggled. Finally, Joel couldn't wait any longer; he demanded, mustering his best French, that the beak-nosed nurse summon the doctor.

"Yes, I think the doctor will see your friend now. He's up that flight of stairs, the first door to the left." She pointed a skinny finger.

Joel lifted the man from the floor and dragged him up the stairs to the door. Kenny seemed to act out his sickness with a wilful intensity. When they reached the door Joel pushed it open while supporting Kenny. "Damn!" It was a toilet.

He glared at the nurse standing by the foot of the stairs. "There's no doctor here." He let Kenny slip to the floor beside the toilet.

"Oh, he's not there?" She replied as if that was an interesting development. "Come with me then, and we shall find him." The other nurse who wasn't as tall but much heavier, watched with shark eyes and an expressionless piglike face, a disturbing combination. Joel left Kenny on the landing and followed beak-nose. They navigated endless corridors. The sick and dying lay everywhere. When the nurse walked by some would raise their hands and cry out in Arabic, but she ignored them, an imperial bird-god on her way to a mysterious business beyond their knowledge. At last she stopped and pointed to a door at the top of another flight of cement stairs. Joel stared at the peeled white paint.

"He'll certainly be up there, I'm sure of it." She smiled sweetly despite her awful nose; then walked away. The air was filled with the stench of rotting fruit, a smell similar to the liquid explosions from diseased intestines. It made him remember having to clean a gut-shot deer when he was young, while his father watched, disapproving.

It was the first animal he'd hunted, and he'd killed it badly. Joel ran up the stairs, taking them three steps at a time.

When he opened the door, the stink was a pressure on his brain, his nose. It was another lavatory. There was excrement everywhere; some of it resembled congealed blood. There was even shit on the walls, and pieces of paper were wadded into the hole where the patients relieved themselves. Joel slammed the door and turned around; the nurse was gone. "You bitch!" He ran down the stairs, through the dirty corridors, past the patients lying like dominoes tipped onto the floor.

A fat, sick woman cried by a staircase, tears streaking her face. Joel ignored her, ignored everything. It took several minutes to find the two nurses who had resumed their places at the front entrance where they talked and laughed. Joel ran up to the one with the nose and grabbed her arm, but she shook herself free.

"Keep your hands off me, you animal."

"What the hell are you trying to prove!" Forgetting himself, he spoke in English. She looked blankly at him; then launched an Arabic tirade.

Joel calmed down and spoke in French again. "Please, I'm sorry. Now will you get the doctor for me?"

"The doctor is busy," the heavy nurse said, her fat face moving slow as she spoke, a pig eating a corn cob.

"If you don't get him, I will."

"Very well," she said, and walked over to a wall phone which looked at least thirty years old. She lifted the receiver and began speaking in Arabic. The beak stared at her for a moment; then giggled. Joel wondered what would happen if he punched her in the face. A man who was obviously the doctor came walking along the corridor. The heavy nurse was still on the phone, but the other one said something in Arabic, and she slammed down the receiver, embarrassed, turning to face the doctor.

"This man would like to see you."

"Ah yes," Joel said, taking the doctor by the sleeve and half dragging him up the stairs to where Kenny lay. The Englishman's eyes were fluttering. He was curled up on the floor, motionless, except for those eyes and the small, panting breaths that escaped his mouth. "It's my friend. He's very ill, as you can see."

The doctor eyed the sick man, took a pad from his white coat pocket, dashed a few illegible words onto it, tore off the slip of paper and handed it to Joel. Then he descended the stairs.

"What's this!" Joel cried, holding up the slip of paper.

"A prescription for diarrhœa," said the doctor without looking back.

"But you never examined him."

"He has dysentery; he'll get over it in a day or so."

"But you never examined him!"

The doctor wheeled around at the foot of the stairs. "You imply that I don't know my profession?" he glared at Joel, hands on hips, lips pursed together. He certainly had a professional attitude. Joel threw the slip of paper onto the stairs, and the doctor walked away in disgust. Joel bent down and lifted Kenny. The sick man regained clarity for a moment.

"What's going on? Is he going to examine me?"

"Forget it. We'll find a better doctor." He helped him tackle the stairs. At the bottom, beak-nose waited.

"That will be thirty *dirhams*, please."

"Thirty *dirhams*, what for?"

"For the doctor, of course."

"You're mad." Joel tried to walk around her. She sidestepped with impressive grace and stood in front of them once again.

"Thirty *dirhams*," she said with an official voice. Joel, full of contempt, pulled three ten-*dirham* bills out of his pocket and scattered them at her feet.

"How would you feel, if you were sick in a strange country and no one helped you?"

She gathered the bills, straightened up, and walked away. "It's not my problem."

They found another doctor. This one had a private clinic. An old woman sat at his feet, raising her hands, declaiming prayers and entreaties. Joel couldn't decide if she were begging for help or singing the doctor's praises. The man prescribed eleven different medications for Kenny, claiming it was an intestinal infection. This brought Joel to the verge of asking what kind of kickback the pharmacies gave, but he thought better. At least there were antibiotics on the list. They might help. The doctor charged forty *dirhams* and told the receptionist to escort the two foreigners outside, where Kenny collapsed on the street with such melodramatic aplomb that, for a moment, Joel wondered if this whole business was an act. Joel stuffed him into a taxi and they returned to the hotel.

Kenny shivered in the bed; he was freezing, lost under some kind of arctic sun. Joel drew the thermal blanket tight around the man's shoulders.

It was barely a few minutes before Kenny hurled the cover away from his body and cried that he was hot, burning hot. He claimed his stomach was a chimney, the flue where the ash and heat escaped from the hospital incinerator. "My lungs are full of burned bodies." Joel draped wet towels over him, and cooled his face and chest with a cheap fan he'd picked up in a tourist shop. Shoddily-painted camels adorned its brown paper pleats.

"I can't see. I can't see!"

"It's alright. It'll pass. When the fever's broken you'll be fine."

Joel usually travelled alone, yet on a whim he'd agreed to share the hotel room with the other man, more out of boredom than for any other reason. Lucky for the Englishman when he took sick, and unlucky for Joel — stuck with the wreckage.

Kenny had amused Joel at first with his precautions and paranoias, his packsack filled with pills and sprays and deodorants, arms stabbed with every injection and vaccination known to the doctors of England. Joel travelled loose, just getting out of bed one day and going, throwing his clothes into a pack. His sole protection a smallpox vaccination, and that because his grandfather's scarred face haunted his childhood memories.

The American couple returned, and they sat on each side of the bed. The woman gave the sick man a motherly look. She took off the wet towel and stroked his forehead with the back of her hand. Joel wasn't impressed.

"He's the same, isn't he?" she asked.

"Yes."

"Have you eaten today?"

"No."

"You should eat and walk around for a while," said the man. "It's not good sitting in this hot room all day, watching a sick man."

"Maybe I'll go to the *medina* . . . you don't mind staying with Kenny?"

"No, go ahead, or you're going to get sick too."

Joel gathered his cigarettes and walked to the door. "I'll be back in a while, Kenny. You'll be fine." The Englishman waved his hand weakly. He had other things on his mind.

After a dinner of speared lamb and onions broiled over an open brazier, Joel drank a green glass of the hot, sweet mint tea and went for a walk; he soon grew tired of the crowded *medina*'s gaudy streets. In Fez, the narrow ways are packed with people and burros. His foot ached, stepped on by a runaway donkey. Fortunately he was wearing his cowboy boots and didn't suffer serious damage. He felt more sympathy for the donkey than himself: the beasts of burden were overladen and undernourished, gaunt animals staggering under mountains of bricks and sticks.

"The world is a sick house of men and animals." He couldn't recall the origin of the phrase. Then he felt foolish; it was his own, pulled from an article he had written years ago when he was twenty, almost ten strange years ago. He was thirty now, at the point where a man's life and thoughts begin to slow down if he isn't careful.

He realized he'd left the core of the *medina*. He was in a grim, silent alley, and ahead a young Moroccan blocked the way. He stopped. The boy had two friends, one leaning against each of the walls lining the narrow, cobbled path. The door of a mosque, shaped like a mouth, towered above them.

"Where's your passport, tourist? I have to check your passport." The boy wasn't eighteen years old and his friends looked younger.

They wore black T-shirts and dirty blue jeans. The leader had a scarred face — smallpox when he was a child; yet a variety of handsomeness reflected behind the skin.

"Let me through."

"Not unless you show your passport. It's against the law to travel without a passport." The boy confronted Joel with a hard, empty face that betrayed his street intelligence.

"Yes, show us your passport," one of the others said. He wasn't as good as the boy opposing Joel — a thin smile crept onto his lips. None of them was more than five feet tall.

"Look, I've about had it!" Joel grabbed the leader by the throat, shook him like a rag doll, and hurled him against the mosque.

Three knives rushed into the light, glimmering in the dim and narrow street. Somehow, Joel found himself on the other side of the boys, and he pointed his finger at them. "If one of you moves, I'll drive him so hard he'll pick his teeth out of his asshole for a week."

The boys ogled him, shocked. He was almost a foot taller than any of them, yet unarmed. A weird silence followed. Finally, the leader broke it. "Punch my teeth down to my bum?" he turned to the others, grinning. "This American, he's crazy."

"A crazy American," agreed the one to his left.

"I'm not an American, I'm Canadian," Joel was irritated more by the remark than the threat of their knives.

"Oh that makes a difference," said the third Moroccan. "Crazy Canadians don't need passports, do they?" He looked at the others. They nodded smugly.

"Aren't you afraid?" asked the first boy, the smart one.

"No."

"Can't you see he's not afraid?" said the one leaning against the wall.

"Do you want to buy hashish?"

"How about my sister? You can make love to my little sister for just a few *dirhams*. She's a real virgin. I know because I'm her brother, and I look after her."

"Sorry." Joel turned his back to them and continued up the alleyway, past the mouth of the mosque, knowing they wouldn't come after him yet.

"Goodbye, crazy Canadian."

"Goodbye."

As soon as he rounded the first corner, he pressed himself against the hot, dirty wall. Now he was scared. The fear erupted, a storm in his belly. He waited. At least the first one would get a boot in his groin. He didn't know what he'd do with the other two.

A few moments later he heard a quiet scraping around the corner. When the boy came into sight, Joel wheeled out, kicking. But it was the leader, and he had the instincts of a cat, leaping backwards into the other two, knocking them down. They scrabbled around on the ground as if they were clowns in a circus, laughing and pushing each other over, sorting out their knives before getting to their feet.

"This Canadian, he's not only crazy but he's smart," said the leader once he'd confiscated his knife from the boy beside him who'd insisted vehemently that it was his.

"No, he's definitely not afraid," laughed the other, satisfied at last that he had his own knife. Joel moved forward and they retreated into each other with mock fright.

"Okay, Canadian, we changed our minds. We're not going this way after all. We'll turn around and go that way and you keep going straight ahead. That way everyone lives to return home happy." The leader had a disarming grin, and Joel couldn't help smiling.

Once again he turned his back to them and continued up the alley. This time they descended the cobblestones, laughing and talking excitedly among themselves until their voices faded in the distance. Joel was lucky. He never should have tried to kick the boy; if he had connected they would have been committed to fight, and he would have been slashed, maybe killed. The incident was like a dream, and he couldn't understand why they hadn't cut him up anyway. Unlucky city. He stopped walking, and absorbed the atmosphere in the empty street. Lucky city.

He looked at his watch. It was late in the afternoon, and he should return to relieve the Americans. Their holiday in Morocco wasn't turning out so great, and he wondered how long they'd continue tending the sick man.

Joel found himself in an courtyard filled with vats of dye. Young children stained purple, yellow, red — all the colours of the rainbow — jumped on and scrubbed the cloths. It was a nightmare vision — the rainbowed children of hell dancing in a stinking beehive, slaving for the gaudy desires of distant people.

He remembered Kenny's complaints on their first day together in the city. The endless harassments and thefts by small children had irritated the Englishman until Joel showed him the empty lot across from their hotel room. Night was approaching, and children collected in the slag, carrying rags that would soon become blankets, a few of the children perhaps five years old. The Englishman stood at the window for a long time before he turned away. "It's their karma."

Joel plowed through the *medina*. He was glad to reach the open streets of the upper town. When he walked by the perimeter walls of the castle, he almost felt good. Even from poverty comes the castle. Or was the poverty because of the castle?

Up ahead, in the square, there was a police wagon beside the fountain. It wasn't far from the hotel. The wagon made him nervous. There was a threatening air about it, as if it were parked there to point something out to him. At first he couldn't discern what was going on because of the crowd collected around the wagon.

The armed and uniformed men were arresting two people. The Americans, stupid and shambling in their ridiculous bathing suits, were being pushed, protesting, into the dim interior of the truck. "Christ!" He broke into a run, shoving his way through the crowd.

The police slammed the door on the Americans. The motor started, and a black cloud came out of the muffler. As he rammed his way forward, the Moroccan bystanders eyeing him with unrepressed anger, he couldn't help thinking "They need a new motor. The piston rings are ruined."

The congregation began to disperse when the truck drove out of the square and up the street. Joel gestured crazily while the crowd studied this new development.

"It keeps on coming!" he screamed. Everyone shuffled away, giving him an open circle.

There was an older Moroccan in a business suit seated on a bench beside the fountain, and Joel approached him. "What happened to the Americans?"

The man ignored him, took a drag on his cigarette, and was thoughtful. He had a cataract in one eye. Slowly, infuriatingly, he flicked his long ash to the ground. "It's against the law to wear a bathing suit in a public street."

"I don't believe it."

"Suit yourself." The crowd, realizing Joel wasn't crazy, moved in close, like secretive animals watching an injured member of the pack.

"Stupid Americans," the man with the cataract said, "they didn't offer a bribe."

"Could I go to the police station and make a bribe there? Pay the fine?"

"No, it's too late now. Once they're registered, the judge has to be bribed, and that means waiting for the trial. Then it gets dangerous — if the bribe is too small, you'll have to bribe him for yourself because he'll have you arrested too. Stupid Americans, the police wanted money. They didn't want to take them."

A man behind Joel laughed.

This grinding, this hellish heat and big sun, this poverty, it makes a man die.

Kenny was alone, sweating on the bed, half-dreaming, or perhaps fully dreaming. The door slammed shut. "Hello Kenny."

It took the invalid a few moments to sort out the dream and the real. "Hello," Kenny said. "They told me they were going for cigarettes, but they never came back. I'm afraid."

"How are you feeling?"

Kenny didn't reply. He was sleeping again.

Joel gathered his possessions. He travelled light; it didn't take long to throw everything into the pack. Kenny woke up with an alertness that illustrated his diseased condition more than his delirium.

"Joel?"

"Yes?"

"Are you leaving?"

"Yes."

"Are you coming back?"

"No."

Silence. Kenny analyzed the dirty ceiling of the room for a few seconds. "Am I dying?"

"Yes."

Joel shouldered his packsack and put his hand on the doorknob as if it were electric.

"Joel, I think I'm getting religion. A while ago I saw Christ on the cross, and he winked at me."

"That's good; maybe he will help you." There was nothing more to do, nothing more to say, so he shut the door; then he strode down the dark and ugly hall, towards the single light in the stairwell.

BAD TIMES IN CASABLANCA

Casablanca, I love you, asshole and armpit of the planet: city of eyeless children, city of smoky dreams. Casablanca . . . Casablanca . . . house with a million white windows called houses, city of cockroaches and piled figs, I love you. All your streets are burning, all your skies are one sky. Only the flies could love you as much as I, city of mud, only the flies could love you . . . Casablanca . . . Casablanca . . . asshole and armpit of the planet.

When Pip awoke, he saw the sun under the crack in the shutter; he knew it was late, and he was terrified. There were more than enough bodies for comfort in the room; warm, sensual bodies wrapped around each other, but the middle bed was empty. Joel was gone, and he wondered where the Canadian was; then he wondered why every time he woke up these last few days, he wanted to see Joel. Joel? Wasn't Joel in the next room, sleeping with a knife? Pip needed to be comforted. But he fell asleep again, dreaming about an urgent, necessary appointment, one that was marked with blood, huge gouts of blood.

***

The sun creased Joel's face with sweat, and he was desperate for a bath, desperate to wash the greasy meat of Casablanca out of his system, but he didn't move from his chair in the sprawling café beside the crowded street.

An urchin in once-white rags clung to the short, iron bars of the fence that ringed the café, gazing at the remnants on Joel's plate, a broken chunk of bread and a half-stick of speared meat.

Joel slid a piece of lamb off the end, and tossed it into the air. The child dived and caught it in his mouth, swallowed and grinned; then he did a backward somersault, almost tripping an old lady shambling past.

Impressed, Joel hurled another chunk of the shish-kebab, and the boy repeated the performance. It was the puppy grin, hypnotic, without pretension or thought. The child might have been nine years old.

Aware that the other diners were watching, Joel ignored the boy, wondering how to end this show with decency. The owner moved through the crowded chairs, zeroing in on the pair causing the disturbance. There was one last piece of meat, and the boy eyed it through the iron grating, his chubby fingers opening and closing on the bars.

"Now bark like a dog," Joel whispered, picking up the meat in his fingers. The boy's eyes clouded, puzzled, and Joel thought he might not speak English. "Bark like a dog." Joel gave a few, plaintive barks. The noisy restaurant grew hushed, and the waiter-owner was closer, blocked by the last tangle of chairs and customers. "Bark!"

The boy's eyes glowed. He barked, did a half-twist on the street as if he were chasing his tail; then he howled, softly and sweetly to the blue daylight sky. Joel tossed the last of the meat over the grate, and once again the boy caught it in his mouth. He gulped it down, and ran away, barking and laughing through the crowd.

A shadow fell across Joel's table. It posed, motionless on the cloth like a new course he should eat for dinner. "I'll have my mint tea now," Joel said without turning around. He'd made a fool of himself, and to save face he had to pretend he hadn't. But there was an ugly question behind this. Why did he have to save face? Why did he always have to look good?

The shadow didn't move.

"My mint tea, if you please."

The restaurant remained quiet. The shadow shook its head and walked away with too much dignity. Joel became a statue facing the street, immobile and expressionless until his mint tea appeared at the end of a hairy arm, the glass bouncing so hard on the table that some of it spilled. Joel lit a cigarette, and drank his tea.

For two burning days and three nights he had cruised the streets of Casablanca and no amount of sweet tea could take the bitterness away.

Everything began at the train station in Tangier.

People pushed and jostled, shuffling crates of chickens and suitcases, old men tried to straighten their sliding *djellabas*, and the street children looked for what they could steal or tried to sell what they had already stolen.

Joel found himself sitting next to two Americans, and the old story began again. Stay with us in Casablanca; we'll get a hotel together. It's cheaper and there's safety in numbers. Aside from one other unhappy occasion he had always travelled alone in Morocco, but he liked these men, and agreed.

Then came the women. Pip found them and they fell for his innocent face. They were perhaps sixteen, French, runaways, and determined to be free. One, Jenny, had red hair that stretched down to her waist and the Moroccan men went wild at the sight of her.

When they arrived in Casablanca it was two in the morning. The fog rolled over the wide street outside the station. Ghostly shadows wandered in and out of the light cast by the pathetic street lamps that spotted the pavement as if they'd been an afterthought designed by an eccentric engineer.

The girls asked an Arab for directions and found themselves encircled when more grinning faces erupted like hallucinations out of the fog.

Joel thought they were in trouble, but two lights flicked on in the distance, and approached, growing brighter in the silence disturbed only by the muttering voices of the Moroccans. It was a taxi. He flagged it down, agreed to the outrageous price the driver demanded, and they moved out of the foggy upper town towards the *medina* where the driver assured them there were lots of cheap hotels.

In the *medina* they paid their fare and the cab disappeared. Every hotel was full. They moved like a caravan from one to the other, collecting a crowd again — discreet and distant at first, but growing lewder and louder. At last Joel found a hotel that was receptive despite being full; the clerk said he knew another place, one that might have rooms. He disappeared into the shadowy antechamber behind the desk to confer with another man, thick-voiced and invisible.

"The flies have found their meat." Joel nodded towards the doorway where a group of men, braver than those in the street, clustered about the French girls.

"They never go away. What do they think they're going to get?" Harold said, leaning against the counter.

"The red hair. It drives them crazy." A short man in blue jeans and a dirty T-shirt had worked himself behind the girls and ran his fingers through Jenny's hair. She didn't seem to notice until he patted her behind. She giggled, turning around, and slapped his hand away. He pinched her.

Harold looked at Joel. "You've got red hair; why don't they want your behind?"

"I'm sure they do, but I'm bigger than they are." Joel hated sounding so tough; it rang false in his ears.

The hotel clerk emerged blinking from the dingy back room and nodded. They clutched the girls and followed the man into the street. The Arabs trailed them for almost a block, gradually losing interest until the foreigners were alone with the clerk, working their way down the narrow, black alleyways, guided by the weak batteries of the man's lantern. Even the fog, Joel noticed, avoided the dark heart of the *medina*.

Pip stopped, revolved on his heels, and looked back. "I just saw a cockroach dragging a melon."

"Bullshit!" Harold laughed.

"Maybe it's in training for the cockroach olympics." Joel pulled another cigarette from the pack and lit it with the one already in his mouth. A chain smoker, he wielded the cigarettes like weapons in his conversation. He flicked the used butt away, keeping his eyes on the girls and the clerk up ahead. His lungs hurt. Why did he smoke so much?

Harold followed his gaze. "Those French girls are something else, aren't they?"

"Them, I don't mind; it's their friends I can't take." He started walking again.

Harold remained where he was, wondering if the remark included Pip and himself.

Once more the girls lured men from the narrow doorways, the men fluttering about like moths around a lamp, though Joel and Harold put their arms around the girls, signalling that they were private property. Then they disappeared as suddenly as they had appeared.

Pip walked alongside the clerk now — two half-men shining in the erratic flickering of the lamp between them.

"Look at that," Harold said. "The windows are full of women." They stopped in front of a building that dwarfed the neighbouring houses. On the second floor there was a row of windows, each backlit from a central hallway or courtyard, and seated by the windows were the women, their veiled faces shadowed and sideways to the street.

"I think we're there," Joel laughed. Pip and the hotel man entered through the big door, its iron gates open to receive whatever visitors the night offered.

The group was assigned three rooms: the women at the end of the hallway, Joel next to them, and the Americans across the courtyard. Payment was in advance, not cheap, and there was no dickering. Everyone was so tired they crashed onto their beds without a goodnight. Joel, grateful that he had drawn the single room, stripped and slid into the cool sheets where he soon found the uneasy countries of nervous sleep.

Time walked through the dim courtyard, accompanied by silence and the occasional patter of footsteps on the tiled floor.

Then the night screamed. It began far off, rolling across the muted air, and came to an abrupt end. Joel's eyes opened as if they had springs, and his hand pushed into the packsack beside the bed. He pulled out the skinning knife, letting the leather sheath fall to the floor. The blade glittered in the tiny louvres of light coming through the shuttered window.

Footsteps dashed across the tiles, followed by more footsteps. Both pairs collided in front of his door, and he heard a moan, a small grunt that began sharply and trailed off into silence.

In the dark, his knife and naked body sliced by the thin strips of light, Joel remained motionless; then he slipped out of the bed, pressing his back against the wall, the flesh of his elbow jammed against the light switch. He clicked it on, and realized too late that was a mistake.

The harsh brilliance of the light bulb flooded the room and, he knew, trickled through the shutters overlooking the courtyard. There was nothing but silence, emptiness, fear. *Why do I always screw up?*

It was cold, yet his sweat made him stick to the wall, and he understood what the fly recognized when it hit the flypaper.

Minutes passed before there were more footsteps. They stopped at the other side of his door; he didn't move. He was stuck to the wall. The silence returned, seeping through the window like gas.

He knew there was a head pressed against the door. He didn't hear anything, but he sensed the listening ear. He let his head slide down, and cupped his own ear against the wood, aware of how strange it was, the two questioning skulls jammed against opposite sides of the panel. "If you come in," he whispered, "I'll cut off your sex and stuff it down your throat."

There was no reply. He waited.

A disembodied voice whispered through the wood. "Go back to sleep." More silence. At last there was movement, the sound of something heavy, perhaps a body, being dragged away.

Through the final portion of the night, he remained against the wall.

When the first tints of dawn struck the outside window he dressed and opened the door. The courtyard was empty, hushed, almost innocent. He crossed it fast, his feet tapping against the cool, mosaic tiles.

It didn't take long to work his way out of the tangled *medina* and into the more affluent section of the upper town. He found a hotel with steel shuttered windows, big gates, and a uniformed man beside the door. It was expensive, but he'd seen enough of the *medina*.

He returned and pounded on the doors of the Americans and the girls.

"What's going on?" Harold asked.

"Pack up, we're leaving."

Soon, everyone was ready to go. They could tell something was wrong.

As they crossed the courtyard, a short, fat man in a business suit appeared in one of the doorways, stroking his moustache against his cheek. "Ah, our guests have risen early."

"Yes, we must be leaving," Joel said.

"I trust you slept well?" That damned silence came seeping into the courtyard from the adjoining windows.

Pip beamed. "I had a most delicious night."

"Yes," the Moroccan nodded, stroking his moustache until Joel wanted to knock the fat hand away from his face. "There was some noise in the night, unfortunately . . . the clerk . . . " His hand began to move backwards against the moustache, bristling the hairs. " . . . the clerk . . . he had a bad dream and screamed in his sleep."

"I see," Joel said, "I thought I heard a scream in the night."

"It was a bad dream. There's no point in discussing it. It was a bad dream."

"Don't worry," Joel said, "I never talk about other people's nightmares."

"That's good. Too much talk can get a man into trouble."

"I understand completely. It was just a bad dream."

As soon as they were outside the building, Harold turned and asked: "What was that all about?"

"Someone got knifed outside my door last night, and I was stupid enough to turn my light on."

"Christ, I didn't hear a sound. Did they kill him?"

"How should I know? I didn't go out and examine the body."

"It could have been one of us."

"Count yourself lucky."

"You could have scared them off."

Joel shook his head as if he'd just heard a great joke. "I'm not that stupid."

Harold became angry. "You'd have left us out there with those flies?"

"It wasn't you, was it? It was a kink."

"You knew who it was?"

"No, of course not, but I had an idea. A kink damaged one of the whores, and they cleaned him out. I heard a woman scream before they got to him."

"You mean that was a brothel!" The realization flooded the American's eyes.

"You're not that naïve?"

"I spent the night in a brothel, and didn't even know it." They began to laugh. But Joel felt sick to his stomach, knowing how stupid he'd been — turning on the light — and hating the way his words and body went so icy when his failings made him obvious.

That was the first night.

He finished his mint tea and ordered another from the owner of the café. The man hadn't forgiven the performance with the street urchin, but he set this glass on the table with a shade more gentleness, not spilling much.

The second night in the new hotel was no better. Joel shared a room containing three big beds and nothing else with the Americans; the girls took the adjoining room.

Next door, Jenny, after washing her red hair, pulled a towel from the rack, and the rack fell off the wall, clattering against the yellow tile counter while a single, astonished cockroach fled into the hole. She laughed.

She even laughed when she and Pauline sat on the bed, testing it for lumps, and it collapsed to the floor, throwing them onto their backs ... laughing ... laughing ....

After an hour they called in the men, still laughing as they told their tale; the room was falling apart around them. Joel smiled and pulled out the lump of *kief* he'd bought for twenty-five *dirhams* in the *medina*. "Try this," he said, "it will make the room fix itself." The

Americans looked at him; their French was too poor to pick up anything said fast.

Jenny took the lump and rolled it in her palm. "Why have you taken us under your wing? You're not like them." She rolled her eyes in the direction of the Americans.

Joel shrugged. The Americans, realizing they were in for a spate of incomprehensible syllables, leaned against the wall like innocent twins, arms folded, shoulders hooked to the ugly paint.

"You want to use our bodies," Jenny said, "and discard us the way you'd discard old rags."

"No, not me," Joel grinned, stuffing his hands into his pockets, resembling a child caught with his fingers in the jam jar. "But you seem to know a lot for a runaway girl of sixteen."

Jenny glanced at Pauline who was on the bed and studying Joel — her hard, small face waiting for something unexpected — and Joel wondered if the girls had some strange plan to set him up, take him down to reality.

"If you have my face," Jenny said, "if you have my face, my hair, my body, you learn a lot on your back, even if you're only a runaway girl of sixteen." On the bed, Pauline smiled triumphantly.

"Then you'll learn different from me. I don't want your body."

"What do you want?"

"I want what I can't have, and right now that includes the drug. Either eat it or pass it along." Sadness filled him, and he wanted to go home, back to Canada.

She smiled and bit into the corner of the tawny chunk of kief, passed it to Pauline who nibbled at it like a timid rabbit.

"Where did you get this?" Harold asked Joel when she handed the drug to him.

"In the street, where you get everything here."

"What did you tell them?" Harold asked, glancing at the girls whose English was as poor as his French.

"That it will make everything better, turn their room into a castle that never needs repairing."

Harold smirked and passed the *kief* to Pip who took far too large a bite.

"Let's go out for some tea," Joel said. He asked the girls, but they shook their heads. They wanted to stay in the room.

Harold nodded to Pip and the three men left for the hectic streets.

They found a hole-in-the-wall café and sat down to wait for the *qahouaji* to bring their tea. In the back room, men sprawled on rugs, drinking Coca-Cola and smoking their pipes.

A boy spoke too loudly to the older man next to him. "If you give me money, you can have my bum. If you don't give me money; then my bum belongs to me." Several customers sniggered at the remark.

Harold eyed the boy and the ugly man who got up in disgust and walked out the door. "They're not shy here, are they?"

"It's just a lover's quarrel."

Pip gulped down his tea, and soon began to fidget. "I want to check out the stall across the street," he said, gazing at the garish collection of clothing and leather displayed around the door.

After he left, the two men were mute for several minutes, sipping their tea.

"You know," Harold said when he finished his drink, "I'm beginning to dislike Morocco."

"The country is alright. It's how you live in it. I had trouble about six months ago in Fez. The guy didn't have the guts to live with the country, and it got him in the guts." Joel sat back in his chair, considering what he'd just said. He'd always spoken this way, making bullshit out of terror.

"How long have you been here?"

"A year."

"You're on the run, aren't you."

"We're all runners."

"Drugs?"

Joel shrugged; then he smiled.

"Are you wanted by the police?"

"I didn't stay around long enough to find out."

"You're not using your real name, are you?"

"Of course not. Want some more mint tea?"

"Sure." Harold examined the dusty street and the bazaar on the other side; Pip hadn't emerged from the interior. "But if anything happened to you, nobody would know."

"Nothing is going to happen to me, and if it did, nobody would care. God, I'm crazy about this mint tea. It goes straight to the sweet tooth."

"You're so cool," Harold said sardonically. "Why do you hang around with innocents like us?"

"I'm not as heartless as I sound."

"You're lonely."

"I miss my home."

"Why don't you go back?"

"You can't go back." Joel sucked on his cigarette, and studied an old man in a *djellaba* who shuffled down the street, mumbling at his dirty, sandalled feet. "And what about you, why are you here?"

"That's the first thing you asked about me."

Joel shrugged.

"It's plain as day. I'm engaged to be married. I've got a job in a bank when I get back to Cleveland. I can't speak for Pip, but this is my chance to live. You know what I mean? I want to have something behind me before I disappear into the grind."

"You don't have to disappear."

"You're sticking with us for the girls. You want to have your night with the two of them."

"If I wanted sex I could buy it on any street in any town in this country."

Pip reappeared from the back of the shop across the street, a man tugging at his sleeve, waving a braided wallet. There was such a wide-eyed look of innocence about the young man that Joel couldn't help smiling. "For all you know, I could be waiting for my chance with him."

Harold was startled. He looked across the street at his dreamy but beautiful friend who smiled innocently while the man praised the wallet as the most precious object made between heaven and earth.

"You can't. He's mine."

"I'm sorry. I've got a big mouth."

"That's alright. Let's go, I've about had it with your mint tea. It's too sickly sweet for me."

Joel lay on the bed, immobile, paralysed, listening to the steady, muted breathing of the Americans. He'd eaten too much kief again. The room was black like the inside hollow of a coal seam, and he tried to imagine working in a mine, until his brain sank into the back of his head and sleep came.

All night there was noise – too much noise. It clanked and hammered against the roof, and he kept waking, unable to move, stoned, listening, wondering. It was the wedding couple. For some reason he remembered the doorman sniggering and telling him there was a pair of newlyweds in the room above, that he surely wouldn't get any sleep at all, but the noise wasn't shaking beds or the movements of love; it sounded like keys being dragged across a floor.

After a while he began to wonder if the conversation with the doorman took place, or if he'd imagined it, and was he imagining those keys, slow, heavy, nuzzling across the floor, and what kind of sex was that?

When he awoke there was light, about six inches of it streaming over the floor. The metal shutter had been lifted. He climbed out of bed and examined the louvres. Somebody had jimmied the thing with a bar, lifting it until the contraption jammed, leaving too small a gap for a man to slip through.

"The keys . . . the keys . . . . It was the metal grinding against the tracks."

"What's the matter?" Harold sat up in his bed, looking lost and scared for a moment. In the other bed, the beautiful Pip slept peacefully.

"Nothing . . . someone tried to jimmy the shutters, but they didn't get in."

"Only an Arab would try to break into a room with three men sleeping inside," Harold sighed, falling back against his pillow.

Joel contemplated the door, one corner of it twisted and broken. He pushed against the metal; it was thick and sturdy. Whoever bent the end, even with the help of a bar, had to be stronger than anyone inside the room.

Harold, his head sideways on the pillow, eyed the twisted wreckage in the shutter's corner.

That was the second night. Joel ordered another tea. Despite the changing crowd, the street remained the same in front of the café, poverty and riches rubbing *djellaba* against business suit, leaving and approaching in every direction. He wondered where the dog child went, if he was doing his act at the next café down the street. The owner brought a third glass, impressed now by the foreigner's speedy consumption of the sweet tea.

"It's a machine," Jenny said, beneath the vent in the bedroom. The clicking, monotonous noise had begun several minutes earlier. It so unnerved the girls that they called the men into the room.

Everyone listened to the ticking thing behind the wall. Joel pulled the cover off the vent and held a lit match against the darkness. The flame died. He tried again. Inside, there was nothing but blackness.

"It's an insect," Harold said. "It has to be an insect."

"No," Joel shook his head, "I can hear metal."

"It's the furnace, and we're all paranoid." Pip reclined on the bed, smoking a pipe full of kief.

"It's a mechanical insect!" Jenny clapped her hands together gleefully, as if she understood everything said.

They opened the windows to clear the smell of the drug, and when the noise continued for another twenty minutes, called the clerk. It took the old, bespectacled man ages to climb the stairs, and by the time he reached the room the noise had ceased. He was dubious.

"It's for ventilation," he said. "There's nothing in it."

"I think someone's trying to put gas in the room," Joel said.

"No one's trying to put gas in the room. You're crazy."

"I know; it's a mechanical insect," Pip laughed, his eyes lit up like big green coals. Jenny guided him back to his room.

The dubious clerk studied the occupants for several seconds, and then his gaze fell on the broken bed. He sniffed once at the air, shook his head, and descended the stairs.

Almost as soon as he was out of sight, the noise resumed. They huddled under the vent, listening, sniffing . . . .

"Well, I can smell *kief* alright," Harold joked. "If anything, we might be drugging the rest of the hotel."

"Call him back," Joel said to Jenny. "There's something wrong."

"Forget it," Jenny said, "we're going to bed."

That was the third night. And for the first time in Casablanca, Joel slept undisturbed. He rose early and walked about the town until noon. By the ocean, he lingered for a while, watching the boys fish off the stone walls lining the beach, hungry for what little the sea would release. On the way to the café he passed the same white-robed group of men he had seen early in the morning. They'd travelled a hundred yards, shuffling forward religiously, while the drum banged each step. The slow power of that movement scared him.

Then at the café, the dog-child, the shadow of the owner, the watching crowd. He had to get out of this country. It was wearing away his bones. He finished the third cup of tea, paid his bill, and returned to the hotel.

As he climbed the stairs, he heard voices in the girls' room. There was a puddle of water blocking the open door, and he stepped over it, puzzled. A condom lay beside their bed, spilling over with liquid that resembled semen. The girls were on the crashed bed, puffy-eyed and unhappy, and the entire room was webbed with black thread.

Harold stood on a chair, passing the thread over curtains, around the light, across the bed posts.

"And what does the spider weave today?" Joel asked.

"See for yourself. You were right about that noise . . . they were drugged."

Joel looked at the girls. "What happened?"

Jenny tried to speak. Then she began to cry.

Harold stepped down from the chair he had been standing on. His hands were shaking. "When we woke up a while ago, I went to collect the girls and go for lunch. There was water seeping out from the door."

He pointed at the puddle by the door jamb. "I thought it was water, but it's piss. Smell it. I knocked on the door and they didn't answer, so I knocked louder. Then I went to get the clerk. He unlocked the door and we found the girls unconscious in the bed, untouched — as far as I could gather. That, where it is." He nodded at the used condom.

"We couldn't wake them for a long time . . . and look at their eyes. They're swollen. Some creep drugged them and jerked off beside the bed."

Joel sat down beside Jenny. "Did he touch you?"

She shook her head. "I don't know . . . . I don't think so."

He turned to Harold. "I've heard of this happening before. Some men here, they don't use dirty magazines. They need condoms and real, sleeping women. It's a fantasy number . . . . What did the clerk say?"

"That creep!" Harold jerked his index finger into the air. "He said this was a good hotel, and if we caused any more trouble he'd kick us out."

Joel surveyed the room, the spiderweb of thread, the unhappy girls. "And I'll bet the door was locked from the inside." He couldn't help laughing.

"That's right."

"You're going to catch the kink with the threads when he comes back tonight, using them as an alarm?"

"That's right."

"And when he hits those threads, your pervert is going to go wild. You want to give him an excuse to cut up the girls?"

Joel walked across the room, his hands ripping the web, breaking the links and collecting the tatter until he held a hairy tarantula of thread in his hand.

Pip grinned and handed his pipe to Jenny who took it gratefully, inhaled several times, and passed it on to Pauline. The skinny American leaned against the chest of drawers, his eyes beginning to glitter. "I'll sleep in this room tonight."

"No you won't," Harold said. "Not alone. I'll stay here with you."

Pip shrugged nonchalantly.

"That's a good idea," Joel said, "and I'll take the girls in our room."

Both men stared at him, but Joel's smile was innocent.

Jenny understood something was going on, and she looked at him with puzzlement.

Harold rested his hand on the bedpost with an air of finality. "You're a son-of-a-bitch."

Joel shrugged and turned away. "I'll sleep here tonight, alone; you can share with the girls if they don't mind."

"Uhhh . . . ," Pip nodded, catching a thought in the haze of his mind. "why does anyone have to sleep here?"

"General principles," Joel said, walking out the door and back to the room he shared with Harold and Pip, taking the pipe. "I'm not going to be harassed anymore in this town."

Midnight came like a cat through the city, the dusk leaping from rooftop to rooftop. Every house gathered in its shutters, and the streets emptied as the shadows padded down the corridors. The fog rose from the sea and painted the air with shades of white, chasing the darkness across Casablanca. The city without innocence shifted into its night mood.

"What the hell is that?" Harold exclaimed after Joel stood up from the bed where he had been sitting with the others, sucking on the pipe and talking. When the knife slid out of its sheath in the packsack, an eeriness shadowed the room. The blade was long and thin and shining.

"A skinning knife; great for porcupines."

Jenny shook her head, as if trying to clear the kief out; but the dull numbing kept her eyes glued half-shut. "Why don't we all sleep in this room tonight?"

"There's nothing to fear." Joel stood at the open door. He winked at the hushed group clustered on the bed, and crossed the hall. Then he entered the empty room and locked himself in.

The ventilator shaft was clicking again, but he ignored it, stripping and climbing into the collapsed bed. He stared at the knife blade — beautiful and ominous in the lonely room, scary, like his father, before Joel had discovered the streets. Then he put the knife under the pillow and lay back, facing the ceiling.

He didn't regret the situation, yet he was sad. It was a convergence of lines, like Harold's twisted threads hoping to catch prowlers in the room of the world.

His head felt comfortable, cushioned by the warm and soft pillow. He gazed at the ceiling for a long time, tracing the cracks, the blotches, making shapes and memories out of the formless disasters that time had worked on the paint and the plaster, and he wondered where the dog-child slept tonight, whether he did somersaults in his sleep or howled at the fog-hidden moon. The clicking, ticking ventilator shaft droned incessantly. He knew he had been wrong yesterday. The shaft was harmless. If anything those girls had been chloroformed by hand, but the ventilator's noises plucked at his nerves. "I want to go home."

***

When Pip awoke, his face was against Jenny's breast. He kissed the nipple and lifted his head. Harold and Pauline were still shrouded with sleep in the far bed. Between the couples was the other bed, empty and unwrinkled. He slipped out from between the sheets and dressed, as if there was an urgent appointment he had to make.

He padded out of the room and stood before Joel's closed door. He knocked. There was no answer. He knocked again.

He returned to his own door.

Harold's eyes jerked open. Pip stood before the hall light, silhouetted, gazing at Harold. "Get up. There's no answer."

Harold pulled on his undershorts, couldn't find his socks, and, disgusted, ran half-naked out of the room.

His eyes caught Pip's gaze. Fluid was leaking under the door.

"Christ!" he screamed, hammering at the wood. No sound issued from the other side.

He rammed his bare shoulder against the door; the jamb splintered, and the door flew open, crashing into the wall.

The room was silent, half-dark. There was another used condom on the floor beside the bed. A puddle of urine at the door. Pip followed him, remembering his dream about the appointment, and the blood, the gouts of blood.

Joel was between the sheets, cradling two red roses, roses bright and beautiful like all the flowers that grow in Morocco, dark roses, roses unfolding on the white cotton, roses of love, roses with petals of blood; one red and bloody rose between his legs, and one blooming gaudily on the sheet tucked around his severed throat.

Casablanca, I love you, asshole and armpit of the planet: city of eyeless children, city of smoky dreams . . . Casablanca . . . Casablanca . . .

THE WITCH

Witchcraft always comes upon us by surprise; it hides behind our consciousness, waiting to make its move, and we never know we are taken until we are gone. She stole my childhood.

I was young but I convinced myself I was getting old during that summer, the one I remember most — her summer. I was a skinny girl, small for my age, studying myself naked in the mirror every morning, waiting for breasts, eager to become a woman although I hadn't reached eleven years yet. Mother said I was precocious.

But that year my world also revolved around the witch. It didn't seem like it at the time, yet now, looking back, I can see that was when she invaded me.

And the seasons have never been the same. I remember an over-exposed photograph of yellow fields, the racket of the crickets, heat that made me sticky, even though I didn't sweat then. Sweating is a craft learned with age.

Now, after more than forty years, the landscape has lost some of its magic, as if my eyes have grown bored. I remember how excited about the world I was. Take blue. I decided that I'd count all the blues. Blue of night sky, blue of dawn sky, navy blues, pale blues, the blue in my father's eyes. I wrote them down in a list, and when I finally gave up I scratched the count on the back of my dresser, so I would remember it forever. There are 278 blues. Now, I seldom think about blue, and if I do, it's a defiant gesture, a desire to return to my childhood, rather than loving blue for what it is.

She lived three blocks away in a tiny house on a corner lot. The house hadn't been painted for years, but it had a seedy elegance. Inside, the rooms were crowded with objects, spidery vases, stained glass lamps, dried flower arrangements, brocaded wallpapers, paintings, lots of paintings, and there was a wall of dusty books.

I knew she was a witch, because only a witch would read so many books. And she did read them. I'd spy on her at night. She would be under the yellow light of a lamp, the withered pages of an old book open in her lap, mumbling to herself as if reciting incantations.

Once, when I was coming home after dark from the fields, I peeked in her bedroom window and saw her dancing. She looked goofy, but she danced well. There were framed photographs on the wall. One was of a couple in togas. Romans. I thought she must have lived a long time. There were more. A woman in a suit. Was she a man too? Another showed a crowd of people standing around in a king's court. And another was of two elegantly dressed people dancing in a ballroom. The real proof was a photograph of three obvious witches, two old ones and one who resembled her. They were all wearing black and they had those crazy hats, and the young one was naked under her dress. The light from behind her showed everything. A sexy witch! A man with a sword and a crown was threatening them. As I said, the young one resembled her, except she was pretty and the witch was ugly.

The witch's face was pushed in as if the hand of God had squashed it because He hated her.

Somehow, I'd known she was a witch for a few years, maybe because she dressed in black.

The flowers she grew were different. Nobody else had anything similar to them. And the plums on her tree ripened two weeks before any others. She'd put a spell on her plum tree.

That didn't stop us from raiding it. The tree was at the corner of the lot, heavy branches overhanging the picket fence. We'd stand on the fence and clean it out, and after we'd eaten too many, we'd have plum fights.

Tommy was the least afraid; he'd climb to the crest of the tree for the sweetest plums. Once in a while he'd break branches. The loud crack would send me and the other girls squealing in every direction. The witch would come out, swearing and waving a dust mop at us. She spoke awful words. If I'd said anything as nasty I'd have been sent to my room. I decided the world wasn't as cruel to adults.

I can't forget Tommy at the top of the tree, shirtless. He never wore a shirt, so everyone could see the big round scar on his belly — actually, it was a series of circles, one inside the other. He'd fallen on an electric stove when he was a baby. I could tell he was embarrassed by the scar, but instead of hiding it the way a sensible person would, he'd take off his shirt as soon as the days became warm, daring the world not to look. Tommy was weird.

I gawked at those circles of burnt flesh through the leaves of the plum tree, and they reminded me of the colour of the unripe fruit a few weeks before.

Then the witch appeared and we fled screaming, filled with a delicious fright, because we knew what would happen if she caught us.

And it did happen. A few weeks later, Tommy disappeared. For a while, the adults around town would sometimes glance with panic at us children, or my mother would stare at me and start to cry, overflowing with love. Then she'd tell me to keep away from strangers, or I'd disappear too.

When my mother said strangers, I knew she meant the witch — keeping to herself, growing her different flowers and pretending they were normal.

I talked about it with the other kids, and they also thought the witch had taken Tommy and cooked him down for his fat — witches liked fat. But we couldn't understand why the police didn't come and arrest her. We concluded they didn't have any proof, even though I told mother about the swearing and the mop, and the witch chasing us.

My mother smiled and said, "Never climb on another person's tree. People need their privacy, especially her." I didn't understand how that justified taking Tommy away. I thought he should have been just sent to his room or something, and I didn't see what was so special about her, except that she was a witch.

That's when I decided to spy on her and find the evidence that she cooked Tommy down to fat.

I went to the library and read about flowers, thinking there might be a hint in what she grew that would give her away. I found out they were mostly herbs, plants that I hadn't heard of until then: Rosemary, Old Man's Beard, Burdock Root, Thyme, Sage, Tarragon. And many of the flowers were of a variety the books called everlasting. Everlasting. Forever flowers. The kind a witch would grow.

One day when I was standing by the fence, studying a flower I couldn't identify, an old man walked past, a friend of my father, and I asked him what it was. He studied the long black stamen and the single purple petal for a while. Finally, he said, "It's a voodoo lily, not much good for anything except attracting flies." How's that for evidence?

I can go on. I can tell about the time I trailed her to the cemetery at the edge of town, how she carried a jar of her everlastings to the graveyard and a broken tombstone near the trees. Most of the stones were shattered. At the time I thought they were put up broken to signify death. Looking back on it now, I realize they must have been vandalized. She stayed by the grave, mumbling to herself, and when she left I crept up and kicked over the jar of everlastings. I didn't want her to put a spell on a dead man. The name on the stone was Peter McLaren, and the birth date was long ago, before the turn of the century. It didn't say when he died because that part of the stone was broken, but it was the same last name as hers and I wondered if she'd been putting a spell on her father. Now of course, I think the birth date would have been near the same time as hers. I don't know why I failed to realize that then. There's so much a child can't add up.

She never drove a car. Once, when the delivery boy parked his truck in her driveway she came out of the house screaming that no automobile would park in her yard for as long as she lived. She walked everywhere in her black dresses, most people avoided her, except my mother, who'd stop and talk to her when they met while shopping, and if I was there, I'd wander off because I didn't want a spell put on me, and often the witch would be rude to my mother.

There's more. We were playing, Sharon and me and a few others, in the forest behind the new houses when we saw her black dress rustling through the hemlocks. We went silent, and followed her down to the bluff by the creek, where we hid behind a tree. Then she did something strange. She hiked up her dress and climbed on the swing. The swing was a big rope hung from an old tree, with a piece of wood fastened by a knot. It had been there ever since I could remember. It was an institution. Whenever the rope broke someone invisible would put up a new one. She straddled the stick and swung out over the creek, and started to laugh, a crazy laugh. It made us scared.

After she was finished with the swing she walked down to the pool beneath and took off her clothes. This was the first time I saw an adult swim in the pool, not counting Billy and Sarah, but they weren't adults then — just teenagers. And they didn't swim much. They went down there to practise for when they got married two years later.

So the witch swam in our pool, and floated, and chased crayfish, I suppose. I can't remember now all of the stuff she did, but it wasn't interesting, not until she got out and started dressing and I saw her front for the first time. She was skinny, yet her belly folded over as if there were extra skin, and then I noticed the scars. They weren't circular like Tommy's; they were thin lines across the waist. The difference wasn't important at the time. But the fact that there were scars seemed to be evidence of her guilt, as if Tommy were haunting her now, showing everyone the scars.

I was trying to figure it out when Sharon got the hiccups. They were loud. Behind the tree, we looked at her with horror, but she couldn't stop. The witch heard and started screaming at us for spying, while she pulled on her dress. Then she chased us through the forest. That was one of the most exciting days of my life, hiding in the trees, listening for the rustle of her dress as she stalked us. Fortunately, she couldn't find anybody, not even Sharon who had trouble hiding because of her hiccups, and ran out of the forest.

That wasn't the only time the witch chased me. The worst was less than a month later. I think I was angry because I couldn't find any evidence. I'd even examined the suet bags she put out for the birds when autumn came. But I couldn't tell if it was Tommy's fat or beef fat that she'd rendered down.

I threw four crab-apples at her window. The window cracked creepily, as if it couldn't decide whether to break or not. The crack didn't start where the apples hit, but at the bottom corner — one slow line spread across the glass. Then I was running in the lane.

I heard her dress rustling. She was behind me, hurrying down the road, and she had that terrible mop. This time she wasn't screaming, but I could tell she was angry.

I ran into the house. It was after dinner, dusk. And my parents weren't there. They went out a lot. My father used to say they were real social lions. Yet they hardly had anyone over to the house. It wasn't until years later that I figured out why they never entertained. Father was embarrassed by the rickety house and the cheap furniture. He didn't like people to comment on how badly the company treated him during what he called his "forty years in the wilderness."

I was alone. I thought I was safe. It was my house. Then I heard those awful steps on the back stairs. The witch, out of breath and moving slower now, wasn't going to stop. I ran into my parent's bedroom and hid in the laundry basket.

The back door opening . . . the sliding steps in the hallway . . . the ominous material of her dress . . . . She went through the rooms, one by one. At last, she came to my parents' bedroom. She walked in and I watched her through the wicker basket. She slid her mop under the bed as if she were house cleaning. She was silent, and that silence scared me more than when I'd heard her screaming.

Then she left.

I climbed out of the basket and sat in my room, waiting for my parents. I knew this had to stop. The witch was closing in on me. The dusk stayed blue for a long time, throwing silhouettes over the rooftops of the neighbourhood. The moon. The first star. Then millions of stars. Millions and millions, and as it grew darker I grew more and more afraid, until finally I heard the car in the driveway, and the release set me sobbing. I ran out and clung to my mother's skirts while she tried to get through the front door.

There was a look of fright in her eyes when she saw me sobbing so wildly.

"She chased me," I screamed. "She chased me into the house."

"Into the house?" My father said, standing behind mother. "Who chased you into the house?" He looked stern, and I knew the witch was in for trouble.

But I was so frightened, and happy at their return, that I couldn't get anything out at first. "That awful woman with the pushed-in face."

I could feel my mother's body tighten, and she gave me a hard look. "What did you do?"

"Nothing. I didn't do anything."

"Why did she chase you?"

"It was an accident. And she's a witch. Now she wants to cook me down to fat."

My father did one of the cruellest things he ever did. He looked away. And I could see he was trying to stifle a laugh. Worse was yet to come. I noticed the same expression creeping around my mother's eyes, but at least she kept a straight face.

"What was an accident?"

"I broke her window, but I didn't mean to."

"How did you break her window?'

I pulled away from my mother, angry. "You don't believe me! You don't believe me!"

"Of course I believe you. But you'd better go to bed and we'll straighten it out in the morning."

"And she's going to come back and get me."

Now it was my father's turn. "Don't worry, no witch is going to come in here and cook anybody down to fat while I'm around." He winked at me. I think he'd been drinking. Mother gave him one of her famous annoyed looks. I realized they'd both been drinking. It must have been a good party at the boss's house, because they didn't drink alcohol, except for a bottle of wine during holiday dinners. Then they were funny to watch and listen to.

Annoyed, and feeling superior, I turned away.

If the witch came back I'd take care of her myself. I felt like a grown-up. After my parents went to bed, I snuck out to the kitchen and got the carving knife and hid it under my pillow.

Things were different next morning. Mother was gone for a few hours, and when she returned she was angry. "You threw six crab-apples at Mrs. McLaren's window and broke it."

It was a lie. I threw four. That became an important point. Adults weren't supposed to lie. "I didn't throw six crab-apples at Mrs. McLaren's window, and the window broke by itself, anyway. Afterwards."

"Don't you lie to me!"

It suddenly became obvious to me that adults could lie, but children couldn't. The old witch — even her windows broke different from anyone else's. I imagined her out there, inventing crab-apples to make it sound worse.

"I paid her for that window, and you're lucky I don't deduct it from your allowance for the next two years."

I'd never considered that.

"And I don't want you going near the Widow McLaren again."

"But she's the liar!"

"I'll wash your mouth out with soap."

"Can't you see, mom. She's a witch. She's a witch! She put a spell on you."

My mother had the art of looking angry. She could give cross glances that made my skin crawl. That was because she seldom got exasperated. This time she did. Her face went a funny kind of purple. Her eyes were terrifying, weird, and for a moment, I thought the witch really had put a spell on her.

When she spoke, her voice was sad, because she was so angry. "Don't you ever, ever call her that again. If you do, you'll spend so long in your room you'll forget what the world looks like. And you stay away from her." Then she said the scariest thing. "You don't understand yet, but one day you will, and then you'll be sad."

I avoided the witch, and a few months later my father got his promotion. He didn't have to spend his forty years in the wilderness after all.

He came home, excited, his face red. "At last we're going to leave this dump. It's the city lights again." He grabbed mother's hand and they did a dance around the kitchen. "And I get a raise!" We were going to move.

When he talked about a promotion before, I always thought it would be wonderful, but while we prepared to move, I became unhappy, as if I understood what lay ahead. The last magic summer was gone, the yellow fields, the pool, and the rope swing. The city. The dirty streets. Things would never look so fresh. Even the blue sky got duller.

Nor did I realize then, though I think I suspected it, that I would change at last, become a woman, get pregnant when I was eighteen, and marry on the summer I graduated from school. The whole shebang. The flow of my life would stabilize, and I'd become anonymous in the suburbs.

It took another few months until we were ready to move.

The day before arrived, and so did the witch. It was the last time I saw her.

There was a timid knock on the door, and I knew who it was. I could hear the rustle of her skirt behind the wood. Mother opened the door, and Mrs. McLaren stood on the porch, holding a pie that smelled like apples. I suspected it was crab-apples, and I wondered if the four I'd thrown were in there, nurtured in her freezer, and waiting for their chance to return.

I fled to my room.

Above my desk there was an air vent that led to the kitchen. My parents didn't know I'd loosened the screws so I could slide out the cover and watch when they got romantic. They couldn't see me through the slots on their side if my light was out.

My mother and the witch sat down at the table and talked for a while. I could hear everything they said.

Mother made her favourite herbal tea, hibiscus, and they talked more, and drank lots of the tea. After a while, I could see the tears in their eyes.

"I missed you, Ruth," my mother said. "I'll never know anyone like you." That was for sure.

"You gave so much support after the accident," the witch sobbed. "And I've been terrible to you, all of you, just because he drank that night."

Then came the capper. My mother tried to smile. "I'll never forget those great bridge tournaments we used to have when Peter was alive. One awful night can't erase them." My mother played bridge with a witch?

"I still dream about it," the witch said, "the lights on the road."

And who was Peter? For a moment I sat down on the desk, and considered the broken gravestone, how everyone called her the Widow McLaren. I was a stubborn kid, I was hooked. The witch had killed her husband. The grave might even be a fake. And I wondered if his fat was in the freezer next to where she'd kept my crab-apples. Then it became clear. She'd put a spell on everybody, all her friends, to kill him, and now she was changing the spell.

When I looked in the vent again, they were crying hard, and they were kissing. I'll never understand how my mother could put her mouth to that pushed-in face. I remember whispering: "She put a spell on you. She put a spell on you."

It was one of the more tearful goodbyes I'd encounter for years. And I was wrong. The witch had put her spell on mother ages before. That was the day she put her spell on me. I was caught.

After she left, I tried a piece of her crab-apple pie. It was so good I had another piece. Caught. I was caught.

And now, the older I get, the happier I become. With an emotion near gratitude, I wore my first black dress when my husband died. Don't worry, it wasn't a marriage of love. I never see enough of the children, but I bake them crab-apple pie when they come over. I put suet out for the birds in the autumn, and I grow everlastings. I think of these things as a private joke.

I want to haunt the summers of every child in the neighbourhood, but I can't. That was her, and I am me. I can't become what I'm not. I know that now, but it took some hard learning. Still, I'm grateful, and I think, I hope, one day, I might yet return to the secrets of the colour blue, or that I will learn to understand the history of women in small towns.

We moved, and it was gone: the magic, the summer.

Yet I can hear the crickets following me across the field. The images flow over each other, mingling, becoming more important, crisper. The witch stalking crayfish in the pool.

I can taste the sweet flesh of the plums from her tree, and see myself rubbing their downy ripeness on my skirt until they shine like tiny hearts in my hand.

CAMPING OUT

The Road Prowler inched up the last rise, rolling off the paved road into the numbered stall. Sam, a tall balding man, pulled on the emergency brake and climbed out, stretching his legs.

"You wait here," he said, "and I'll scout the grounds for a better site."

He strolled through the park while Ginny ushered the children out of the mobile home and inspected the campsite. There was a nice fire grate and picnic table. The trees were open to the east, so they'd get the early morning sun. West, the flat grey waters of the Pacific began their journey to Japan.

Ginny breathed deep while little Sammy and Virginia tracked a squirrel that had skittered down from a pine to beg for handouts. Ginny sucked in the air again. She needed so much of it, that clear salty wind scented with pine needles.

Sam returned. "There's a whole passle of campsites at the other end," he said, out of breath, "and way over in the north there's a big one, but I like this spot. The nearest camper is fifty feet away, and isolation is what I came for."

It didn't take long to unload the lawn chairs and settle themselves into the site. Ginny cooked lunch on the stove in the Prowler. There was no firewood. A sign said it was sold after five o'clock near the washroom facility.

Dinner finished, they had a glass of whisky while the children explored the forest. "Don't go too far, kids," Sam said, "there might be bears."

The children stopped, eyes wide as they glanced back at the clearing. "Bears?" They were so innocent.

"Sure . . . bears . . . Indians . . . rattlesnakes . . . . We're in the wilds now. They don't call this Fort Defiance for nothing. You've got to be tough to make it here." He winked at Ginny.

Growing suspicious, little Sammy scuffed a piece of moss, but neither he nor his sister wandered out of sight.

The whisky warmed Ginny's stomach, and she grew comfortable. It was good to get out of San Bernardino. She'd been anticipating this trip more than she'd admit to Sam. But she couldn't free her thoughts from the drunk on the Seattle freeway.

He had the thick red face of a man who'd spent too long facing whisky bottles. For some reason, he'd tried to cut across the freeway with a cart full of groceries. The metal cart must have overturned mounting the divider. Ginny watched as Sam pulled the mobile home off the road while the man scurried among the cars to gather the remains of his groceries. A plastic bottle of bleach exploded under a cadillac's tires, the owner of the car waving a fist at the old drunk, but not slowing down.

That's what it is — running to pick up the remains after you've made the wrong decision. She tried to put the man out of her mind.

"I suppose," Sam said, "tomorrow I'll take the Prowler to the garage in Coupeville, and see if they can fix that grinding noise."

"Is it bad?"

He poured himself another drink. "Naww, I think it's a wheel bearing — shouldn't be more than an hour's work."

"Will you take the children?"

"Sure, we can tour the town while the Prowler's getting fixed." He smiled, knowing she was desperate to be alone. He was a thoughtful man.

Later, they explored the campsite, and further. Ginny was surprised to discover how small the grounds were. From Sam's first description she'd expected a massive park.

They found the gun emplacements built during the Second World War. The bunkers were cavernous, buried in the banks overlooking Puget Sound. Cement. Dark tunnels led to the camouflaged slits that used to hold the barrels of the big guns.

Ginny was afraid to enter without a flashlight. The dank, narrow walls. Sam took the kids inside, scaring the hell out of them, telling gory tales of dead war heroes. She was proud of the way he sauntered into the black and foreboding maze, daring the kids to look for the skeletons of lost soldiers.

After they scouted the abandoned base, they returned to the heart of the campgrounds. Most of the people sat in their lawn chairs and contemplated the trees and promenaders on the road. Outside of exploring the ruined bunkers, there didn't seem a lot to do. It struck her as strange that the state would convert useless army bases to campsites, but she supposed it made sense financially. And there was a wonderful poetry in the killing grounds turned to playgrounds, though it didn't seem a very wild wilderness park.

Actually, besides the relics of the base, there'd been a fair amount of work done. Most of the brush was cleaned out beneath the trees, and, she guessed, a lot of trees had been removed. Still, that didn't seem to satisfy all the campers.

On the way back from the bunkers they passed an elderly pair of women, one of them speaking in a brassy southern accent. "I don't understand why they've left so many trees here. They get in the way of the view."

"But dear," her friend said, "I think the trees are supposed to be part of the view."

"You can hardly see the ocean. And it's so claustrophobic."

"That's true. It is kind of scary."

There was a coldness about the place, Ginny thought, but she couldn't figure it out. The designers of the park had certainly put a lot of thought into it. She liked the way they had paved everything to make it convenient, and the many lights would be comforting at night. That way everybody could see what was going on, so there wasn't any danger of axe murders or that sort of thing. It was also clean. She liked that. There weren't piles of toilet paper behind stumps, or newspapers lying alongside the road. And the colour-coördinated display board was very informative about the region. The central complex was a big, cinder-block square, painted yellow, nestled in the center of the park, well-lit, with showers and lots of toilet stalls. No outhouses.

Unfortunately, by the washroom courtyard, Sam was outraged to find the fat boy in the truck wanted six dollars for a tiny bundle of firewood.

He was still grumbling as he lit the fire. "Six dollars for ten pieces of wood. It's robbery."

"I think it's wonderful that they give the contract to the local handicapped society. It's for a good cause."

"Don't get me wrong. I wouldn't knock them, but camping out just to get ripped off by the local retards, it doesn't rub me right. Tomorrow, I'm gonna chop my own tree."

"You can't do that." She was horrified. "It's a government park. They'll throw us out if you get caught."

He fanned the flames with his baseball hat. "I'll go over the hill and cut one. They'll never catch me."

When the stars appeared, Sam explained the constellations to the kids, pointing out the configurations, telling their stories. "And Andromeda, chained to the rock, waited for the sea monster while Perseus rushed to save her, flying through the air with his magic winged sandals."

Ginny had no idea where he learned this. It was hard to imagine him considering the constellations behind his desk, designing advertising campaigns. Yet, he had these secret places, unexpected things he knew.

The darkness grew, and they roasted marshmallows over the fire, conserving the few logs they'd bought, Sam sighing as he threw each one onto the coals. Ginny liked her marshmallows burnt, flaming beyond the fire until extinguished by her breath, so she could suck out the small, sweet core. He cultivated his, roasting them with care, each toasted square rising from the flames immaculate. The kids kept dropping theirs in the ashes.

That night, in the Prowler, she awoke, her legs trembling. They were cuddled under the down quilt, and she wanted him. But the children weren't far away.

He snored softly at her side while she lay motionless. It would be easy to reach down and stroke him. The night was silent, creepily silent without the noises of the city. A perfect night for love. Too bad.

In the morning, after breakfast, he bundled the kids into the vehicle. "Why don't you take the day off, honey. Go to the beach and catch a little sun."

She felt guilty.

Her world flooded. She was too short. Her skin was too white, and her breasts too large. She wanted to squeeze them against her chest. Damn him. He always knew. "That would be nice."

He winked endearingly as he climbed into the driver's seat. "You'll be fine, babe. The world is changing and there's adventures waiting for you out there."

"Thank you," she said, grateful for his understanding.

Her descent began slowly, steering through the high, dead grass of summer. Then it grew steeper, and hidden prickly pears stabbed at her fingers as she groped for a handhold. At last she came to a bluff, eight feet high. She was trapped, and she wondered why she'd been silly enough to try the cliff instead of the long path that led down to the sea.

Above her, the hill now seemed unnaturally steep, and she didn't want to go back through those cacti.

She hesitated at the edge, swinging her body until it built up rhythm; the jump. Her foot caught on a branch. She landed awkwardly, the knee twisted, but somehow her body sorted itself out, her leg hurting at first.

Then she realized she'd lost her shoe, and she cast about in the rocks, looking for it.

She gawked at the shrub in front of her. The dead bush was adorned with both her shoe and her shoulder bag. "How the hell?" It was amusing, the shoe and bag in the branches above her head.

Crawling through the branches and retrieving them wasn't easy. Then she slithered down the short distance bridging the bluff and the beach. The surf thundered louder than voices, and she was alone.

It didn't take long to find a heap of boulders which she could hide behind, and she took off her blouse and pants, revealing the auburn one-piece bathing suit.

The beach rumbled with the roll of the surf. Out in the grey-green sea a few boats, fly specks, trolled for salmon. She studied the near-empty horizon and after some thought, peeled off the bathing suit, hanging it like a flag from a raised fork of driftwood.

Ginny felt wicked, lying on the blanket draped across the rocks, listening to the surf while the sun glazed her skin with heat. It was a good kind of heat, warm, yet not suffocating – a cool wind from the sea.

Her head against a log, she examined her body, the pale whiteness of her skin, unhealthy looking. The small triangle of orange-red hair below her belly seemed unnatural against the pasty skin. *Too long in the suburbs.* She didn't like the contrast, and then there were those breasts that refused to sag even when she lay down, rising like pyramids from her torso.

Angry, she turned onto her belly, and enjoyed the sun striking her buttocks and back, knowing she'd have to be careful with this deceptive breeze and cold burning sunlight. It wouldn't take long to burn. She read from the romance she'd picked up at the drugstore near Breeze Bay, and sipped a beer she'd brought in the shoulder bag.

The steady drone of the surf lulled her, and she turned over again, sleepy, her eyes shut, feeling the sun on her eyelids and nipples – worried they'd burn.

When she opened her eyes, there was a man standing beside the boulder, and her body went rigid with fear.

He leaned against a wooden staff, wearing nothing but cutoffs and sneakers. An Indian, resembling a refugee from a lost civilization, which she supposed, thinking about it, he was.

The Indian was silent, gazing at her. She squinted. He was so dark, silhouetted against the sun; without sunglasses, she couldn't decipher him.

Animals hung from his left arm. Dead animals. They resembled large, furry rats.

Ginny watched him stare at her, realizing how she looked. The orange patch of hair, her spread legs, yet she didn't move.

She closed her eyes, her skull numbed by the surf sound and the pressure of sunlight. It was too late to move. The wicked feeling again, and she enjoyed it, letting her legs untense. There was a noise, faint, the tick of the wooden pole being laid against the boulder.

When she opened her eyes he was taking off his pants. He kicked his sneakers against the rock and stood above her, naked except for his sunglasses, and she wished she hadn't mislaid hers. The sun was too powerful. She closed her eyes again, imagining the lonely glasses on the antiseptic counter of the rest area by the freeway . . . .

Her eyelids squeezed shut, she listened to him kneeling. Something long and fleshy touched her belly. His hands massaged her breasts.

She peeked at the hands, so dark, almost black against her skin as they manipulated her. She tried to look at him but the sun was over his shoulders, and she grinned, letting him see a bit of her tongue as she took his glasses off and put them on herself.

Now she could see him better, admire the smooth unruptured skin and black hair.

Then he was on her, pressing into her belly, and she realized she must have been wet to let him in so easily. A distant plane hummed across the horizon, and she wondered how this would appear from above, the dark line of him against her, while her white legs wrapped around his buttocks, squeezing him closer.

He was so large inside her, and slow, unlike Sam; as if the waves were pushing to get in, the rhythms rising and falling together. She wanted to take it all inside . . . ocean . . . beach . . . man . . . all of it. Yes, it was just like the novel.

When they finished, he lay against her, admiring her, but she couldn't endure his scrutiny, and choked on a sob.

He felt the shudder passing through her body, and stood up, pulling on his dirty cutoffs and sneakers. He picked up his pole and the string of dead animals, and turned away, without a wave, walking down the beach.

Ginny lay motionless for several minutes; then her nervous hand slipped down her belly and felt the stickiness between her legs. A giggle she couldn't suppress. She started to laugh and her eyes went liquid.

She sat up suddenly, and searched the beach. He was gone.

But the evidence lingered. She climbed to her feet and picked her way over the slippery rocks to the surf.

She squatted before the waves, watching them rise and break, pour over the rocks, sand trickling between her toes. The fifth wave, the big one hit, and the water rose, icy. It sent a shock through her body as it touched her thighs and sex, washing the remains of him away.

Pulling herself open, she let the finger of the wave clean the tender skin. It was painful.

Ginny returned to the nest she'd made among the boulders and lay on her belly on the blanket, allowing the sun to soothe her back. She knew if she thought about it, she'd start to cry, so she forced her mind to go blank. The giggle returned. "Think about nothing . . . think about nothing . . . think about the red-faced man on the freeway." There was a stubbornness in his eyes as he counted the remains of the groceries once he'd got the cart off the freeway, even though there wasn't much left. Sam unbuckled his seat belt. She knew he was going to give the derelict money. She shook her head. Sam would have been generous, he always was, but the drunk had that obstinate expression as he added up his battered groceries. He was still alive, proud.

When she awoke, she knew she was burned, though the sun had not moved far. She'd been asleep less than an hour, but she could feel the heat seeping into her shoulders. "Damn!" She sat up, and realized why she'd wakened. A young couple with two children were strolling down the beach, less than a hundred feet away. Ginny pulled her bathing suit off the stick and stuffed herself into it, knowing they'd seen her.

At least the couple had the decency to ignore her embarrassment. They nodded casually as they strolled by. Then she heard the young boy exclaim to his father when they'd passed: "Boy, she sure put her bathing suit on fast." And she couldn't help grinning. It must have appeared funny.

Then she was afraid — what a fool she'd been, thinking none of the campers would descend to the isolated beach. That made her consider the situation. "I cheated on Sam." Oddly, it didn't make any difference, and she realized she was more upset by her foolhardiness than the event. It occurred to her that she might catch a disease, or worse, insects. She refused to think about that anymore.

Remembering the awkwardness of her descent, she decided to walk the few miles down the beach to the trail and take the easy way up the cliff.

But it was further than she'd expected. After more than an hour scrambling over the slippery stones of the beach she still hadn't reached the trail, and was impressed by the couple dragging small children on so long a hike. She began to fret, increasing her pace. Sam and the kids would be at the campsite.

Then the cliff sucked in around the corner, and it made her think of a fat man bent in sleep, the crease a wrinkle in the belly of rock.

There was a government sign, and people.

A man in a uniform was talking to a an elderly couple beside the sign, and they were examining something by the foot of the post. Ginny saw a red object, and ignored the path, joining them.

Two animals. Skinned. They reminded her of an aborted foetus she'd seen once in an educational film.

"How awful," the old woman said.

"What is it?" Ginny asked.

"Skinned muskrats." The ranger studied them for a moment, with obvious disgust. Then he noticed Ginny's eyes were full of questions. "The hides are worth money. It must have been an Indian from the reserve that borders the park. He left them here so I'd find them and know he was trapping in the park. They think they own the place."

Ginny grinned at the last remark, and the ranger grew embarrassed, realizing what she thought. "They might have once, but they don't anymore. And it's time they learned."

On the way up the path, she stopped, out of breath. It was a steep climb. Surrounding her, monstrous trees. This must be the decadent forest that the forestry engineers always talked about when refuting the claims of the environmentalists who wanted to save everything. It was pretty, even though it was obvious there was a lot of wood going to waste. She enjoyed the smell of decaying wood; the lushness of the place, it seeped into the pores of her skin.

Sam was already at the campsite. He watched her climb through the path to the clearing, a curious look on his face.

"Where'd you get those sunglasses?"

She was startled. "I found them on the beach."

"Did you hear that, kids? Treasure. Your mother found treasure on the beach."

Little Sammy and Virginia rushed out of the camper. "Treasure?" Virginia asked. "What kind of treasure?"

"The secret kind," Sam said, "the best kind, and there you are, hiding in the camper when there's a world of treasures waiting for you."

Once again they analyzed him with suspicion.

"Did you see any Indians?" Sam asked.

Ginny shook her head.

"No Indians? Too bad." He glanced at the kids. "But there's Injuns here, I can smell'em. This sure seems like Indian country to me — rattlesnakes — and bears too!"

"There ain't no bears here." Ginny grinned. "You read the notice on the board by the toilets. It said there ain't no bears."

"You don't believe everything you read, do you? I think there's bears here — despite what they say."

"Awww, you're joshing us." Little Sammy pouted.

"Don't believe it then, but don't blame me if you get surprised."

The kids wandered into the camper again, to play the video games on the TV.

"Now don't you run the batteries down," Sam warned.

Ginny sat by the dead fire.

"You got problems, babe?"

Ginny nodded.

"Anything I can do?"

"You're more than I could hope for, Sam. It's me. I've got a few things I have to work out."

Sam leaned back in his lawn chair, surveyed the trees, the blue sky beyond, sipping a glass of whisky. "I understand, babe. You're free."

Once again she was proud of him. He knew so much, and he was so easy to deceive. His most endearing qualities.

"But me, I got a tree to chop down."

"O Sam, you're not going to do it, are you?"

"You betcha. I'm a secret son of the great north woods."

He took the axe from the side compartment of the Prowler. "By the way," he said, "you ain't going to believe this; the flush toilet's jammed." He tested the axe blade with his fingertip. "I've got to go back and get that fixed now. I just had a big crap and the bloody thing wouldn't flush. I think we bought forty thousand dollars worth of scrap metal."

Ginny had a vision of him spending his entire three-week vacation taking the Prowler to garages along the coast.

"The toilet's not important. Why don't we forget it?"

"A machine's gotta work right or it ain't a machine worth having." He had a defiant expression, and she knew there was no point in arguing. "I'll be back in a while — gotta gather the fire."

He trudged along the path leading along the side of the bluff, the same one she'd used to return from the beach. The children poured out of the camper, following.

The next hour was punctuated by the sharp retorts of the echoing axe. Every blow made her anticipate the ranger.

But the campsite ignored the axe. And she was grateful when he reappeared at last, arms full of wood, little Sammy proudly carrying the axe.

"Mom, he cut a big tree down!"

Sam grinned, nonchalant, dumping the load by the grate. "'Twas nothing."

"A live tree?"

"I wanted real wood."

"Your hands?"

He stared at his hands. They were bleeding. And for a moment he looked guilty. "You understand, babe, don't you? Son-of-a-bitch." He squeezed them together, trying to make the pain go away. "Never thought I'd turn into such a pansy. My hands are soft."

Ginny searched out the bandages in the Prowler, and wrapped his hands up.

She cooked dinner on the stove again, because the green wood didn't burn well, even though Sam insisted it was a great fire.

Ginny had to light his cigarettes for him, and pour his whisky — she'd bound his hands so tight. She enjoyed him helpless. And he made it seem funny, a joke.

Then Virginia had to relieve herself. The little girl studied the night, the cold, rising stars, and announced she couldn't make it to the washroom complex.

There was an expression of compressed terror in the child's eyes, and Ginny led her into the shrubs behind the site, pulling her pants down with a practised gesture.

The child squatted beside the salal, studying the bush, as if waiting for danger. Too many of her dad's stories. "I can't now."

Ginny smiled, kneeling at her side, resting her hand on the girl's bare knee. "Yes, you can."

Virginia grunted, reassured by her mother's hand. The small stream jetted to the ground, steaming in the cool air.

Her daughter's face was so earnest, concentrating on the task. Ginny felt a wave of affection, watching the urine splatter to the earth, that white skin — like her own — and the smooth slit between her legs.

Ginny had never cheated before. Sam was the only man she'd known. But it had happened. Suddenly. Unconsciously.

She didn't feel guilty. Now there was a magic between her legs, a secret, one that was her own.

"I'm finished," Virginia announced.

"That's good, dear." Ginny pulled up the girl's trousers, and patted her head. "Let's go back and have some marshmallows."

Sam and Ginny remained by the fire until late, as if there were something they wanted to say, but couldn't. They were too comfortable to break the rapport.

They drank half the bottle of whisky. Then Sam tucked it into the locking compartment of the Prowler. "Don't want the local lads getting tanked on my whisky," he said knowingly. "They cruise the campsites, checking for bottles on the tables."

She recalled the slow cars that had come sliding down the night road, headlights stabbing at the trees. Kids looking for booze. The campsite was an easy place to prey upon people who thought they were alone and safe.

It was cold when Ginny awoke; the down comforter had slipped aside. Her shoulders were hot from the sunburn. Sam lay still, a lump of meat beside her, and she could hear the quiet murmurs the children made in their sleep.

The silence was overwhelming. The world seemed huge around the camper. Camping out always made her feel small in a big world.

There was a moon; the windows on one side of the camper crystalled with a silver pattern, the other side soaked up the blackness.

Why did this always happen in the middle of the night when she went camping? She never had to get up at home. Sliding out of the bed, she dressed. It was difficult finding her clothes even though she was sure she'd laid them aside with care before going to bed. Every move made her swollen bladder uncomfortable, made her think of Virginia huddling in the salal beside the campsite, and she wondered why she hadn't taken the precaution then of relieving herself.

She unlocked the door, and stepped outside. It was a graveyard. Nothing stirred. Her first step found a twig, and the snap frightened her. She laughed. But she was so tiny in this dark world; for a moment she contemplated squatting in the bushes beside the motorhome, like Virginia. That would be an admission of weakness and she refused it.

She should have brought the flashlight, but there were street lamps on the paved road. She surveyed the campsite. It reminded her of a wagon train, the trailers and mobile homes, circled around the brilliant core — the safety of the toilet house with its lights and hot showers.

The washroom complex was lit up like a Christmas tree, the lights humming with electrical noise as she stepped inside. It was empty, cavernous.

When she had finished, she stood in the bright halo of the building and contemplated the road, then the shortcut that led through the bush to the site. Defiantly, she strode down the trodden path into the dark.

It didn't take long to regret it. Away from the bright safety of the road and the washroom complex, she was swallowed in darkness.

She was close to the camper when her regret took on a new note. Terror. The underbrush rustled. She stopped.

Silence.

She stepped forward, quietly, and it resumed. She stopped again. More silence. She couldn't tell where the noise came from, and she rushed down the path blindly. Then she came to an abrupt halt.

The bear was standing in the moonlight, beside the trail, shovelling a branch of huckleberries into its mouth. It froze, jaws dripping berries and juice.

Either it hadn't seen her, or it decided there were more than enough berries for all, because it resumed yarding the branches forward, scraping the berries into its maw. The unconsciousness of the bear made her remember her father trying to describe a sharp-witted friend and getting everything screwed up. "He's got the ears of an owl and the eyes of an elephant." That about described the animal. The bear was ludicrous, erect on its chunky hind legs, mouth dripping — reminding her of the derelict on the freeway, the same stupid expression, only the bear wasn't beaten.

Ginny, almost fondly, watched it stuff itself — as if she'd discovered one of the children doing something cute. Yet it stood giant and black in the night, and it was single-minded about the berries. Then she remembered how dangerous they could be, and she knew she'd become terrified as soon as she retraced the darkness of the trail.

There was no choice. She stepped backwards. The crack of the branch breaking under her foot echoed through the campground.

The bear gave a startled woof, and dived into the bushes, crashing and grunting, and she was surprised at how violently it reacted. It made her feel guilty, disturbing it and the silence of the forest.

Then she was proud. The animal was nothing but a big pussycat. "That was easy." She flexed her arm like a muscle builder, and hustled across the clearing, through the final leg of the trail to the campsite. There, she realized her heart was pounding, and she knew how scared she'd been.

Creeping into the motorhome, she locked the door behind her and undressed, crawling in beside Sam's leaden warmth, shivering.

She knew she wouldn't tell him about it. He'd never believe her. Besides, the best things are always kept to yourselffelt.

The alarm rang, irritatingly, and even as she struggled to awake, Sam hauled his long awkward body out of bed.

"Rise and shine," he cackled. "It's nearly dawn and many miles of adventure are ahead." His blisters, which she'd unwrapped before they went to bed, had dried, and he flexed his fingers.

She grinned sleepily, and sat up, scratching at her hair. Her gown had opened up during the night, and her breasts hung exposed.

Sam winked lewdly at her; then she heard the children stir and she pulled up the blanket. Sam sighed, turning his attention to the stove, which was tricky for him because his hands still hurt.

She sat in bed, watching him, feeling the warm weight of her breasts, thinking how strange it was that he had been the only man to handle them in her entire life, and then she had let a stranger play with them. The memory made her desire Sam. Usually, she wasn't this way. It was the air. It had to be the fresh air coming from the sea. These thoughts made her recall the time Sam bought her the edible underwear, spun from red licorice.

She was too shy to wear them for weeks, but she did at last. Only, that night, Sam dallied downstairs as he locked up the house and shut off the lights. By the time he arrived upstairs, she was uncomfortable. When he climbed into bed she couldn't restrain her giggles. "They melted."

Sam thought it was the funniest thing he'd heard in ages. He told her it was because she was so hot for him. She thought it was cheap licorice.

"We're heading out today," Sam said. "That's why I set the alarm."

"So soon?"

"Yup, I've got it figured out. When we reach Deception Pass, it won't be far to a garage. I can have the toilet fixed easy. Besides, there's salmon fishing, and better swimming. It's not as boring as this place."

"Boring?" She studied him with amazement, repeating the word to herself while he fussed around the stove. How could he ever think this place was dull? "Boring?" She restrained the laughter lurking in her chest. "Boring?"

When they'd finished breakfast, they toured the site, checking for objects left behind. The sun hadn't begun to rise in the trees standing guard above the sea. The morning was a grey promise.

Ginny hated these early mornings, but she knew it was a long drive and they were going to the popular grounds at the peninsula – they had to get there before noon to find a good site.

The campground was hushed, tranquil – a tomb of motor homes and tents. Since there was no fishing at Fort Defiance, none of the campers had reason to rise early except those who were moving on.

Sam eased the Prowler around the narrow curve by the gates, his hands light on the steering wheel because of the blisters. A lone figure stood at the crossroads to the reserve. Ginny recognized him. It was the Indian. The same long stick. And a dead animal hung from his free arm.

"Indians!" Sam shouted, gearing down the Prowler to a crawl. The children woke and peeked out the window from their bed in the back. Sam gave a jaunty wave to the man as they drove past.

The Indian nodded his head slowly, and smiled like a real Indian.

Then he recognized Ginny and stared at her. She squeezed her arms together across her chest, terrified he'd wave, but he remained motionless as the truck idled down the road.

"Well, we've seen an Injun . . . but no bears . . . ."

"And he was holding a dead animal," little Sammy interjected. "What was it?"

Navigating the Prowler around another corner, Sam grew thoughtful. Caught. He didn't know.

"It was a muskrat," Ginny said.

Sam was impressed. "How'd you know it was a muskrat?"

"There are things I know that you don't."

They'd driven less than a mile when Sam pulled off the road. They were at the last section of bluff before the road dipped into the valley. The kids had fallen asleep again. Virginia glanced up sleepily as Sam climbed out of the truck; seeing nothing of interest she fell asleep again. The sun was rising.

Ginny followed Sam as he walked to the edge of the cliff beside the road.

They stood at the bluff while the sun broke over the southern rise, turning the morning and the sea red, briefly glutting the landscape with colour. Sea birds rose in a mass below the cliff and wound into the spectacular clouds like specks of dust into cotton candy.

"Strange," Sam said, holding her shoulder as they watched the sunrise.

"Strange?" She looked up at him.

He gave her an affectionate squeeze, contemplating the silent turbulence of light. "I've got everything I need, and I still want more. Do you know what I mean?"

At first it made her sad. Then she pressed against his body, her chest flattened into his stomach. She loved the smell of him. "Yes. I think I do." Behind her the last spectacular fireworks of the sunrise faded into the almost normal light of day.

CROW AT LONG BEACH

Cool, green, and awesome, the forest above him — everything that makes the world contained within the austerity of the evergreens — the energy concealed behind the motionless fronds of the hemlock . . . the scaly, ripped trunks of the cedar . . . the tall crowns of the fir.

The trail led through the sword ferns to water. He swung the pail at his side, happily thinking about nothing.

If he had eyes like a camera, he could focus on the shadows, drive his vision through the evergreens to the one animal thing, the eye of a crow. The black eye contemplated the man passing beneath it.

The well was clear, an invitation to drink until his ribs hurt with the sweet cold. He found himself facing the smooth stones and moss, unaware of how long he had been there.

He filled the bucket and returned down the trail that led to the beach.

A black thing rushed at his face. Startled, he raised his hand and knocked it away as if it were a leaf. The crow landed on the earth, and shivered.

Crippled, it flapped a wing against the ground, but the sky was denied to the bird.

"Why did you do that?"

It stopped struggling and lay motionless on the dirt. He heard the movement of other wings, the hushed sound of crows converging on the path.

The bird studied him . . . helpless, and its steady gaze made him think of another time, another bird, on the beach at White Rock.

He was walking with his wife. Evening had arrived, that brilliant moment of sunset before the real dark. They found the cormorant in the dunes, the ribbon of its neck stretched across the weeds.

The bird tried to raise its head, coiling and uncoiling its neck. For ten minutes they watched, until he couldn't bear the pain anymore.

He grabbed the bird by the head as if it were one of the geese he slaughtered when he lived on the farm. He swung it around, becoming a human windmill; then snapped his arm and the bird shuddered into extinction.

He picked up the crow, and while it attempted to dig its beak into his palm he slapped it against a tree. The bird didn't die. He hit it again. The thing was still alive, struggling in his hand. He slammed it again and again at the tree. When he stopped, the remains oozed in his palm.

He opened his fingers; the one black eye stared at him, dead and accusing.

In the near trees a crow cawed. He heard wings moving everywhere, but they were invisible. Then he dropped the body and continued down the trail, wiping his hand compulsively on his jeans.

When he reached the beach he saw the packsack on its side by the lean-to, and he started to run, splashing the precious water against his thigh, his toes digging into the fleshy sand. He'd been robbed.

Only the coffee remained intact. At least the birds couldn't open glass jars. He studied the hundred tracks that told him of this pillaging by a flock of crows. They wanted him to eat sea, sand, and air.

"Well, I'm not resourceless," he thought, ignoring the innocent birds preening themselves in the stand of hemlocks above the beach. There were the eggs he had buried in the sand, and inside the lean-to was a bag of sunflower seeds; the doorway was undisturbed.

After he relit the fire he checked inside to make sure they hadn't touched the seeds. Then he set the frying pan down beside the fire and looked for the eggs. He dusted the sand aside until he saw the smooth white sphere of the first one — intact and rising whole from the sand as he brushed it clear; but when he lifted the egg the weight was wrong. It was hollow. There was a small hole drilled near the bottom. Two more eggs were hollow, and the rest were broken. Underneath the shattered shells the sand was sticky.

He sat back on the end of a log and was lost in thought.

***

As soon as he switched off the light he knew this was a mistake. Darkness swells the sensuality. They stood there, alone, bodies in a pit, inhaling the animal smell of each other. She had asked to watch the darkroom work, a chore most professional models showed no interest in. After the morning's session in the studio he had invited her through the door, casually, and turned off the overhead. "We can use the safe light once the negatives are developed," he explained.

Her fingers were cool and dry. He took them, tried to be gentle, unsure of the pressure, so that instead of holding her fingers he seemed to caress them as he touched them to the plastic reels and pointed the film in for her. She wound the roll.

Then he led her to the tank, holding her wrist, and was surprised again by the coolness of the skin. Her touch made him think of beaches and the ribbed stretches of sand washed into patterns by the surf.

For a moment he was inside a dream. There were two rocks on a beach. It was dark at first; until the light fanned over the foreshore as the sun rose and the rocks were distorted by the shadows and the dawn revealed that the rocks were lovers, naked on an empty beach.

He tightened the lid of the tank; then stood too long in the dark. "Where are you?" she said. He could have slipped his hand under the loose blouse, opened her up and joined with her.

"I'm here, beside you." He took her hand again. A mechanical, invisible desire kept pushing him closer, his fingers running over hers even as he heard the footsteps of his wife on the floor above. The children would be home soon.

When he hung the contact sheets to dry he asked her: "Will you let me photograph you naked?"

"No." She laughed, "I only model naked in my bed."

"I didn't say here."

As she was leaving she wrote her address on a sheet of paper. "Come tomorrow night."

Now he was alone, camped on the beach.

Night came. Unimaginable night. No stars shone through the blanket of clouds surrounding the sand and ocean. He curled into his sleeping bag, nude. Nothing seemed to be working right. His head was open and expanding, encompassing the wooden lean-to, the gone stars, his home, his love, all of his love.

He couldn't sleep. Already hunger was pressuring him. On the other side of the driftwood shelter the waves slapped against the beach. Huge. Endless — every wave followed by another wave.

Her cool limbs flowed around him, pale in the darkness. He held her tight, running his hand down her thigh. There was something he had to reach, a glance that hooked him to her belly and made him want to push inside. Then a large shape moved against the lean-to and he stiffened with fright.

The heavy steps thudded against the sand. It was big. It tapped against the wood . . . tick . . . tick . . . tick . . . before it moved away with a queer kind of rustling noise. He lay quiet in the sleeping bag, pretending he was a rock.

The animal pushed at the driftwood, testing its sturdiness the way a dog would test a gate. It shoved harder. The shelter swayed, threatening to break apart. The roof bent down.

Like rubber, it sprang back. The thing was jumping on the key log. The lean-to shuddered, and the wood made a terrible cracking noise that obliterated the sound of the surf.

Inside his elastic life-raft he was afraid to breathe. His hands dug into the sand, clawing for support as the structure whooshed and wheezed and twisted.

Then a flapping wing disturbed the outside air, hurling sand through the cracks between the logs. Quiet descended, and the sound of the surf returned.

He awoke, afraid. He thought he had heard the wings again, but it was morning and he was safe. The sun sent thin rays of light through the driftwood surrounding him, and instead of a house of wood it was a prison barred with light.

He pushed the tarp aside and stuck his head out. His back was sore. His chest ached. The sun reflected on the grey sand, and no clouds wandered across the sky.

The sole evidence was the tracks. Small, delicate prints of a crow where the bird had hopped across the damp sand until it reached the lean-to and evaporated into air.

He crawled out of the shelter, still naked, and scuffed sand over the pathetic tracks. The evergreens were bristling with crows. His stomach was tight and empty, a knotted circle of muscle. It would be so easy to walk back to his car and drive to the nearest grocery store.

But if they wanted him to eat air and rock and ocean, then he would eat air and rock and ocean. He'd live off nothing until he became like the air, like the sky, nothing made of nothing, without enemies or friends. "I'm not afraid of you!"

Several crows took off in hurried flight, winging towards a newly remembered appointment at another place. "And besides, there isn't a crow made that can turn wood into rubber."

They were cold. Yes, even her lips were cold, and her mouth was small. He pressed his tongue against the edge, and through, beyond the teeth, into the depths of her while their faces crushed together.

His tongue passed along the surface of her tongue into the accepting throat, down, into her, filling her œsophagus and voyaging through the twisted linings of her stomach. His tongue swelled up inside her lungs, discovering every cavity of the sweet interior until she was permeated by him.

It felt the insistent beat of her blood within the heart, and the throbbing of her womb which waited for him to enter the door between her legs. He opened his eyes and her face was the sky.

The rocks of the outcrop chewed at his back, yet he didn't move. The pain was a counterpoint to the massaging sun. The sea wind played with his face before it passed into the trees.

Had he spent forever on this ridge overlooking the Pacific? The stone was growing into him. Soon his skin would erupt black and craggy. He glanced down the long stretch of beach and counted seventeen crows.

They were following his tracks, a broken string of birds. Amused, he watched them hop along the winding line of the route he had taken from the shelter in the morning. The calculated tracing of his footsteps in the sand made him think of Texada Island where he lived when he was young.

Often he'd walk from the farm on the High Road to the old couple's house on the Low Road. They kept dairy cattle, and the milk from those pampered cows was always good. The sunlight drummed at his forehead until it throbbed. His hair clung to his skull in rat tails, irritating the flushed skin made tender by sweat and heat.

Near the field he watched the crows gather. Hundreds clustered about a stump. They resembled black lumps of coal flung across the meadow. One crow stood on the stump jabbering and declaiming in harsh crow-language while the others watched, occasionally breaking into a raucous chorus of encouragement. It was a crow convention.

When he got the milk he was so hot he drank both quarts before he was halfway home, lining his mouth with the cream. He loved the cream best, the way it rose to the top of the cold bottle; and the sliding, inviting coolness as the milk flowed down his throat.

For dessert he followed the wild strawberries up the side of the burning road until he reached home empty-handed and happy, stained with cream and strawberries, greeted by the chagrined laughter of his mother.

He was hungry. He inspected the sky, but it didn't look edible. Then he returned his attention to the crows tracing his steps. "Maybe I'll eat crow."

Last dinners. Great dinners. It had to be lamb, the leg braised in the oven and smothered with mint sauce, sitting open on the table in a nest of endives. Beside it a Caesar salad. He carved the lamb, shovelling it onto his plate. Then he scooped the clear green mint jelly onto the meat. He cut a chunk, spread more jelly over its surface, and brought it to his mouth.

"Maybe I'll eat crow."

He climbed off the rocks. One by one the birds flew away as he retraced his footsteps to the driftwood lean-to. It was a long walk and his stomach felt tight with hunger.

The sunflower seeds were outside the tarp, shelled and stacked in a neat pile beside the empty plastic bag. He was stunned. There wasn't a crow in sight, or any tracks around the campsite. His eyes searched the trees; then turned to the surf where the green heads of foam rose and crashed against the shore a hundred yards away. The distant heartbeat filled him with grief.

"When will you come home?"

"When I'm ready. I've got a few things I have to sort out in my head." He felt guilty, throwing his pack into the truck, abandoning her, breaking for the first time the rapport they'd built between them for too many years.

No, he wasn't ready yet. There was something wrong, a stickiness that he had to unstick. He had been married eight years. Was it that long? Yes. And she was as fair to him as he'd been to her. They fitted together like a fist and a glove, like a dream and a nightmare.

He threw the sunflower husks into the embers of the fire. They caught the dying heat and smouldered. Then he heaped a few splintered ends of driftwood over them, hurrying to burn out the shells.

When night came he retired to the shelter he'd built on the first day. The pain in his belly had become a piece of dull, dead wood around which the muscles tightened.

It's easy for a man to tell himself he isn't frightened, but that doesn't drive the fear away. Conscious of his belly and his salt-caked skin made dry and itchy by the ocean spray, he waited, listening to the surf and the rustling, night trees on the hill.

Shortly before dawn he heard a different sound. It took him a while to realize it was his own body shivering against the nylon sleeping bag.

The animal didn't come.

As he climbed the trail, the wind caught the hemlock boughs, a forest of green arms shaking above his head. It was steeper than he remembered. Every step difficult now. The rain during the night had made it slimy.

The mud slithered under his sneakers, and he tried not to glance at the filthy, fly-gathering corpse of the bird, but he couldn't keep his eyes away, and even as he stared at it he thought of stuffing his belly with food.

This time the water was bitter. It hurt his stomach and numbed the lining of his throat. He drank until his bloated gut ached; then he drank more.

"You didn't come"

"I couldn't."

"Will you come tonight?"

"No, not tonight."

"You won't at all, will you?"

"Yes, I will. Now stretch your arm to the left, open your fingers. That's it." He circled her, studying the angles as if his eyes were the camera. He tried to be casual, unaffected. This was business.

There were so many years of repetition behind this, so many models. It was mechanical, despite his being a few feet from her, standing over her as she coiled and uncoiled, a long-necked bird on the divan. It was for the camera — the magazines that filled their pages with stereos and clothing, with dishwashers and night tables. All for money, all for nothing.

"This is becoming a negative experience."

"You're not funny. Turn your head back, let your hair touch the couch. That's not enough." He lifted her chin with his hand. She was so cool to the touch. "Great. Now don't move. Stay like that. Forever."

Long Beach. The summer of 1967. Nothing is moving except the line of waves banging their heads against the endless sand. It's big. It's wild. Very few come here. Very few will come here for at least two more years.

Sitting with his back against a log, he contemplates his hunger. "This beach will change me."

He watches the pile of driftwood across from him. The patterns begin to shift. The wood is moving; the dark comes out, the light goes back. And there's a new buzzing in his ears, a deep, swelling sound.

The gun-metal sky hangs over him, and the air drips with moisture. It's so damp on this beach that it rains inside the skin.

A low winging crow rushes along the beach, two feet above the sand, passing in front before it disappears beyond the rocks. He gets up and follows it like a drunk. "You bastards."

The world is grey, and the incoming tide stammers to a halt within arm's reach. "You bastards." Never mind — he will eat air and stone and ocean.

Cool. Dry. Inviting. His lips traced a passage between the small breasts down to the valley of her belly, towards the legs.

Her eyes were open and watching as she waited for him to continue while the footsteps of his wife made their statement on the floor above them. Her hand spidered down his back, and he wondered what she was thinking as his mouth touched the moist center of her. He wondered what she was. A troubled girl, he'd been told, uneven, always running to her psychoanalyst. Yet there was nothing in those eyes that suggested she needed anyone else to tell her what her life was, or should be.

What was she thinking? Was she unsure if it would ever happen? Did she care?

"Will you come to my house tonight?" The endless, endless refrain.

"I'll come tonight." The endless, endless lie.

But he didn't go. He didn't go. Standing on the rocks, he hurled a stone at the surf. The head of a wave swallowed it, and the stone disappeared.

"I should kiss the sky."

He vaulted off the ledge and walked around the steep point's corner, farther than he had gone before. It was a small bay, walled with high, black stone. The cliffs were harsh rock and impossible to ascend.

The mouth of a cave rose between the forked edges of the bay, overlooking the sea. He sat down and ignored the waves, allowing his body to be lulled by the perpetual roar as the tide moved closer; it touched the rocky point and entered the gap. The time of the ocean had arrived.

Inside the cave it was dark, glistening and damp. He touched the walls, and they resembled flesh — cool and wet. He sat beside a tidal pool, wrapped his arms around his knees and began to cry.

He started shaking — a shiver at the back of the spine that grew stronger as it surged over the empty belly and struggled against his chest. Then it came out — the sobbing, the expansion of pain to the surface of his skin.

The tears rolled down his cheeks to the corner of his mouth. He stuck out his tongue, running it across his upper lip, drinking his own salt agony.

Now he'll never have her.

When the crying stopped he realized the surf was close. And he became aware of the animals. The cave was full of living things. Sea anemones clung to the walls and seemed to drip from the ceiling. Urchins waved their slow, gloomy spines in the corners. It was a cave of life. The rhythm of their moving triggered a reflex, a gear within his brain.

"Now I am inside your womb. It's deep and dark and warm. Marvellous animals live with me here, secret in your secret womb. We move slow if we move at all. We listen to the pulse of your heart; we feed on the darkness.

"It's soft. It's cool, a sweet request; home, and I'm going to stay here forever, deep within your belly, admiring the walls and the glitter of dampness, the waving spines of the mysterious creatures that live with me here in the safety of your belly.

"In the safety of your belly I will never think about my wife. I will think about darkness, the sea-beat of your walls. I will think about glittering things within the obscure life of your belly.

"You make me whole. You make me a cell within your blood where I am contained with the other living cells. You are my home and my safety now, and outside is nothing but crazy chances. We live here, protected by your blood and belly without need to enter or exit, because our tentacles and sticky appendages know their limit. Confine me. Close me up and never let me out."

Somewhere west a crow flew into the sky. It rose higher and higher, thought itself a hawk or an eagle. It climbed into the ragged edge of clouds and was swallowed from sight. The sun poured through the hole in the sky and onto the earth as if searching for a crack in the rocky mantle above the cave.

The parting clouds rippled like old cloth. The sunlight struck the ground and found the crevice that led to the cave, and the feeble strand of light expanded inside, reflecting the damp, crystalline walls.

The ray exploded. Darkness became incredible light. The sea anemones shivered their tentacles and attempted to retreat from the sudden, painful illumination — the watery walls the interior of a crystal with the man at the center.

It was too bright, and he staggered outside, rubbing his eyes — that sharp moment of brilliance and rainbowed animals etched into his brain.

He fell on his knees, and a wave crashed over him. The foam engulfed his head, filling his mouth with the cold salt of the Pacific Ocean.

Soaked, he raised himself and stared.

Now the ocean was dangerous. He looked around. The sheer wall of rock was behind and on both sides. There was only one way out.

He got to his feet and charged into the surface, and was knocked back by another wave. He jumped up again, flailing against the water as he fell forward.

The wave uncoiled over his head, towering, green at the base, foaming at the crown. Then he was underwater and whirling around like a slow, crazy top without solid contact.

The world turned green, cold, and it stretched forever into nothing. It rolled and churned, filled with a steady roar that condensed into a heartbeat.

His heartbeat. He lay on the sand beyond the point, listening to his chest pound. Here the waves were gentler because they weren't confined by the bay. Or because he was safe?

He contemplated the leaden sky for a few minutes. When he moved, liquid gurgled in his belly. It was water, salt water. He was sick to his stomach, but little came out — a long greenish dribble that was strangely fascinating.

When he reached camp he heaped dozens of logs onto the fire so that the flames reached high into the night and bruised the sky. He remained cold. There was ice in his veins.

Dawn. He awoke with a start, sure the animal hadn't come.

He sniffed at the air, inhaling the wind from the beach, trying to fight the fear back. There wasn't a single log on the west side of the driftwood shelter. The plastic rain-cover slapped lamely in the breeze from the ocean.

After he climbed out of the sleeping bag he splashed water from the pail onto his face. The fire smouldered, and he eyed the log-ends jutting from every side. Had he burned the shelter in the night? Or had something come and taken half of it away? Unreal. It was time to go home.

He went for a walk on the beach and discovered mussels in a crevice at the point. With a sudden passion he jerked them out, cutting his hand, and smashed them open — then he gulped down the soft, salty insides. The viscera of the creatures reminded him of a substance he couldn't quite figure out until his mind wandered, and he began thinking of her again, naked, what she looked like undisguised by the advertiser's fashions.

She stepped behind the screen, tossing out the blouse, the pants. It wouldn't take long to slip into the graceful caftan, but those seconds she spent behind the screen were painful.

"I want to see you naked."

She appeared, unclothed, ran her hand along her thighs, her proud little chest thrust forward, and then just as suddenly darted behind the screen. "That's all you get."

"It wasn't enough."

The mussels made him ill as they rebelled against his empty stomach. Fortunately, he had only discovered a few. He wandered back to the campsite and found himself a comfortable place with his head on a log and his feet half-buried in sand.

The sun came through the clouds, and he let his skin soak up the warmth. The moment was becalmed, unreal, permanent, and too short. When he woke up there was a crow seated at his feet, between his outstretched legs.

The bird was quiet, almost loving as it snuggled in the sand, its casual gaze surveying the beach. He remained motionless, and the bird didn't mind him at all.

After a while the crow got up, stretched its wings and walked away, circling the log he rested his head on. It disappeared behind.

He became frightened. The beach was quiet except for the impossible waves which beat their heart rhythm against the sand. He couldn't stand it anymore — he sat up and looked behind the log; the crow was gone.

Now it's night again, the last night. That perfect sky fading under a wash of mist — the rosy star of evening was the last to go, winking out like a fading torch carried across a meadow.

When he tucked himself into the goosedown of the sleeping bag he was afraid. Even the fire illuminating the open side of the lean-to didn't reassure him. Beyond the flickering light lived a planet of darkness.

He waited for the animal to come, but the beach was silent except for the dying fire and the roar of the surf. "Someone should stop the waves, give us a change." He fell asleep. Then he woke up, uncomfortable, hot, nervous.

Very still, pretending he was a dead bird, he remained in the sleeping bag. There was nothing outside but the sea and the night. There wasn't a human being around for miles — no companions in this gloom.

He felt light-bodied, and he was hurting inside. It was his belly, the pain mushrooming from his bones and through his meat. He was changing, the hunger consuming his flesh, eating him from inside out. He moved his wrist. It felt buoyant and odd, distant.

His legs floated against the top of the sleeping bag. "My bones are hollow." His left foot jerked. Grotesque jolts of pain spurted through the nerves. Then the right foot.

He heard a scratching sound. It was his toes pushing against the sleeping bag, the nails growing sharper. Another spasm shook his legs, and they moved back and forth as if they were organic pistons. Every time they moved they changed.

The sleeping bag split open like the belly of a deer being cleaned, and the claws erupted into the open air.

"Don't do this!" he screamed. Then his head twisted, shivered, and distorted.

A certain kind of calm developed in the moon-filled landscape, a calm made more real by the pounding of the sea with its forever noise that finally became no noise.

Against the expanse of sea and stars coming back through the disappearing mist, against the trees and the hollow moon, the shelter was pathetic, a dot on the unrelenting beach — until it exploded. The roof and the remaining side flew into the air, heaving driftwood in every direction.

The black bird of dreams, the big black bird of the night, the real bird stretched first one wing and then the other, slowly, lovingly. It shook its beak at the sand. It flapped its wings, once, twice, awkward at first, before it flew into the unreal darkness.

The house sat on a bluff overlooking Semiahmoo Bay, a relic from a pioneer past, among a forest of evergreen on a large lot. She lived alone within her island of evergreens. The house could only be called an inheritance, a lovely one.

The door opened and three panes of glass shattered with a sound like wind chimes in a high wind. Whispering air blew down the hallway, pushed by the thing scratching across the floor.

At the other end of the house she was asleep behind the French doors that led to the bedroom. The front window overlooked the bay and the ocean lit by the full moon which tonight decided to resemble a sea shell. The other window, the tiny one, was a porthole to the forest of whispering evergreens that sheltered the house.

The douglas firs, clustered together, were like small children in a night playground, whispering. The cedars stood tall and separate, their crowns peering over the others, whispering. shivering in the midnight wind. Whispering. Branch scraped against branch, soothing, almost affectionate. A few dead needles fell to the carpet of green underneath. If one could talk the language of trees, one would think they were talking about a particular thing. A certain sound repeated itself, slipping through the open window. A whisper like a distant caw.

It drifted through the window and over the sleeping figure of the woman in the bed. It disturbed the gauzy curtains on the French doors separating the bedroom from the living room.

Except for the conspiracy of trees the air was muted; life had gone down for the night in order to recover from the wounds of the day. She was motionless, the covers pulled up to her neck, an arm draped over the blanket and reflecting the icy light of the moon which shot a single bolt over the waters of the bay, up the hillside, through the window, across the room, and onto her arm.

The stillness of her sleep and the tranquillized expression on her face suggested she lived a happy life and slept a happy sleep. That was a lie — one suggested by the drugs she took every night to shut her body down, the drugs that brought her close to a state resembling death.

Yet she's far away from her death now. She's young; she's got a heart bursting to make something beautiful in this world if she could only figure out what beautiful was, what beautiful meant, what beautiful did.

The black shape emerged from the confines of the hallway and scraped across the dining room. For a moment his wings hungered to release themselves, and one fanned out, catching a green vase on a table. The vase teetered; then crashed to the floor.

She didn't wake up. She was far away in the dream planet where beautiful is.

The beak of the crow lunged through the French doors, jammed for a moment between two worlds. The doors flew apart, sending glass and splinters of wood everywhere.

Now she struggled to awake, knew it was there — powerful, dark, in her room. Beautiful disappeared. It blew out the window with the wind.

Her arms slammed against the bed and lifted her into the air. Her mouth opened, trying to frame a word, an exclamation that would chase it away and bring beautiful back. She exposed her upper torso, unconsciously returning as sexual prey, her breasts bathed in the uncaring, seashell light.

The woman's senses had rushed off. She remained on the bed, wordless, struggling to comprehend.

The powerful beak enclosed her neck, bore her down onto the bed, twisting her spine, hurting. She reached up and clutched the bony wings. She squirmed like a young, white nestling, a song bird in the beak of the crow. Her throat hurt. She couldn't breathe.

It covered her, beating its wings against the sides of the bed, sending a wind around the bedroom and out the window where beautiful went.

She pounded her fists against his breastbone. It was futile, desperate. The beak released her. She was pounding on flesh. The bird was him. A moment of stillness entered the room. She glared at the tortured photographer. "It's you?"

He ran his fingers through her hair, enclosing her face between his palms. "I love you." Their lips met, and he tasted her mouth.

She was trying to formulate a question, understand what happened to beautiful, but his lips pressed against hers, his tongue entered her mouth, and her hands unconsciously slipped down his back.

"This isn't right. This isn't real," she said as his tongue withdrew. His lips trailed down her neck, transmitting skin messages through her body. She hugged him against her.

"I waited for you. I wanted you." She arched her back. "I thought you'd never come. This isn't real."

"You're beautiful," he said, and for a moment he seemed covered with feathers. Then he hurled the blankets off the bed, and she spread her legs.

At last the morning came, cold and clear. She awoke with the first rays of the sun pouring across the bay and over the windowsill. Startled by the hard light, she sat up, letting the sheet fall to her waist. Then she saw the shattered French doors.

The room was a mess. She fell back. She felt dirty, defiled. She looked down her body's length and analyzed it mechanically — her breasts, nipples erect and sore; her neck, which she couldn't see, hurt; her belly, white and breathing freely. She knew her thighs, hidden by the sheet, were bruised. She lifted the sheet. Yes, they were bruised, but not raw. She felt between her legs where she was most sore. There was no blood. The hair was hard and sticky.

Disgusted, she threw the sheet aside and lay motionless, looking at the sun.

A cluster of images hovered in her brain. She remembered a crow. A man. She remembered wings and arms and claws. The bottom sheet was ripped. Even the mattress was ripped, and the stuffing was coming out. She remembered bending and twisting, holding him in her mouth, and his wings beating at the air.

She crawled out of bed and stumbled into the living room; then into the dining room where she saw the broken vase on the floor. Down the hallway the kitchen door swung back and forth with the morning breeze. Then she noticed she had cut her foot walking out of the bedroom; there was broken glass everywhere.

She shut the back door. The wind ignored her. It blew through the holes. Walking into the bathroom, she left a trail of blood across the rug and the tiled floor. She looked at herself in the mirror.

A loathing welled up in her, a disgust she couldn't place. It wasn't him, the bird, or the strange and evil night. It was the hard day that came now, filling her house with the shattered light of dawn. The morning made her feel a dirtiness that drove her to the shower where she scrubbed her skin until it was raw and red.

Once she had washed, she tidied up the house as best she could. She found a knife on the kitchen counter, and couldn't recall leaving it there the night before. Could she have used it to rip up the bed?

She'd suffered violent dreams before, but never like this. Later, she'd make an appointment with her psychoanalyst, even though she already knew what he'd say about so obvious a dream. And what would he say when she told him it wasn't a dream?

Then she made coffee and moved out to the sundeck. Still naked, she sat on the canvas chair facing the beach, hidden by the protective evergreens from the eyes of her too-wealthy neighbours. The sun sank into her skin and warmed her flesh. The coffee soothed her belly, heating her from the inside out. She was comforted by the reflecting expanse of water; the sun fondled her like a lover. She shut her eyes, absorbing warmth while it moved higher in the sky, and the trees rustled with the inshore breeze.

Everything was so far away, that night, last night. Now only the arms of light seemed real. She was still hurting. Her womb felt sticky, filled, and the sun kneaded her body with its heat. A spasm welled within her belly, caused her to shudder, and she spread her thighs, letting the sun roll over her. Vaguely, she wondered what she'd do if he did come now. She wouldn't open the door. She'd never talk to him again even if he had another job for her. It was crazy, fooling around with a married man. Lots of men wanted her. She could take her pick. The sickness. The sickness of it all . . . .

At Long Beach the sea lions were moving even before the sun rose above the horizon. They slid across the rock; then poured into the water like snakes out of a jar, searching for their morning meat. The sun came up fast, warming the flattened wasteland of beach while those areas shadowed by the rock outcroppings were left in cold and a semblance of darkness.

The sun crept around the last of the rocks, soaking the ribbed sand with light. It discovered the naked back of a body, and massaged him with its warming rays.

He was half-buried. Scattered bits of sand coated his back. His feet had left marks that clawed into the beach. For a long time he did not move. He knew he looked cold, white, defenceless.

He lifted his head; his cheeks were flecked with sand. He propped himself on his elbows. His mind felt remarkably clear. He was sore, but not tired. The chill of the beach was in his bones.

He rolled over and let the sun hammer at his eyelids until green and purple bars of light stabbed his brain. "I raped her. I raped our dreams."

Shakily, he stood up and dusted some of the grit from his body. Then he walked to the water to wash away the remainder of the sand in the icy sea.

After he'd splashed around a bit, he returned to the remains of his camp — shivering convulsively.

Everything here was surreal. His goose-pimpled skin, his ripped sleeping bag, the exhausted fire — it was all far away, dead. The whole last week was dead.

He dried himself and started a new fire. Once the flames rose he burned his sleeping bag; it was useless now. It sent up a cloud of black smoke visible for miles down the beach. Then he made himself coffee — the last from the small jar.

As soon as he was in dry clothes and settled down with his coffee he dealt with the memories. There wasn't much evidence, yet it had happened. He knew it had happened. He glanced down the length of the beach, and there wasn't a crow in sight. Weird birds. He stared into the burning embers, thinking.

A crow walked around the log and sat at his feet, between his legs and the fire. The crow made a nest in the sand and huddled, watching him. They all looked the same, but he suspected it was the one that had sat at his feet before.

He set his coffee on the log and considered the bird. They'd taught him his lesson, alright. He knew he'd never see the woman again, even if she was crazy enough to want him to return.

"I'm sorry I killed your friend, but it was an accident."

The cold black eye ignored him.

The bird stood up and stretched; then darted aloft and onto the log, between him and his cup. For a moment, he wondered if the bird was going to knock over the coffee. "Go ahead," he said, "finish off the job." It eyed the steaming mug balefully, but turned back to him.

The bird brushed its beak against his shirt, almost affectionate for a second; then it hurled itself into the air and flew away, disappearing beyond the cowl of evergreens above the beach.

Picking up his coffee, he took a sip, thinking of the birds, the woman, the return home. There wasn't much left to pack — his guilt and a bit of clothing. The night seemed distant already.

He remembered night-winging in a cloudy sky over the cedars and mountains of the island. Then he was the lone, big bird above the waters of Georgia Strait. He flew low over a party in a pleasure boat, a crazy late-night affair that went dramatically silent as the unfolding shape floated twenty feet above their heads, out of the darkness and into the darkness.

Then he was in the bay, among the trees, striding to the door. He was through the door, through the house, on her.

He shivered even though he wasn't cold. His stomach felt soothed, as if there were food in it. "I think I ate crow." He recalled her small, beautiful breasts and the sweet taste of her mouth, the way she wrapped her delicate legs around his back and pushed against him, his body pressed to her skin — wanting to hold her and love her forever, his black wings beating against the bed.

THE PEACOCK

Silence. Pure silence, broken by the snow crunching under his skis — and the world was white. Pat had forgotten how bright the mountains were in winter. He'd forgotten a lot of things.

He was awkward again, as if he'd returned to being a child. Ten years ago he wouldn't have ended up with the tips of his skis impaled in the snow bank at that last turn. Nor would it have taken him so long to extricate himself. He grinned, glad that no one had seen him. Now he was on the Pine Tree Flats and travel was easier. He used to hate this stretch — it was so boring; today, he was grateful for it.

As he skied along the tracks made by the groomers, he noticed how beautiful the pines were, saddled with snow, and he couldn't remember thinking that before. He'd been too full of energy then, eager to reach the open hills and push his luck on the steep, trackless slopes. Those were the days when, to amuse himself during the boring stretches, he'd talk to the ravens. He had a natural ability to mimic them, and they often answered back. He'd carry on conversations for several minutes with the dark birds.

After he got tired of their conversation he'd cry like a peacock, the lonely call echoing through the forest, surprising the skiers on the other trails. It must have been strange for them, hearing that eerie cry on the slopes, expecting the exotic bird at every corner. That was a long time ago, and he didn't have the nerve to make the call anymore, as if he were embarrassed at himself.

He was. He looked ridiculous. It had been foolish to buy this new ski suit. Pure white. He'd wanted to blend in with the snow. But it was too tight, and his belly stuck out. It accented his fat hips. He thought that purchasing a snug one would make him lose weight faster, and he ignored the unconcealed smile of the salesman who'd recommended something less flashy, not as constricting. The asshole. Pat was not inclined to appreciate salesmen these days.

The hills seemed a good place to start, always lots of loose ski bunnies around; however, he had the sense to know he was in no shape for downhilling so he'd decided to start working out on the cross-country circuits. Besides, it was better exercise. He was astonished at his decline. He'd thought it was just fat, yet now his legs were rubber and his suit was slimy with sweat.

The terrain began to change, more hemlocks, the forest growing thick as he made the slow descent that culminated at the foot of the open hills. His skis glided over the dog tracks on the trail. The woods unnerved him, and he wished he could have talked one or two of his friends into coming; unfortunately, they were all married now. And he didn't want wives or families. He'd never pick up girls travelling with a bunch like that.

The trail opened at the foot of the barren slopes. And he stopped to wipe dry his glasses, fogged with sweat. It was a long way up that first hill, and he wasn't going to enjoy it. He slid forward, his tips digging into snow. The crunch. The ominous silence of the mountains. Beyond the slopes lay the peak of Silver Mountain. He'd always wanted to dare its dangerous runs with the helicopter skiers – a goal to push himself towards. One day. Never again would he let his body decline. "How easily," he said to the empty hill, "we let ourselves go when we think we're safe." We're never safe. Ruth had shown him that.

Halfway up the hill, he stopped again, panting. He might have to sidetrack, but he'd always herringboned here, and he was determined to make it. He was a stubborn man. He felt slimmer already.

The summit at last. The sharp air blew against his cheeks as he descended, until he hooked a tip, and before he could clear the ski, he was tumbling sideways, over and over. He leaped awkwardly to his feet, and fell again. He stood up once more, angry; then embarrassed. He studied the forest at the edge of the barrens, hoping he wasn't being watched. It was empty.

He glared at his crossed skis, and wanted to cry. He was tired, and he would fall more often now. This was as far as he was going to get today.

One more hill. He skated across the flats, conscious of his trembling legs, yet trying to look good in case anyone else was approaching the empty hills.

When he fell again, there was a loud crack, and a report, and as he lay in the snow he wondered if he'd broken anything. Is that the sound of a leg snapping? No, it was too loud. It sounded like gunshot. He lay face up in the drift, grinning. I'm making angels in the snow.

Was it a gun?

He was paralysed.

Am I shot? No, it's just fear. Get up.

He couldn't. If someone had shot him, they wouldn't be able to see his white suit buried in the snow. Now he was grateful he'd bought it.

You're being silly. No one shot at you.

On the other hand, if it was true, only his pink face ringed by the cowl of the suit would be a different colour. And it wouldn't be visible from the forest.

Should I turn? Should I look?

I have to. This is paranoid. Not only have I jellied to fat, I'm a coward.

He moved his face by fractions until he faced the forest. That had to be where the shot came from — if there was a shot.

Nothing. Trees. He was about to get up when he saw the man holding the gun, wearing a black ski suit, leaning against a tree, virtually invisible.

Aww Christ! I've been shot.

Pat wanted to disappear into the snow, snuggle down deeper, but he was growing cold, the sweat turning icy on his skin.

Am I shot?

He lowered his eyelids, examining the suit. No blood. He wasn't hit. He knew he had to look because a friend of his, a Vietnam veteran, told him a man never feels the bullet that connects — he goes into shock as soon as he's hit. He never even hears the gun. It's as if the body, the ears, reject the wounding bullet. Hadn't he heard the shot? That meant he wasn't hit.

What do I do now? There's a maniac with a gun, and I'm alone.

He inched his face around again. The man was still there. The gun was lifted, pointed in Pat's direction.

The man lowered the gun.

Does he think I'm dead? Even with the gun, he wouldn't come out in the open. There must be other skiers around, and they'd see him. I'm safe if I don't move.

The black-suited man continued gazing in Pat's direction.

Where the hell are all the skiers? Usually, these trails are crawling with cross-country fanatics.

The cold ate at his bones.

How long can I remain here? I'm trapped.

The fear turned to anger. It was Ruth. She'd got him stuck here by running off with that sleazy stereo pusher. Safe? He whimpered. There's no safety. Your woman can run off. Your car can take you over the cliff. There's always a maniac with a gun.

I'm not safe. I'm going to die. The man will ski out here and shoot me. Or worse, he might see my stupid, flushed pink face from the trees.

Pat imagined the silent shot. The fatal one. The terrifying invisible bullet puncturing his forehead, skin, bone, scrambling everything and leaving a mess of brains and blood in the snow behind his body.

I just wanted to look good and meet women.

A man can't live alone. A warm bed. Another body to fondle, listen to your troubles, comfort you, look up to you.

What an asshole I am. No wonder Ruth left. She didn't run away, I drove her away. I became fat and sloppy because I thought I was safe. I never cared about what she was doing — I listened to the television more than her.

The enormity of the last ten years overwhelmed him.

I'm a monster. Shoot me.

The black devil was watching.

Go away and I'll be good.

Never again.

Frostbite soon. His hands were numb in their gloves. That death in the bush might remain there until Pat became too cold to move; then he'd be a real angel in the snow.

How long do I wait?

As long as necessary.

Will he go away and then kill me when I return through the flats?

He might.

When will it be safe?

Never.

Am I going to die today?

Yes.

Cold. Bone-biting cold. Flesh-freezing cold. He sobbed, and hoped that his shaking belly didn't show.

Then he heard a sound, distant, scary. An animal howling. A wolf. He'd never heard one before, except in films, yet he recognized it immediately. The films hadn't captured the thrill of that wail, the iciness that travelled through his veins. Wolves now. What next? He imagined a pack of them coming over the rise and ripping him apart.

Wolves? What if the gunman had shot at them and not me? He began the slow shift that would take his gaze back to the trees again. He'd had enough of staring at the blue, endless sky. The man was there, leaning against the pine, watching.

A terrible embarrassment overcame Pat.

How could I possibly get up now? If the man hadn't seen me and shot at one of the wolves, what would he say when he saw a fat man stand up, shivering in the snow? I could never look at myself in the mirror again without recollecting his astonished laughter.

Pat remembered the dog tracks on the ski trail. They weren't dog. They were wolf. The gunman must be a ranger, hunting the wolves so they won't attack skiers. A rogue pack that drifted too close to civilization.

The gunman stayed where he was, and Pat's heart began to sink. If he was hunting them, their voices diminishing, he'd be moving across the hills. The only way for Pat to know for sure was to stand up and offer his belly as a target. If the bullet didn't smack into his flesh he'd know he was right. If it did, it wouldn't matter.

Great choice.

There was nothing to do but stay in the snow, die in the snow. A human icicle loving cold, embracing it, smothered in a white variety of death.

Then he heard the sirens, mechanical whining voices beckoning him home, and his heart raced. Their sweet whine flooded his brain with ideas.

Sing, sisters, and drive away my enemies. Find me and take me home.

The whine of the sirens grew louder, backed by a whup-whup sound he thought he'd never be so grateful to hear.

I could be going helicopter skiing yet.

It was far away, yet it was closing. It would cross the hills to reach Silver Mountain.

This was his chance. He'd have to stand up and wave. They'd be coming in low, and they'd see him. The gunman wouldn't dare shoot if he was hunting humans. Unless he shot the copter too — that would be dangerous, taking down a helicopter full of skiers.

Gawwd, what if the man shot at them? Would I be the one that lured them to their deaths? Bait.

Am I dangling on a hook?

I'm a worm.

Come over the rise and look at me. The white worm.

It was getting closer, fast. One hill away. His heart was pounding so loud he was afraid the gunman would hear it.

Now! Make your move.

Pat sprang to his feet; his skis snagged and he tumbled forward. He scrambled upright again, waving his arms, skis sliding in all directions as he attempted balance. The machine howled over the rise, veered and ascended the mountain while he stood there, helplessly waving his arms. They hadn't seen him.

His hands fell to his thighs. He felt naked. Doomed.

Where's the bullet? I'm set up. A target.

There wasn't any bullet. Slowly, he turned to face the pines.

The gunman was gone. Pat wondered if he'd just receded into the trees, made wary by the helicopter.

Nothing.

Pat picked up his ski poles, still expecting the bullet.

Nothing.

He climbed the rise, sidestepping this time. He didn't care how he looked. There was a bullet waiting for him.

Nothing.

Then down the slope. A miracle. No falling. He sped across the flat between the first hill and the second hill, and he fell twice, when it should have been easy. Everything was confused. There was no black gunman in the trees, not yet.

No bullet. Nothing.

Up the last hill, sweat fogging his glasses. When he was on the crest, he couldn't remember climbing it. Telemarking, he took the slope like a professional. He knew he looked good, was proud, even as he awaited the bullet between his shoulder blades. Nothing.

He collided with the first tree beside the Pine Flats Trail. Fool. Wasting time. He was up almost before he was down — as if the collision were a foregone conclusion, and he was already planning his recovery before he hit.

He heard a branch break, and he stiffened, pretending he was a tree, yet knowing he was a target. The gunman? The wolves circled back? Neither. Too much snow on a limb. He raced down the narrow trail, looking for a home he'd never believed in before, followed by the nightmare wolves of his imagination.

Every yellow pine concealed a death. Every snow-shrouded clump. The silence of the flats was louder than gunfire. He'd never seen so much threat, never realized the caw of a raven could possess such terror. The worst of it was that nothing happened, so the threat increased as he traversed the gentle trail.

Figures in red glided around a corner, and he choked on his terror. But they were red, and they weren't wolves; a young couple slid past the curve. They didn't speak as they passed him. Yet he knew what he looked like, sweating, red-faced, fat. And they couldn't contain their laughter a few yards down the trail as they sped out of sight.

He stopped. Christ! He should have warned them. There was danger beyond here. Wolves or a gunman. If he was a decent man he'd turn around. He turned around. He should follow them, call them back to the safety of the lodge. Still, they had laughed at him. And they'd laugh to watch him struggle after them. He turned again. And for the first time since the shot, calm invaded his system.

I've had my test. Let them have theirs.

That's when he realized he was close to safety, the lodge. He was going to make it. He slowed. There was danger behind every tree, but now it was in his mind and not his blood. There was a buffer between him and that weird death beyond Pine Flats, the young lovers in their matched red suits.

Evil. He was more evil than a maniac hunting humans. How could he think of them as a shield? The lovers were entering the danger zone as he was leaving it. He heard cars skidding up the road to the lodge. And what about the couple? They were gone.

If they die, I will be responsible. My terror, my fear killed them. Yet they laughed at me. They were pretty and they laughed at me, and if I read in the papers that strange deaths occurred on this mountain, I will be responsible. Can I live with that?

Yes.

His pushes with the poles were slower now. The sound from the lodge grew louder, and he remembered a story his father had told him. His parents were living at the bay on the east coast of Vancouver Island, their house overlooking the beach.

The eagle came down like an arrow among the gulls, pierced one, and ripped its neck open. The flock scattered, fluttering a few feet into the air. Once the birds saw the eagle had its victim, they settled down again. In a few minutes they were picking at the sea worms too plentiful to ignore, while the eagle, a king on a rock, calm, arrogant, plucked the feathers from the gull it had killed.

Pat's father could never understand those gulls that ate at the feet of the eagle plucking their brother.

Pat could. It was easy. He'd just become another gull.

There were no shots. There were no wolves. He slid over the last hump onto the road, and was back in a snowy world of wonder. He sucked in his stomach and pulled off his skis, hefting them over his shoulder, strolling up the side of the road to join the growing crowd that approached the lodge.

Then a mug of mulled wine on the upper deck among the excited, red-cheeked skiers. Ski bunnies. Those large girls who'd stuffed themselves with too much hormone-injected chicken for years and developed so soon.

They never had bodies like that when he was a kid. It had to be the chicken.

He'd survive alright up here. All he had to do was lose the paunch. Work, yes, but he'd worked before. He'd lose it. The hot wine went to his head, and it was more than an hour before he staggered out to his car, exhilarated, leering at the well-built little chickens. And he knew that when he returned, and he would return, the hills would echo with the cries of the peacock.

He remembered his friend, the Vietnam veteran, in the Legion bar downtown, discussing the war. "Once you've been shot at, your life is easy. Nothing else seems significant."

Everyone should be a target, at least once in their lives, and it'd be a hot day in hell before he'd tell the police about this. The black gunman would be his gift to the world.

ALIEN NEAR THE STREAM

Summer had passed like a rainstorm that washes a landscape clean, yet Collin felt dirty. It had missed him, and now he wanted everything before winter.

They led the horses up the rubble of the trail into alpine country, abandoning the last pine ridge, and further below, the brilliant orange of tamaracks breaking into fall colour.

A cinnamon marmot, fat and pompous on a boulder, whistled at the horsemen's arrival, like a voyeur admiring the juicy hindquarters of the horses. A cluster of heads popped out from the rocks and the family surveyed the intruders. Deciding the men were headed in the right direction, away, they resumed their play in the avalanche zone among the burning scarlet of the kinnikinnicks.

Hank stopped and rolled himself another cigarette.

Collin held up his horse, contemplating the older man and the marmots beyond him. Hank played his part to the hilt. Skinny and grey-haired, his face seamed by mountain winds, he was worth his pay just to watch him perform, as if he knew all the cliches, and cultivated them. His eyes showed that he'd seen horses break their legs in godforsaken places, that he'd nearly filled his pants more than once — surprised by a sudden grizzly, or sliding on a slope that plummeted to nowhere.

Collin had always wanted to believe the tall tales of mountain men finding God beyond the next ridge.

Every so often, Hank would direct his attention to interesting displays, a cluster of shaggy manes, a tree where a grizzly had sharpened its claws, late-blooming gentians on what appeared to be a dirtless rock face, as if it were his duty to give nature lessons as well as hunt sheep.

When Collin won the wild game lottery, he was more excited than if he'd won money. For years he had entered, never thinking his fortune would appear. Then, his name drawn, he became one of the twenty allowed to hunt sheep in the Howling Range.

The chance to return to the town he'd left behind and find the man he remembered from his childhood — the silent, reclusive farmer who could track everything. The idea of the hunt had come when he'd heard from his parents that the farm had become unprofitable and Hank had taken to guiding strangers into what was once his private landscape.

Hank, like most of the local guides, was suspicious, fussy about who hired him, and he asked Collin if he'd hunted high country before and where — what he'd bagged. Collin didn't lie much.

Collin didn't tell him how he danced with a shotgun pointed at his face when he was nineteen, but he did recount the time the dead mallard shot off his finger, the limp head hanging out of the back of his mackinaw where he'd stuffed the bird. He'd hooked a twig from the blind in the barrel, and when he flicked it away, the jerking motion caught the beak on the trigger of the supposedly pumped out twelve-gauge. He didn't hear the gun fire, but he noticed the powder stains on his hand, and the stump of his finger that resembled a piece of chicken-bone. He couldn't find the finger, lost in the sunny potato field, where, no doubt, later on, a duck would discover a tasty morsel.

"Just what I always say," Hank laughed. "There ain't no such thing as an empty gun."

Reciting this mishap for some reason made him acceptable to Hank, and they set up their schedule. Real hunters seem to enjoy their misadventures more than their successes. Collin didn't tell him about his last hunt, ten years ago.

They mounted the horses at the top of the rise, the plateau stretching before them under the metallic sky. A few hours' ride, and they'd make camp beneath the scree where the plateau dipped back into the timberline. Hank said there was a good stream flowing down the divide. Clear cold water that made the teeth sing.

The horses climbed through a narrow gully near the end of the plateau. The sun hung above the scraggly pines by the timberline, growing bigger as it approached the day's close.

The whisky jacks, feathered beggars, followed Collin relentlessly. He had a package of crackers in his saddlebag and fed them from the horse, the brazen birds landing on its head before jumping into his hand, taking the piece of cracker, and flying away. Hank had spent enough years in the mountains to ignore the birds, and they ignored him, but they knew a victim when they saw Collin.

The men halted, before the rising plateau behind them cut off the view. Here, they could see hundreds of miles in each direction. South, the Cloud Range led to the U.S. And north, there was a big valley, beyond the frosty skull of Anarchist Mountain. A few elk grazed west on the plateau. So far, Collin had not seen any of the rams that made this region famous. There'd been a small herd of sheep on the first day, but the young rams barely had a curl on their horns and when he pointed at them, Hank smiled.

"I leave those sheep for the Americans intrepid enough to hike a day from their cars. They think they're doing good when they bag one of those; that way they leave the real sheep for us."

Another fifty feet down the last gully, Hank stopped again. His horse became motionless, as if it knew what was going to happen. "What's the date?" he whispered over his shoulder.

"September the fourth." Collin answered too loudly, and Hank shushed him as he pulled a slingshot from his rear pocket.

"That means we're legal." Hank inserted a ball bearing into the sling and pulled it back. Collin followed the line of his sight. A ruffed grouse sat on a boulder, nearly invisible against the mottled stone.

Hank released the rubber. The metal ball whistled through the air, knocking the grouse off the rock. "Fool hens are too stupid to waste a bullet on." He dismounted and picked up the dead grouse, and stuffed it into his saddlebag.

Collin was sure the old man put on the same show for every new hunter he took into the mountains, but said nothing. It was a good show.

"Where'd you get that slingshot?"

"Made it fifty years ago, when I was a young chicken. Had to replace the rubber a few times, but it comes in handy."

Beyond the ridge, near the treeline again, they found the stream and Hank set up camp on a bluff two hundred feet away.

"How come we're pitching our tent so far from the water?"

"Getting too old to feed the blackflies." Hank lit a fire and began another impromptu dinner that would make a French cook evil with envy. "Besides, I like the view."

There was a sudden flutter in his saddlebag. Hank looked up with displeasure and walked over to the nervous horse. He pulled out the revived grouse and snapped it against the air. It sagged in his hand. "Damned birds are too dumb to die even when they're dead."

The men stared at each other. For the second time since they'd met, there was an uneasiness between them. And Collin recalled when Hank threw that first casual diamond hitch over the pack-horse, displaying his skill while Collin made a point of ignoring it. Hank had frowned. No doubt, twenty years ago he'd have unpacked the horse and said: "Shite, I'm not taking out a chechako with something to prove. Don't want to get shot in the back." But times had changed.

After dinner, Hank made a point of gathering the grub into a sack, then enveloping the sack in a plastic garbage bag to hold off sneaky rains. He threw a neat loop over the overhanging limb of an old lodgepole pine by the stream, and pulled up the sack above the deep water, beyond the reach of even the most intrepid bear. Very mechanical and efficient, smooth — the way a man would wipe his ass in the bush. He was doing his best to keep up his side of the show.

There was nothing left to do but stretch out beside the fire and talk. Collin didn't know how to tell him he had a bottle of whisky tucked into his saddlebag. Collin knew the guide was a man who thought whisky had its place, and it wasn't in the bush. For the first two nights, he'd left it there, but tonight he had to pull it.

Hank watched as he slipped the bottle from the leather and settled it beside the fire while the slow sun cracked on the horizon.

"Seen a few hunters miss their shots, hung over with that stuff." He rolled himself another cigarette, his big concession to addiction — the tobacco, the rolling, the forever relighting of the stub. Collin shrugged.

"And I seen a few high on the stuff, belly-shooting a moose and me tracking it through the willows while they polished off their bottle."

"There's only one bottle, Hank, and we're going to finish it tonight."

"I wouldn't have let you bring it if I'd known." He was weakening.

"It's Glenfiddich, and we're going to drink it tonight."

"Glenfiddich? The expensive stuff?"

Resting his head on the saddle, Collin nodded, ignoring the bottle by the fire.

The guide studied the first stars for a while as he sucked on his cigarette. "Well, I guess we'd best get busy. We got a good day ahead of us tomorrow. "

The mountain's silence was broken by the snap a cap makes when the bottle opens. Collin poured a small one.

They gulped it down quickly, savouring its smooth warmth while the stars grew brighter overhead. The whisky jacks had disappeared into the surrounding trees where they planned their dawn attack.

Hank contemplated his empty tin mug. "Are we going to admire that bottle, or drink it?"

The younger man poured a larger shot into Hank's mug, and into his own, thinking, "Here we go."

"You're not the ordinary city kid?"

"Do I act like one?"

"Nope. It seems to me the country has gone to the city."

The cups were empty already. Collin filled them halfway to the brim.

"What are you going to show me, Hank?"

The hunter was thoughtful for a bit. "There's a ram over the next ridge. A day away. I've been watching him. He must be forty-nine on the curl."

That wasn't what he wanted to hear. Collin had done his reading, and he knew the world's record was fifty and an eighth. He didn't reply, but was disdainful of the boasting.

"Sure, that's the whisky talking, and you're not here for whisky talk, are you? Pour me another."

The bottle was half-gone.

Collin sloshed a quantity into the wobbling mug, and then more into his own.

"Alright, tell me your story."

Collin knew what Hank meant; he'd wanted to tell him about the hunt since they started out. It was hard.

Ten years ago. A still-hunt with his father.

His father had left him for his own spot while he sat in the clearing, a jumble of burnt wood overgrown with young alders. It was on Vancouver Island. They were looking for the small blacktail deer, a better meat than could be found in any store.

He sat so long he began to listen to the caterpillars dining on green shoots. A bee flying overhead terrified him. The nearby forest carried the silence only the marsh coast can create, made more real by a sudden bird's flight or a rotten branch falling.

Collin's hearing had become confused by the hours of listening; he thought it was a man approaching. A deer couldn't make that much noise.

The deer poked its head around a cedar. Collin pointed the .275 Savage. The head appeared on the other side of the cedar.

Immobile, he waited for the browsing animal to approach, but it fed behind the tree, often popping its head out to study the clearing. Collin was so motionless he was invisible, and the wind ran right.

It was a variety of Egyptian dance, the head sticking out from one side of the wide trunk – then the other – and he wondered at the limber-necked animal. He couldn't manoeuvre the barrel fast enough to catch it when it appeared. He set his sights on the tree's left edge, deciding the next time the little deer stuck out its head, he'd fire.

The head   the perfect gentle silhouette. He pulled the trigger and the gun kicked. The brush crackled as the animal stumbled away. It wasn't a clean shot. He ran after the deer, snapping the lever up and pumping another bullet into the chamber.

The deer crashed through the brush while he followed, whipping his face with branches until he arrived, breathless, beside its fallen body. The tiny thing convulsed and lay still on the moss and branches.

It was a fawn. Blood oozed from the wound in its neck. He was horrified. How the hell? Then he recalled the Egyptian movements behind the tree. It wasn't one deer, but two — a doe and her fawn, and he had been so wired he hadn't noticed the difference.

He'd passed his twenty-fifth birthday that spring, and he'd lived on his own for seven years, but the first thing he did when he saw the fawn shudder into stillness was cry. Then he ran to get his father in the next clearing.

The old man had heard the shot and was already scrambling through the bush towards him. They met in the clearing where he'd waited out the hot afternoon.

"I shot a fawn."

"For chrissakes!"

"I didn't know it was a fawn!" He'd become a child again. He needed a father to tell him what to do.

"You don't shoot what you can't identify."

It was the wrong answer. He felt even more abject. Now he was a fool in his father's eyes.

The old man saw the tears streaming down his face. "Where is it?" He turned into a father again, taking on the weight. "We won't waste the meat."

But when Collin showed him the spot, the fawn was gone.

"It was here. It fell here."

"You've lost it."

"No, it fell here, and it was dead." There was no sign of blood on the littered forest floor.

His father couldn't hide the disgust that travelled across his face.

They searched for hours, but never found the body of the fawn.

Hank threw another chunk of wood on the fire and lay back against his saddle, thinking about this for a while. Behind him, the ghostly silhouettes of the hobbled horses browsed on the ridge. "You ain't hunting for ram, son; you're hunting for God."

Collin laughed. "I wouldn't ask you to guide me there, Hank." Collin thought about everything for a minute. "But I couldn't leave it. I had to come back."

Hank nodded, his cowboy hat dipping solemnly. "That I can understand. When you get burned, you have to go back to the fire."

"Not the fire. I want to go back to the river."

Hank was disgusted. "Sounds like poetry to me. You can't go back to what wasn't there."

Collin went silent, embarrassed.

"That's enough bullshit. Pass the whisky and tell me a good story this time."

Collin hated himself for wasting the alcohol, but he knew he'd run awry, so he entertained the hunter with a few tales he'd gathered from the times he'd spent in the woods. He told him about a grizzly hitting the wires on a tent in the middle of the night, and flying into a frenzy of scuffed dirt and wires and stars.

Then he told him about his uncle, saddling up his first horse in the high country, kneeing it in the gut so it'd suck its belly in tight for the cinch. The horse turned around and almost bit his ear off. Hank liked that one.

The bottle was gone and a lot of stars had bedded down beneath the horizon when they crawled into the tent. The horses were asleep on their feet, and the night was as silent as a stone.

The whisky whirled Collin around a little, but he was soon settled, and for the first time, wasn't irritated by Hank's soft snore. Then the dizziness returned, and he had trouble deciding if he was awake or asleep.

After a while, he realized they were not alone in the tent. There was something with them, at the foot of his sleeping bag.

It waddled forward, displaying the green sheen of feathers around its neck before it nudged the flap aside and left the tent.

Collin was motionless for several minutes. Finally, he couldn't stay in his bag any longer.

Outside the tent, the sun seared the stubble field. The mallard lifted its beak, pompously, and trooped through the dead stems. There were round things — blistered, odd lumps scattered on the ground. Potatoes.

The duck ignored the potatoes. It was chasing a white slug in the stubble. Collin's finger. The duck caught up to the finger, picked it off the ground, and swallowed it. The bird glared defiantly at Collin. Then he saw it wasn't a duck; it was a busted-up, giant potato on the ground that, oddly, had the same shape. The potato had been shot.

When he blew his finger off, he didn't hear the sound of the gun, the shock was on him so fast. Then he noticed the powder burn, the broken chicken-bone at the end of his hand. He held his finger above his head, and the blood gushed less. Walking across that potato field was the most intense moment in his life — in shock — drunk on the spurting blood and the blue sky. He found his father, smoking a cigarette on the other side of the dyke, and said: "Take me to the hospital. I've shot myself."

"You didn't."

Collin held the hand out and the stream of blood squirted into the air.

The protection system called shock ebbed from his body and the stark, ecstatic world of the potato field turned into pale skin, blood loss, nausea. He was dry retching when they stumbled through the halls of the emergency ward, followed by the receptionist intent on learning his birth date and medical number, while his father argued with the nurse, until the doctor flung him onto a stretcher and shot him full of Demerol.

The needle changed everything, made it good again.

Collin watched the surgical clippers trim the bone — the doctor pulling the flap of skin over it, sealing the wound with stitches. Collin's father stalked the nurse, accusing her of callousness and stupidity.

"It doesn't matter much that you never retrieved the finger," the doctor said. "I never could have sewn this mess back together."

"I looked for it. I couldn't find it."

"The ducks will have their revenge, probably eat what's left of it."

Collin was so high on Demerol he spent the night playing poker with his family, trying to assure his father that nothing had changed while the old man contemplated the bandaged hand dealing out the lucky cards. "I'll never take you hunting again."

Something clicked and he was aware of the nervous whimpers of the horses in the meadow. The night was cool, eerie, silent except for the rushing stream. He peeked out of the tent, but could see nothing. Hank continued his snoring, enjoying the after-effects of the Scotch.

The silhouettes of the horses shuddered on the rise. They were afraid. Down below, by the stream, there was a clatter. His heart froze.

He nudged Hank and the whispering breaths stopped. Collin could feel the vibrations as the man's hand slithered out of his sleeping bag and clamped onto the rifle.

"There's something out there."

In the dark, his bright blue eyes lit up, reflecting the moonlight through the flap, and Collin could see he was suspicious.

"Listen."

They sat in silence while the moon played tag with a few scattered clouds, silvering the landscape. He could tell Hank was ready to return to sleep, thinking this was just another skittish city kid after all. Then they both heard the splashing in the stream.

Hank rolled around, leaning out of the tent.

For a moment, Collin felt helpless behind him. They were thinking of bears. Even the most hardened guide is squeamish of being caught in his tent by a curious grizzly.

One of the horses neighed and stepped behind the bluff.

Something glinted down by the stream. "What's that?" Collin pointed at the shining object.

Hank squinted, trying to follow the line of the finger, still fighting off the scotch.

The light again; there was something there, something unusual. Collin thought of spaceships. Men in glittering suits. The reflected moonlight wasn't natural. It was creepy. The men stared at the gleaming alien near the stream.

"There's one sure way to find out."

The rifle shot crackled through the empty air, and there was a crash, the sound of an object falling into running water.

"Son-of-a-bitch." Hank gazed at him in horror; then looked away. The gleaming thing by the stream was gone. "That's the first time I ever fired at anything I didn't know."

He climbed to his feet, suddenly old and tired. The too-much-whisky expression fled from his face. "We'd best see what damage I've done."

Collin crawled out of the tent and pulled on his pants and boots. He found the flashlight where he'd left it on the other side of the dead fire. If he'd brought it into the tent he might have saved a lot of trouble.

Not far from the stream, they encountered the first tracks, small with long claws. He shone the flashlight as Hank stretched a hand beside it in the mud, his white hand and white face in the piercing light. "Wolverine, a little guy, a cub; enough to make the horses spook."

"Is that what you shot?"

"Wolverines don't shine in the night."

He pointed downstream, and Collin realized why the man was so depressed. His flashlight played on the tree and the empty rope dangling above the black, rushing water. Their food was gone. "It was the moonshine reflecting on the garbage bag!"

"If the boys in town hear about this, I'll never live it down."

The beam fixed on the broken rope, a piece of garbage bag fluttering at the end. "You shot it through the knot." He was impressed.

Hank grinned. "Not bad for a quick shot in the dark."

Collin ran the light along the banks; there was nothing. The deep, ominous water had taken all of it. "What are we going to do now?"

"Go back to bed and sleep."

When Collin woke in the morning, his mouth felt like an ashtray, and he was dehydrated. Hank didn't seem much better. They got up without a word and walked down to the water to wash up and check out the damage. There was nothing at first. Then a few feet from the lost cache, Hank spotted something white like a dead slug draped across a rock. It was a strip of bacon, floated free from the can he'd opened yesterday morning.

The guide picked it up and washed it off. "I surely do love my bacon in the morning."

The whisky jacks appeared even as the old man lit the fire, and that made Collin remember the crackers left in his saddlebag.

Hank found the tea he kept for short stops when he didn't feel like unhitching the food from the packhorse.

Collin felt guilty waving the whisky jacks away, but they weren't going to get more treats from him. A few remained, searching around the fire for unburnt bones from the grouse eaten last night. There was nothing with meat on it, and they soon disappeared. "What'll we do now?" he asked as Hank dropped the lonely strip of bacon into the skillet.

"Don't worry, I'll share it with you."

Hank turned the bacon over, admiring it. "After breakfast, we can go back if you like. I'll hunt up some meat and there's a few greens around, berries and wild onions, shaggy manes. We'll be hungry, but it won't do us harm."

"Or?"

"The sheep are a day away. We can still hunt if you're willing to tighten your belt."

"We'll hunt."

"That's what I wanted to hear. There's wild onions by the stream. We'll collect them on the way back. Otherwise we'll be farting so bad no self-respecting sheep would let us in shooting range."

One of the whisky jacks fluttered down and landed beside the fire. Before either man could move, the bird hopped into the frying pan, grabbed the strip of bacon, and flew off.

Collin was stunned.

Hank watched it fly away, the bacon hanging from its beak. "These mountains, they never forgive an amateur."

After they finished their breakfast of crackers and tea, Hank climbed the ridge, and stood there for a long time, surveying the country with his binoculars. Collin remained at camp, smoking cigarettes and thinking, strangely giddy, as if he were still drunk.

When the old man returned, he made another pot of tea. "Well, our luck's on the up and up. They've moved in. We're a few hours of hard climbing away from that ram I was telling you about. We'll have mutton for dinner."

At the ridge, he pointed out a sheltered ledge where they could crawl upwind of the sheep. Far below, the animals were almost invisible in the rocks. Hank wasn't joking when he said hard climbing.

"Once we reach the ledge, we'll have to sit and check out the thermals. The wind gets tricky when you're high up; if they get a whiff they'll be gone. And keep low, they can damned near see through rock."

They climbed across the hot morning, stopping, full of sweat at the end of the ledge. The sheep were close now, but out of range of the .275. Collin didn't see a big ram.

As if reading his mind, Hank said: "He's behind that rock. You'll spot him once we get around the rubble on the bluff." He pointed to a small pile of broken stones at the next crest, and Collin wondered how he figured they were going to get up there.

"It's belly work now." The old man inspected him for a moment. "But you're lucky. See that thistledown — the way it blows across the slope on the thermal, away from them. They won't smell us."

Collin nodded, but he couldn't see anything floating in the wind. And he had good eyes. He suspected he was getting the great hunter routine again.

It was a hard climb, trying to keep low all the time. At last, Collin peered over the rubble and saw the ram standing sentry, its horns bent around its face. He'd never seen one like it. The ram was oblivious to their presence, not feeding, surveying the mountains.

"We got lots of time. He don't know we're here. Rest your rifle on the rocks and fire when you're ready. It's a turkey shoot."

Collin heard the guide cocking his own rifle, in case it wasn't a killing shot, and that made him feel more insignificant than anything Hank had done or said. The animal snorted, turning to face the men, still unaware. "Bang, you're dead," Collin whispered.

Then he dropped the gun and stood up, pulling his red bandanna off his neck and waving it at the animal. The bighorn's eyes widened.

The sheep leapt into the air as if its legs were springs, poised for a moment above the precipice; then it was gone, descending to a ledge invisible from where the men were perched. The herd disappeared like soldiers fleeing a rocket attack. The men were left alone on the mountain.

Hank threw his cowboy hat onto the ground. "Shiiite . . . ." He did an angry war-dance around it. Then he stopped, realizing how silly he appeared. He composed himself. A wry smile emerged as he untensed, and his shoulders sagged. "Good shooting, son."

"I don't know why I did that, but I think this is the hunt I wanted."

Hank wore such a wondering expression that Collin wanted to laugh. Then the wonder disappeared, as if the man realized he'd been hired to fail, and the thought made him shake his head. "You've paid for this hunt. And if you're having a good time, by God, then so am I."

"You know," Hank said, deciding to talk about something else, "you're the second man to turn down that bighorn, and I'm not including me. There must be some magic in him. He's near the end of his time, the old codger. There ain't more than a year or so left in those old bones."

Collin nodded casually, feeling good.

"I don't think I'll take anyone else up this trail until he's gone."

"It would have been a good trophy, but tough mutton."

"Better than marmot." He studied Collin. "You get to shoot the first one."

"Sure. I never ate marmot before."

"You won't enjoy it," Hank said with disgust.

They began descending the slope, taking the easy way now that the sheep were gone.

Halfway down, Collin stopped and inspected the mountains, the string of clouds scudding across the blue sky. "You know, when you got pissed off because I ignored you tying that diamond hitch on the pack horse, I thought this was going to be a great hunt."

Hank grinned ruefully, contemplating a diet of wild onions and marmots for the next three days. It was obvious he knew what Collin meant, and that he felt sorry for him. "It's looking good, isn't it."

AMARYLLIS

"Last night, I dreamt about mountain lions," he said, his eyes open and contemplating the textured white surface of the ceiling. A wind rippled through the gauzy curtains, and a shaft of sunlight fell on the side of the bed where she would have slept, so that she seemed replaced by the golden air. The sheets were disturbed on her side, as if she had just risen, leaving only light behind. "They were full of passion and they cried in the night — it sounded like babies wanting their mother's milk."

He sat up, interrupting the light, and it gilded his chest. "It's a fine day for shovelling shit."

Going through the dresser was an exercise in poverty. There was nothing inside except a pair of stretched undershorts, and two lonely socks with holes in them. "I might do the washing this month," he said to the empty side of the bed. "The mountain lions were wonderful . . . on a bluff among the madrones. I think I was one of them."

He found his shoes under the kitchen table where Ricky ate his favourite breakfast of cereal topped with chocolate milk. "Your shoes are under the table," the child said between mouthfuls.

"I've found them. They must walk around on their own." Jeremy sat down and lit a cigarette. Usually, he didn't eat breakfast. His stomach was too tight in the morning — ready for the hot, driving hours of the day. "Sometimes, I think everyone's shoes walk in the night. When our eyes are closed, they stomp away, go for a walk in the park, make love in the bushes; then head off to the night shift where all the shoes reproduce themselves so there'll be lots more to buy the next day."

"You're pulling my leg." Ricky giggled into his cereal bowl.

A dignified but smaller version of an adult, the child finished off his cereal, and then drank his milk — white milk. There was something spiteful about the way he put the chocolate milk on his cereal and the white in his glass. When his throat finished swallowing in that magnificent way children can swallow food they love, he asked: "Is it a good site you're working on?"

"Big. Lots of bucks." Jeremy stubbed out his cigarette.

"Does that mean you'll make enough to register me with the soccer league this year? Two weeks from next Saturday is the last day to sign up."

Jeremy shrugged. "We'll see. I think so. Sure."

"I want to play soccer."

"I want your mother back."

Death makes everyone more dignified, especially children. Ricky examined his father. "Mother is dead, and you're a fool."

Jeremy turned the ignition key and the old motor struggled to life, rumbling and banging under the hood before it finally discovered the rhythm of a good engine that refuses to die. He let it warm for several minutes. There was no use pushing his luck with the machine. The rusty, once-white Ford pick-up pulled out of the driveway and onto the morning street.

It took almost half an hour for him to reach the Bench home, as they lived beyond the valley, and there was no direct road to the mansion on a rise overlooking the green plain. He pulled into the driveway beside the steaming load of manure the truckers had brought in on the first haul of the day. He turned off the motor and sat behind the wheel. Moisture rose into the air from the pile. Behind it, the Japanese-style house merged into the landscape, its clean lines blending with the azaleas and rhododendrons of the foundation planting.

There was a pink-flowering dogwood in full blossom, its powerful trunk warping above the path. Resembling a bonsai, but at least eight feet tall, the tree graced the sidelot – a gardener's dream. Good plant material was always a fighting matter for landscapers in the sawdusted pathways of nurseries, and they coveted the idiosyncratic, the immense, the rare things they found on their projects, for no other reason than the ability to sell them with pride to the next customer.

The house was almost modern, yet the Japanese design gave it a timeless quality, as if it had been born old in the landscape. Jeremy had been impressed on his first visit by the quality of the grounds, and when he had returned to confirm his quote, the plant material had surprised him even more. There were so many he hadn't noticed. Species rhododendrons, rare azaleas, schliffenbachias, Himalayan poppies – even jack-in-the-pulpits sprouting in the warmer yet shaded western exposure above the cool valley.

Around the back, the planting reached an ethereal quality, ringing the pool shielded by the horseshoe shape of the house. And he wondered about the amaryllis-lined solarium that protected the pool, installed at least twenty years ago, he guessed, when plants were not so fashionable.

It was difficult to correlate the impeccable taste of the grounds and the house with the owners. The woman was slim, and must have been beautiful at one time. He could see this even though nearly sixty years lined her face. Her husband had settled into his age differently. He was fat, thicker than the prize breeding-hog that Jeremy's parents had kept on their farm. Even the man's nose had a flattened, piglike quality, and Jeremy wanted to oink every time he talked to him. He remembered their first encounter.

"You need some soil in your soil."

Bench tried to figure out this statement. "What?"

"You need soil in your soil. Manure." Jeremy bent down and scooped up a handful of soil, letting it trickle through his fingers to the ground in front of Bench's expensive shoes. "Shit. That's what you need, some well-aged cow shit. This soil's been leached. Too many chemicals over the years have sucked all the life out of the earth. It's gone to sand. I'll bet you've been using nothing but 6-8-6, maybe even 10-14-10.

"But it'll smell." Bench surveyed the garden, nodding.

Jeremy knew he'd just cut the throat of the last gardener who'd obviously been piling chemical fertilizers into the beds. That was alright; anyone who'd exhaust such a good base planting deserved to be sacked.

Bench's expression grew more pained. "It'll smell, won't it?"

Jeremy turned to the conservatory where the old man must have spent a few weekends puttering about with his prize geraniums. There were varieties that even Jeremy hadn't encountered. "How do they do when you put them out in your annual bed at the front?" He didn't say that he thought a bed of geraniums and hollyhocks didn't relate to the rest of the landscaping, because that was an aesthetic question, the owner's right. He might bring it up later.

Bench nodded, and nodded again, reminding Jeremy once more of his father's prize hog at the trough. "Inferior. They've been inferior for the last three years."

It was Jeremy's turn to nod. He attempted to look as wise as possible. At this point silence would work better than fast talking. And it did.

"It won't smell, will it? Important people come here. I don't want it to smell bad."

"Good, well-aged manure don't smell."

As if it were a conversation he didn't want to continue, Bench turned away. The exorbitant quote didn't seem to concern him at all. He had other things on his mind. "You seem to know what you're talking about. Do what you think's best."

That was that and now this is this. There was nothing to do but get to work.

He let his muscles settle into the shovelling, feeling the blade grind against the soft excrement as he twisted, heaving a shovel-full into the wheelbarrow, and when he got closer to the center of the stack, little puffs of steam were released into the sharp, morning air. He enjoyed the way his body curved every time he drove the blade into the small mountain, his laterals lengthening and then tightening. Lifting the shovel moved the weight to his arms, biceps, triceps, shoulders, deltoids, and across the chest, pectorals; next the turn and the slight knot in the abdominals. This made him think of when he was first married, how Miriam ran her hand across his washboard abdominals, now concealed by an irritating veneer of fat.

Every time he filled the red wheelbarrow and lifted its handles the compaction in his back and shoulders reminded him of what his life was about as he moved across the yard, top-dressing the bed.

He almost had the mountain beat when the dump truck arrived with the second load. He felt the old despair as the pile returned to its former size. It was a massive garden; there were three more loads yet to come. This life, this vision of the steaming, endless shit was also a kind of death, and it made him think of Miriam again.

At the funeral, his hands were helpless. There was nothing for them to hold, and he kept stuffing them into his pants as though they were guilty secrets while his mother held onto Ricky's quaking shoulder. The black-dressed crowd, human crows, milled about, those closest to him, unable to speak except with meaningless phrases. Everyone lined up beside the hearse.

On the other side of the fence, the grass stretched over the hill, speckled with thousands of little squares that reminded him of toadstools, each one bearing names and dates. "Names and dates," he mumbled, "the things that matter the least." Miriam's sister heard his soft-spoken words and came to his side, but he didn't want anyone at his side. He didn't want to talk. He wanted to think. *They should have written that her smile was no mask. They should have written she cried real tears of love when I was inside her; they should . . .*

He heard a shout, and turned. The dog. He had told Ricky not to bring it, but the boy had begun to cry. Even the dogs of the earth should say goodbye. Even? The dog had as much right as everyone else. It was her friend.

It trotted jauntily down the road; a charred bone, suspiciously resembling a human thigh bone, dangled from its jaw. The mourners in their black suits or black designer-dresses, mostly relatives of Miriam, edged towards their cars, as if they were afraid it would contaminate them. The dog wagged its head, shaking the thigh bone at the assembly, and continued down the narrow lane past the cars, happy, moving towards the freedom of the street. A man appeared from the rear door of the crematorium, lost, unwilling to chase the dog past the mourners, yet the dog had the bone. Finally, another man shouted:

"Stop the dog!" And the spell was broken. Jeremy began to laugh, too loud, and his mother turned away from him while Ricky took the bone with its charred end from the dog and handed it to the man who ran the crematorium.

Jeremy knew he'd made a fool of himself when he'd laughed, yet he'd do it again, now. The questions behind loose and charred bones at a crematorium, dogs, and dead loves could never be answered by meaningless ceremonies where everyone attempted to be solemn.

When he began the east bed, he noticed that the solarium centered in the horseshoe back-end of the house was open to the outside. It hadn't been on the last two visits. The whole section fronting the pool was a series of glass doors that folded back.

On the south face of the hill, the temperature was warmer and the couple obviously took advantage of it during the sunny days, although Jeremy wondered if they weren't taking chances with the precious, temperate plant material within: the orchids, the bougainvillaea, the passion flowers, and the massed pots of still-blooming amaryllis. Up here, above the valley, the nights would be cool for another few weeks.

Then he saw her standing among the tall hibiscus in the dragon pots. She was naked.

Immaculately naked.

Tall, small-breasted, wandering between the controlled planting above the pool and the house. It was the distance that made it work. She was too old to be so beautiful.

He grovelled backwards among the tree peonies, ashamed of himself for spying, although she displayed herself without concern.

As unobtrusive as possible, he patted the manure around the stems of the plants, until he realized how foolishly he was behaving.

He stood up, grabbed his shovel, and threw it into the red wheelbarrow where it landed with a resounding clang. Careful to keep his head turned away he pushed the wheelbarrow back up the path to the now immense pile of shit. The third load had arrived.

He was leaning into the last shovel of shit for a load when he became aware of a noise behind him, a purring, a motor, running sweet and smooth. He straightened and turned.

Bench climbed out of the coffee-with-cream-coloured Jaguar and inspected the pile that dwarfed the driveway and his entrance to the two-car garage. He sniffed at the air disdainfully.

Jeremy regretted there hadn't been a chance to mention that manure smelled a little when first turned. The odour would disappear soon.

Bench squatted by the pile. "It's full of sticks and twigs."

This angered Jeremy. "It's good shit."

"It's full of twigs and straw and sawdust." The portly man straightened up.

"Filler," Jeremy said. "It gives air and texture, allows the soil to breathe. It'll break down soon, making a good loam. Do you want to study books on soil structure? I've got a few in my library."

Bench smiled ruefully. "No. No. Go right ahead. You're my man. I trust you."

Unfortunately, at that moment, the fourth truck arrived. Honking twice, the unconcerned driver backed up and cranked his dump into the air, unloading a particularly smelly and enormous pile behind the wheelbarrow while the two men watched with mixed emotions.

By the time Jeremy had turned from the now departing dump truck Bench was already entering the house, so he walked the wheelbarrow back to the tree peonies.

In a few minutes, he heard loud voices from within the solarium. Jeremy decided to call it a day.

At home, Ricky was waiting. "How'd it go?"

"As smooth as shit."

"You gonna make money this time?"

"I always make money."

"Yeah, but your costs eat it all up. That's what you say."

"You're starting to sound like my accountant."

"What's for dinner?"

"Dinner?" Horrified, Jeremy realized he'd forgotten to do the shopping. "Yeah . . . well . . . dinner . . . ."

"You forgot about dinner, again?"

"Who thinks about dinner when they're facing four dump loads of shit?"

"I could."

"Yeah, you're a kid. You always think about food. I guess that means I'm buying. What's your favourite take-out?"

Ricky's eyes glowed. "Chou's Chinese!"

"Me too. I love my stir-fried. I'm glad we agree on that."

How unfortunate that the azaleas had grown so close together. He'd have to remove a few, maybe plant some small ones to give this section of the plot depth. It was a well-aged planting, and the shrubs had character. He'd get a solid price for them on the next job. One of the side-benefits of cleaning out an aging landscape.

He wrapped the second azalea in burlap, cinching it around the root ball. With this unseasonably warm, bright weather, the shrub would suffer; still, he had collected good root, and it should survive.

As he worked, he felt guilty again about the impressive smell of the manure. He should have told Bench that there'd be an odour at first. It made him feel like a cheat, and he liked to think he always played a straight hand. The old man wasn't too bad, despite his resemblance to a pig.

A red Volvo pulled into the driveway. There was an arty, painted sign on its side, advertising Maria's Reflexology and Massage Therapy. Below, in smaller type, it said: Life Engineering and Biorhythmic Projections. An anorexic and ashy-faced women climbed out of the car and rang the doorbell.

He smiled, and decided on more wheelbarrowing. The manure pile wasn't going to get any smaller unless he worked it.

By the time he'd hauled the seventeenth wheelbarrow load down to the south bed, he began to wonder why he was in this business. He'd already removed his shirt; there was nothing left but his cutoffs and sneakers, and he was cooking in the warm air. He should have taken on a helper for this garden. It was starting to appear larger than his estimate.

There was a movement by the pool. The two women. Both of them naked. Mrs. Bench was on the divan by the waterfall, her slender limbs being manipulated by the skinnier Maria.

Enough with the wheelbarrow. He'd prune the three laburnums by the patio. It was late for pruning, yet they were in desperate shape. He couldn't help himself now. The situation was curious, flagrant, and the magnet in his blood drew him to the top of the middle tree, though he knew they could hear him, see him.

As much as he tried to work on the awkward limbs, he kept looking at the women. It was if they were displaying themselves for him, and he almost felt relief when he heard the dump truck pull into the front yard and drop its load. "That's the last one," he said to the smooth branches of the laburnum.

Below, the women ignored him, engrossed in their actions. Maria was rubbing oil over Mrs. Bench's belly, manipulating her small breasts. The black nipples stood out against her white skin, and Jeremy grew aware of the erection in his pants. "She's older than my mother," he whispered, chewing furiously with the loppers at a misguided branch.

After another fifteen minutes of the performance at the divan, Maria gave Mrs. Bench a kiss on the cheek, and picked up a pile of clothes beside the pool. Donning them with a business-like precision, she smiled and left. He heard the Volvo pull out of the driveway.

Her abrupt departure disconcerted him more than the semi-erotic display he'd just witnessed. And Mrs. Bench wasn't moving. He returned to his ministrations on the laburnum, but he soon became aware of her gaze upon him.

He looked down.

"Whenever you're finished," she called out, "torturing that tree, would you like a drink?"

"Sure." He hung his loppers on a branch and clambered down.

"You cut out a fair share of that laburnum," she said, reclining luxuriantly on the divan, pointing those black nipples at him, her legs crossed.

"Well, the last one who worked on her must have been a disciple of Charles Manson. I had to cut her back properly. Even if it's late in the year."

"Charles Manson?"

"Yeah, the hack and slash school of tree pruning."

She smiled. "Alfred said you were a witty man."

"I cultivate my garden."

"And you even quote Voltaire. *'Dans ce meilleur des mondes possibles . . . tout est au mieux.'*" She raised an eyebrow. "How about a gin and tonic?"

"Sounds refreshing."

She climbed off the divan, artfully displaying the silvery bush between her legs, and, with a slight limp, walked up to the bar beside the patio doors. "Does my nakedness bother you?"

"Yes, in an odd sort of way."

She arched that eyebrow again. "Do you enjoy our garden?"

"It's very beautiful. One of the best I've worked on."

"Here's your drink." She handed him the gin and tonic. "I want to show you something."

"I'm nothing but eyes."

She entered the house, and he followed behind. Down the hall, there was a room overlooking the terraced section to the west of the house. The walls were lined with photographs, drawings, paintings. All of dancers.

He stopped before a photograph of a naked dancer whirling gauzy scarves on what seemed to be a sand beach. The face was hard to discern with the odd flash the cameraman had used, but the body was unmistakable.

He didn't have to ask, yet the words popped out. "The limp?"

"Ruptured Achilles tendon. It never healed well enough to walk right, let alone return to the stage. Dancer's disease, I suppose."

"I'm sorry."

She shrugged. "Why? It's nothing to do with you."

"I'm always sorry when someone can't fulfill their expectations."

"No one can fulfill their expectations," she snapped. "I saw the way you examined the house and the gardens. The way you looked at me. The way you talked with my husband. You've got too much contempt."

"Uhh, I don't like the way this is going. I should get back to my trees."

She smiled. "You love them, don't you."

"I couldn't live without them, in more ways than one."

"I didn't mean to be sharp. It's just that I could see the contempt in you. And I heard you mention your late wife to my husband." She was thoughtful for a moment. "I used to have no money, and I was alone, until I met Alfred. I lived for the dance, but my leg was ruined. He gave me the support no one else could. He's a better man than he looks."

"I can't get into this, Mrs. Bench."

"Sylvia."

"Sylvia." She was blocking the doorway. There was no escape.

Abruptly, she turned and marched off. "Let's go back to the pool. I love it so much. Especially the amaryllis."

He followed dutifully, watching her naked buttocks, the untouched drink in his hand. *Ricky is going to hate me for this.*

At the pool she turned again, and pushed him sharply onto the divan, using the tips of her fingers, and he was surprised by how easily he sagged into the cushions.

"Young stud asshole." She smiled. "Wearing nothing but your sneakers and shorts."

"Whups," he said, gazing up at her, sinking further into the cushions.

Then she put her hand in front of her mouth, and her teeth popped out. It was unnerving. She held them in her hand, her face shrunken, yet somehow even more beautiful. She dropped the teeth into his gin and tonic, and they settled to the bottom of the glass.

The moment called for a gesture, and he was lost at first. He picked up the drink and took a sip. "You know, it gives it that *je ne sais quoi*."

She arched that devastating eyebrow again, and smiled, her lips shrivelling into a zero. Her fingers crawled up his thighs to the cutoffs and tugged at the zipper, her shrunken mouth approaching. *If Miriam ever saw this, she'd never let me live it down. The teasing would go on for centuries.*

On the other side of the house, there was the sound of a sixth dump truck unloading. *Six? Holy Christ, what are those idiots doing?* Then he forget about the manure.

The embarrassing moment, his cutoffs around his feet, while she went to fix herself another drink. "Uhh, I should get back to work. I have to phone my suppliers."

She smiled, nodding towards the kitchen where a phone hung on the wall above the heavily chromed gas range.

He pulled up his pants and climbed out of the divan, attempting to look sexy and business-like at the same time. He wanted to start laughing, but he pulled the sliding door shut behind him. *This is not a funny business.*

He dialled the number and waited, listening to the clicks and beeps on the telephone.

A twangy, male voice spoke. "Big Valley Soils and Trucking."

"Hi, Mac?"

"Yeah, who's this?"

"Jeremy. I ordered five loads of manure, right?"

"Let me check." The noise of slamming desk drawers and rustling papers echoed over the receiver. "Right. So?"

"Well a sixth just got dumped."

"Six. How the hell'd that happen?"

"How should I know?"

"Okay, I'll tell the boys to cool it. You just got a free one. Hope you can use it."

"It's a big garden. But my back ain't what it used to be."

"Alright, that's all you get. See you around."

Jeremy cradled the receiver. Now he had to get back to the garden. This time she was sitting on the divan, still naked.

He poked his way timidly through the sliding door. She'd taken her teeth out of his drink. "I've got a lot more pruning to do." He tried to sound apologetic.

She smiled serenely at him. "Of course. There's always tomorrow."

He felt like a young girl at beauty pageant sauntering past her, pretending his attention was on the loppers in the high branches of the old laburnum. There was nothing to do but start climbing.

"So how's the job?" Ricky asked, spooning down a mouthful of curried eggplant. East Indian was his next favourite food to Chinese, and he made no secret of it, nor of his gratitude that Jeremy had done the shopping and made one of his great dinners, like he used to before mother died. Food was one of Jeremy's obsessions. No matter how broke, no matter what happened, agreeable food was a necessity.

"Good, real good." Jeremy was tired. It had been a long day. "A little more than I expected, though. A lot of plant material."

That awkward silence the boy knew how to use so well. "It's going down the tube, isn't it?"

"You might say that."

"You aren't going to make any money."

"I'm going to make money. Eat your curry. You're in the soccer team. I wrote the cheque when I got home. Take it to the tryouts tonight. I hope after all this fussing you make the team."

"I'll make the team."

"Yeah, I know you will."

"This is awful, isn't it?"

It was Jeremy's turn to grow silent. "Yeah, it's awful. She's dead, but we're alive. I'm going to find you a new mother."

"I don't want a new mother. I want Miriam."

"So do I." Jeremy knew this was going to be tricky. "Still, if her ghost was standing here, she'd say to me I should go out and get laid. I should find another woman, for me and for you. We're both young. We can't shrivel up and waste away because she died. People have this thing in them; it makes them hungry, and it takes a lot to fill it."

They finished their dinner in silence, and then washed up, chatting a little to make it easier for each other, yet the awkwardness was back. Jeremy even watched television for a couple of hours, while Ricky was at the tryout. It was a pastime Jeremy usually hated, but he wanted to dull his mind, forget the day.

He picked up Ricky at the field, and the boy was beaming. He'd made the team, so they went home and celebrated with mangoes and ice cream and ice mixed in the blender, a milkshake they'd developed together.

When he went to bed, Jeremy faced the emptiness of the pillows next to him, and he slept badly, dreaming and waking, dreaming and waking.

Then the sun again. Another good day. The light, once more, was upon her pillow. "Last night I dreamt about a beach full of white stones, and there were two black stones glowing among them. You don't have to tell me what it was about. I know."

The steaming mountain of shit faced him with an obstinacy that was terrifying. "Yeah, well take that!" He rammed his shovel in and began spooning it out.

There were beds to be top-dressed, plantings that needed thinning, suckers to be removed, a garden that demanded work, and it was a beautiful day brightening in the heart of the year.

Before noon, he gave up on the monstrous pile, and began weeding the hostas and the Solomon's seal and the jack-in-the-pulpits in the west bed, taking shelter from the heat and the sun. He'd done his share of shovelling for the day.

Then he heard the ominous rumble of a truck on the asphalt road, the beep as it backed up, and he dropped his hoe, sprinting for the front driveway.

"Hold it!" he shouted. "What the fuck are you doing?"

"I"m dumping my load, what the fuck do you think I'm doing?"

"Not here you aren't."

"Whaddya mean, not here?"

"I'm already one load over. Get that stuff out of here before the owner comes home."

"One load over?" The driver put the truck into neutral and picked up the clipboard beside him. "It says here this load's yours."

"I don't care what it says. You know what you can do with your shit. And when you get back, tell the rest of your gang. Tell them no more."

"Take it easy, feller. If they put you through again, it ain't my fault. I'll haul it back."

For the first time in weeks, Jeremy felt vaguely satisfied as he strode around the back of the house towards the west bed while the truck drove away. Then he saw Sylvia, naked again, by the pool, holding a glass in her hand, her black nipples standing.

"You didn't finish your drink yesterday," she said.

It wasn't long before her legs were wrapped around his back.

He was driving into her, working his way towards the short strokes, when she cried out, the sound startling him for a moment, making him recall his dream of the mountain lions. He wondered about the life within her, the glow in her eyes as she began to peak. The past. So much history. He pushed harder, as if he were trying to ream out the secret core within, until, above her cries, he heard an even more terrifying sound: the distant beep beep beep of a truck backing up, the clang as the dump lifted, and the slide of another seven yards of manure.

For a moment, he froze. Then he rammed harder. *God is telling me something.* There was a surprised look on her face, one that said, this is unreal, but give me more. She became a kind of madonna, ageless, her expression deathlike, yet ecstatic, as she clutched his hips and shuddered.

He expelled and sank onto her shoulder, thinking of Miriam, the night he admitted he could hardly gaze at a woman without wondering how she looked with her legs up. Miriam had given him hell, told him he was sexist, that there was more to women than what was at the top of their thighs.

"Sure," he'd said, "but I can't help liking that part as much as the rest." And Miriam, being Miriam, had given him a devilish glance and lifted her legs.

Jeremy climbed off Sylvia and slid back into his cutoffs and sneakers. "I'm never going to get this garden done."

"Your shovel work is magnificent."

"Don't tease me." He grinned. "I've got to use the phone."

"Do you always have to use the phone after you make love?"

"You're a strange lady."

"I'm not strange. I'm very normal. It's you who needs the phone. *'Le travail éloigne de nous trois grands maux, l'ennui, le vice, et la boisson.'*"

He shut the sliding door, picked up the receiver, and dialled.

"Big Valley," the dull voice said.

"Macintosh. It's me again, Jeremy."

"You didn't get another load?"

"Not only did I get another load, but I barely managed to chase one off. He was supposed to radio to his friends to give it up. What are you trying to do, bury me in shit?"

"Cripes, Jeremy. I'm sorry. Do you want me to send out a backhoe to shovel it up?"

"Naw, I'll use it. Free, of course. You guys are embarrassing me. This is a posh place."

"Alright, I promise you. No more. You gotta understand. We have problems. When we amalgamated with South Valley last week, that gave us almost fifty trucks. Shit, I don't know half the drivers. Then the receptionist dropped her baby two months early, and we can't get a temporary for another week, so I gotta answer the phone. I'm up to my ears here."

"Okay, Mac." He hung up, and tried to make a graceful exit past Sylvia.

"I"m beginning to think you're not enjoying our garden," she said.

He stopped. "That's not true. And it's unfair."

She looked away, her grey hair outlined against the pillow on the divan. "Isn't it?"

There was the sound of a car in the driveway, the Jaguar. Jeremy hotfooted down to the wheelbarrow and picked up his shovel.

Soon, he saw Alfred on the deck by the pool, glaring at him, and then back at his wife, naked by the pool. Sharp words Jeremy could not make out echoed in the sultry, late-afternoon air.

Ricky was waiting at the door. "Your cheque's no good."

"What?"

"Mr. Ryan, my social studies teacher, he's the soccer coach. He took me aside after school and said he had a problem when he went to deposit the cheque at the bank during lunch hour. They wouldn't take it. There was no money. He didn't tell anyone else."

"Whaddya mean?"

"The cheque bounced!"

"It can't. It couldn't. There was money in that account!"

Ricky, realizing he'd pushed too far, went silent.

"It's a mistake. That's all, a mistake. The money is there. I'll straighten it out in the morning with the bank and then I'll phone Ryan. You won't be embarrassed. Don't even think about it."

It turned out the bank had deducted his backhoe loan from his personal account because there was no money in the business account, or so they thought, because they hadn't counted the receipts in the night deposit yet. It was all very illegal and he let them know it. They promised to honour the cheque and even phone up the schoolteacher and explain how it was their fault, so that was that. The only thing that worried him was that one of the deposited cheques might not be good. It was from a disgruntled client who objected to the number of shrubs Jeremy had removed while reorganizing the garden — a yuppie fool who didn't understand that rhododendrons lost their fullness crammed against a fence.

When he arrived at the Bench job he vented his frustration on the bamboo planting by the property line, trimming out the excess, yarding them with great effort through the clinging tendrils of the morning glories which had snuck in from the hillside. What a mess. Soon his shirt was off and he was sweating, his bare skin sensitive and scratched by the thin edges of the leaves. A Japanese effect demanded sparsity among the trunks of the black-leafed bamboo.

Then, ominously, the distant clang of a truck unloading. He froze. "No. Please. No." A few seconds after the rumble of the slide, the truck drove away. He hurled his loppers out of the bamboo and kicked over the wheelbarrow, striding onto the grass where he jumped up and down, screaming "No! No!" with great dramatic effect, torn by the knowledge that now he was going to get money back on the manure, but he'd also have to shovel it.

He stopped his tantrum, aware that he was being watched. Up the hill by the pool sat the couple. The old man must have taken the day off. They both seemed to be naked, seated in lawn chairs, their drinks in hand, watching him; Alfred, an enormous Buddha, and Sylvia — a skinny, Christian saint. Their stoic gaze unnerved him for a moment. Jeremy's eyes focused on the black circles that her nipples made on her chest.

"The shit just keeps on coming!" Jeremy didn't care any more. He strode up the hill to the couple, almost out of breath by the time he reached the pool. They remained motionless. He couldn't get the notion of saints out of his mind.

"Do you mind if I use the phone?" he asked, watching her eyebrow arch.

"Having a little trouble with our suppliers, are we?" Alfred asked, his voice infuriatingly understanding.

"Nothing I can't handle."

"You know where it is," Sylvia said.

Jeremy slid the door shut and locked it. He picked up the phone and dialled. "Mac?"

"Jeremy?"

"Yup."

"It's you again?"

"It sure is."

"You're pulling my leg."

"Nope."

"I'll shoot the fuckers. Honest to God, I don't know what's going on. I told everyone I met, but we're very busy here." There was a long enough pause to make Jeremy wonder if the line had gone dead. "You really got another load?"

"Yup."

"Uhhh, we're in the process of changing our work orders to a new format. You know, with the amalgamation and all, we gotta streamline."

"Don't give me that shit, Mac."

The sound of papers shuffling. "I think we already did."

"Mac, what are you telling me?"

"I think the order for five loads went out again."

"Mac, if one more shows up, I swear to God, I'll shoot the driver. I can't take it any more. The owner has a thing about manure, and I don't want him to know we're this screwed up."

"Alright. Alright. We'll deduct each extra load from what you ordered. So you're only going to pay for two. It's cheaper for us than sending a backhoe up."

"Thanks. But remember, another driver shows his face, and I'll bury him in it. I mean that."

"Look, I'll even post a notice in the lunch room. That way everyone will know, for sure. And Christ, the order can't go through again."

"You won't forget. You'll post a note for the new guys."

"I promise. Cross my heart. Talk to you on your next job."

Jeremy hung up the phone and made for the pool, ready for their comments now, but they were gone. Both of them. He stopped, almost frightened by their casual disappearance, before he returned to the bamboo, wondering.

There was nothing except the bamboo and the morning glories — objects he could fight and defeat. He picked up the machete near the loppers and began thrashing at the tangle like a madman cutting down enemies.

When he woke up, and it seemed so much like waking up, the sun was low on the horizon, and the unforgiving bamboo were conquered. The mess would take a little cleaning, yet he'd done more in an afternoon than a regular crew would have done in a day. Satisfied, exhausted, he staggered out of the grove and kicked his tools into a pile. "So there," he whispered.

After getting his breath back, he heaped the tools into the wheelbarrow and pushed everything to the side of the house where he'd leave them for the night.

Alfred was in the conservatory, his huge naked frame draped over a tiny chair, among the masses of geraniums. He was eating a grapefruit.

Jeremy stopped, impressed by the sight, this enormous man, his fat almost wiggling, delicately sliding out small pieces of grapefruit from the half-shell.

The old man looked up, and glared at him a moment; then beckoned with a finger for Jeremy to enter.

Jeremy dutifully pushed aside the wheelbarrow and walked into the greenhouse. He realized Alfred wasn't naked. The man was wearing a dingy pair of underpants, but he was so fat the skin hung over them. Rolls of skin and fat.

"Did you sort out your suppliers?" Alfred pushed the grapefruit away, hiding it among the geraniums, and wiped his chin with a grimy hand.

"Sure. No problem. Got an extra load. But you can use it down in the south bed among the hydrangeas."

Alfred nodded, uninterested. "Why don't you have a boy do the heavy work? You can pay unskilled wages and spend more of your time on the finer details. Better profit in it. An intelligent man like you shouldn't be hauling shit."

"I like the physical work. I guess that's why I'm a gardener and not a businessman." Jeremy couldn't, of course, admit that he regretted the loss of his last helper, a strong boy who worked hard, but quit when two paycheques in a row bounced. The worst part of it was that it wasn't Jeremy's fault. The bank. Goofy clients. Bureaucratic nurseries. The endless chain of working in the real world.

"You prefer to sweat, don't you?"

"Yeah, it's good."

"I know. I sweated when I was a boy. My father wanted me to know how the other side of the world lived. Now all my sweat's inside my head. Do you love your work?"

"Everything I do is for love."

Alfred nodded. "Me too."

Jeremy turned away. He had to get out of here.

"Inhale this," Alfred said. He plucked a scraggly leaf from one of the geraniums.

Jeremy stepped forward and took the leaf. He sniffed it. "Lemon?" He looked at the old man.

"Yes, a good one, developed it myself from one of the standard lemon-scents. Thought I got a whiff of the ocean in it. What do you think?"

Jeremy grinned. "Yeah, there's salt water."

"Try this."

"What's that."

"Apple mint."

"Apple mint? That's getting real finite, isn't it?"

"Try it."

Jeremy rubbed it against the inside of his wrist and sucked on the smell. "Yeah. Hey, you're pretty good."

"I spent years on these little monsters. Here. Suck on this." Alfred stuck a leaf in Jeremy's mouth. It tasted like lamb with mint sauce.

"Wow. Who needs to kill sheep when they've got this. You developed it yourself?"

"How about another? It's an oak leaf, but it takes you into coffee country." Alfred rubbed the geranium around Jeremy's chin and cheeks.

Jeremy collapsed into the chair beside the fat man. "Coffee. I don't believe it. A coffee-scented geranium. You've made it . You're in the big time."

"It's a wonderful garden we live in, isn't it?" Alfred beamed proudly. "But I didn't grow that one myself. I bought it. Here, this is one of mine, a good rose, I think." He rubbed it onto Jeremy's chest.

Jeremy took the leaf from his hand and rubbed it onto the old man's flabby breast muscles. They sat sniffing their chests for minutes.

"Yeah, it's rose," Jeremy said, finally.

"Definitely a rose. A good job well done."

"You've got the touch. Guys breed these for years and go nowhere."

Waving a magnanimous hand at the pelargoniums to his left, Alfred grinned. "None of us goes anywhere. We're merely having fun along the way." Then, dramatically, he said: "Are you ready for the cinnamon?"

"I take whatever comes to me."

Alfred ripped a handful of leaves off a nearby geranium, and began to rub them lovingly on Jeremy's arm. He pressed them into Jeremy's hand, and the favour was returned.

And once again, it seemed as if Jeremy had just woken up. He'd spent more than an hour, rubbing green leaves against another man's skin, inhaling the perfumes of genetic adventures. He lay back like a drunk in his chair.

"It's like that, isn't it?" Alfred said, nodding. "A good drunk."

"I'm high on geraniums."

Alfred nodded again, stupidly. "Aren't we silly?"

"Sure are. I love it." Jeremy climbed out of the chair, gave an exaggerated drunken wave to Alfred, and left the conservatory. He'd forgotten the machete at the bamboo. He didn't want to leave it for the night, so he returned to the grove. The sun was setting, streaking the lush garden, burnishing it. He picked up the machete, so cold, so icy on the grass, a scary tool in the cultivated wilderness of a rich man's garden.

But what do you say to your son when you come home near nightfall and he's hungry? As soon as he pulled into the driveway the guilt filled his guts, made him clench the wheel.

"I'm hungry, dad. It's not fair."

That was a good opening. "No, I guess it isn't."

The next two days became even more a dream. Miriam. Her ghostly face on the pillow in the morning. The old lady with silver hair between her legs, desirable, yet incomprehensible, and always demanding. And the fat man who loved geraniums. Worst of all, despite the free manure, there was the diminishing profit, the work done for nothing, because the work kept on coming. Every job was like this; there was always more than he imagined, estimated, planned, calculated . . . .

He stood above her, his pants on the slate beside the divan. She was also naked, so wonderfully naked, old and naked. "I would have liked to watch you dance," he said.

"You have."

"I suppose I have."

"You're all finished here." She reached for her bathing suit while looking beyond him, to the garden.

"Yeah. You could say that."

"That's good. Your work is very beautiful."

"It depends on your point of view."

"I don't think so, but you should sort out your bill with my husband."

The mention of her husband made him cringe, and he turned from her. For a moment, he felt alone among the struggling stalks of the late amaryllis, all rising from their pots like a flock of demanding phalli.

"Put it in your pants," she said, "and sort out the bill."

"He's here?"

"He's in his office at the front of the house."

So he put it in his pants, and wandered through the house, knowing that he resembled a shirtless Adonis searching for the right door, and he was both embarrassed by and proud of the thought.

Alfred was inside his office, his bulk bound up in a suit as he pored over sheaves of papers. He didn't look up as Jeremy opened the door. "Come in young man, come in."

"I'm finished, sir." Jeremy sat down in the chair, feeling half-naked, feeling too young, too pretty, and he didn't think he was finished.

"Well, you can send me your bill then, can't you?"

"Actually, I have it here." Jeremy pulled the slightly crumpled piece of paper out of his back pocket.

Alfred smiled and took the receipt, sniffing at it for a moment as if he half-feared it would smell of manure. "You know," he said, "I usually get my work done by professionals, big companies who do a good job."

"I figured that, sir."

"Yes, I guess you would have. That's why I let you have the job. It's not a great deal for me, but I suspect it was for you."

Jeremy nodded dutifully.

Alfred looked out the window, almost posing. "But they haven't been doing a good job. I suppose I needed a real man. I'm impressed with what you've done over the last three weeks."

The cheque. The cheque. Please, I need the cheque.

"I haven't," Alfred said, "enjoyed myself so much in years as the other day in the greenhouse. It was almost sexual."

Jeremy nodded again, this time smiling. "It was the plants. They were good."

"You know I love my wife."

Jeremy seized up. *Here it comes.*

"I've been with her a lot of years. She's an amazing woman."

"That she is."

Alfred sniggered. "That she is. And I decided when I met her that I was going to make her happy. I'll do anything to make her happy. I'm an old man now, and she's old too, but she's still got the life in her; you know what I mean. This is a bit awkward, but I like the work you've done in our garden, and I haven't made the money I've made by being a fool."

Jeremy tried to fight back the wave of bitterness. "No, I guess not, sir ... Alfred."

"Don't be pouty," Alfred said, wagging his big jowls. He pulled out his cheque book. "I'm working my way to it. You cut your own throat with your estimate. I'm not a stupid man. But I liked you. And I took it. And I've no objection to your work in the garden. It's good. There are things I wish I could do, but I can't. Too fat. Thyroid problem. Actually, I guess my wife knows the real me. Anyway ... enough .... " He waved the cheque at Jeremy. "I'm not a generous man; didn't make my income being generous, but I pay my bills. Is this cheque sufficient? I'd assume it is."

Jeremy looked at amount on the cheque. He tried to appear businesslike, but his jaw sagged. The guilt and the profit were too much.

The old white truck swayed easily down the road, packing nothing but the tools: the loppers, the machete, the wheelbarrow, the weedeater, the electric pruner. "Yeah, it's good." Jeremy almost ignored the road as he swept the truck through the meandering turns to the valley below.

She was in the front yard when he'd left with the cheque in his hand; she looked older, wizened, withered by the years, almost beaten down, and it was hard to imagine that he'd loved her with a lust, a mechanical drive that Miriam had never known. The beautiful eroticism behind old bones. She raised that eyebrow as he left, and he'd waved the cheque good-naturedly at her.

Then he was into the truck, and gone. "So, shouldn't I feel like shit? A prostitute?" He grinned, thumping a cassette into the tape deck that was worth almost as much as the old truck, and the new Neil Young cassette pounded at his ears. "Yeah," he said to the road. "I can buy that decent stereo at last, and the kid gets new soccer boots."

At the light where the highways intersected, he gazed dreamily at the clouds on the horizon for several moments before he focused on the trucks making a left turn onto the road that led up the mountain. There were three of them. Big Valley. That sure looked like manure. He didn't recognize the drivers.

The dump trucks from hell roared past him while he sat paralysed at the wheel. It had to be another site. They wouldn't have sent the order through again.

Jeremy's hands were hooked into the steering wheel, and he ignored the green light until a horn tooted behind him. Awake again, as if from a dream, he jammed his foot onto the gas, and the pick-up sped through the now-amber light. Whatever. He'd get to the bank real quick and cash that cheque. He started to laugh as he raced down the winding road that led to the shopping mall. Across from the bank was the Audiotron store, and once the cheque was cashed, maybe he'd go shopping, buy a new system. He couldn't stop laughing. He turned the cassette up louder, drowning himself with sound.

THE BALINESE WEDDING DREAM

Another day reached shut-down on the west coast. The blue sky turned off like a switch, and the stars clicked on. I remember kicking the sheets aside before the weight settled into my skull. A voice, distant yet recognizable, said, "Open your eyes." My own voice telling me that I had crossed over. "Open your eyes and look at the world."

It was a simple room in a simple house.

I was lying on the couch, listening to Lee describe the carp that ate out of his hand as he fattened it for the wedding feast, how it loved to have its scaly back scratched, the way it oozed through the lilies of the pond and surfaced when it heard his footsteps. Is it possible for a fish to love a man?

Kim entered the room and sat beside me. She was silent, but that wasn't unusual; she had never talked much even as a child.

As her cousin continued his fond tale of the carp, I realized, I think for the first time, how much Kim had grown in the twelve years since I first attended university and rented the family's tiny basement suite. They were from Bali, but of Chinese descent, and had fled to Canada when racial tensions had grown too strong on the island.

After I finished university I kept my ties with them, half-fascinated, half-repelled by customs that to me were exotic and disappearing. They were caught in a curious warp, one beyond that of their Chinese ancestry, the lost world of Bali, and now the even more lost world of western Canada. I think, in the end, like everyone else, they wanted to blend into the world, any world, but each culture made them outsiders.

Lee said something that demanded a reply, and embarrassed, I had to admit I wasn't listening.

Kim wore a red brocade robe that buttoned down the front. It was embroidered with dragons. The scarlet didn't clash with the unusual paleness of her skin.

I disliked the dragons and would have preferred cranes. In many ways she reminded me of one. Birdlike, she was long and thin and had sunken cheekbones offset by the circular glasses she wore.

Kim unbuttoned the top button of her robe; then the next.

"What are you doing?"

"She is unbuttoning her robe," Lee answered. Kim still hadn't spoken.

There were now four buttons undone, and the collar parted, revealing the creamy skin.

"Why?"

The robe undone to the last two buttons, she opened it casually into a V that reached her navel. I looked at her, and then at Lee, but they were silent.

She smoothed the cushion and sat beside me again, this time closer.

"Is she not beautiful?" Lee asked nervously.

Kim smiled, her eyes lowered, a flush on her cheeks. I should have got up and left the room. I remained on the couch.

It was impossible not to admire her, the narrow body, the almost revealed breasts, the glossy blackness of her hair that contrasted against her skin.

"In a few hours," Lee said, "she will marry a man she doesn't love, a man with cold hands. She would like to be your lover now, because she doesn't want this man to be the sole lover in her life . . . when he has such cold hands."

"I've talked with her parents and they also think this request is madness, but they love their daughter very much . . . and they've never before refused her anything." Kim slipped her hands into the side pockets of her robe.

Annoyed at being invited here to be offered this kinky business, I glared at Lee. "Why don't they just call off the marriage?"

Lee was shocked. "That's impossible. The contract was signed years ago when she and the man were children. It would not be good for the family."

She pushed her fingers forward, like mice beneath the scarlet robe. I realized the pockets were slits and her hands were sliding along her flesh. Then she looked up at me. I averted my eyes, and Lee smiled.

"Isn't the solution worse than the problem?"

"Not at all. Kim likes you very much. And besides, the man might reject her because she'd made love to another man . . . and then we could be indignant . . . call him a fool . . . say he doesn't know a virgin from a fish."

My gaze followed the mice into the zone between her legs.

"Kim likes you."

That was obvious, but I didn't say anything.

Lee stood up and shook my hand. "I'll leave you alone now." There was a coldness in his black eyes as he shut the door.

I turned to Kim, but she was too far involved in her body. Her legs opened and the mice scurried about her crotch. She bent forward, her black hair cascading between us. She was intent on the pleasure and too shy now to glance at me.

She moaned. I thought of a pigeon cooing in its nest. Her belly began rising and falling, and I was afraid her robe would open completely.

"I can't, Kim. I can't." My hand reached out to comfort her; then snapped away.

Her knees moved with a quiet rhythm, and I felt sorry for her; so lovely, wearing her glasses and the revealing robe, her body flushed with love.

The robe separated as her thighs spread even further, her legs still covered at the site where the mice danced. I couldn't help staring at those naked knees.

She released another tiny moan.

Her thighs shuddered, I put my hands on her knees. The flesh was warm and firm.

She glanced at me, grateful. Drops of sweat trickled down her temples, and her glasses steamed up, but she didn't take them off even when her eyes disappeared behind the misty circles. I pressed against her knees, pushing my fingertips into the flesh. "Quickly," she said, "I'm going to come soon."

I didn't speak, holding her knees until her belly swelled as if inflated inside. Then she was motionless. The glittering drops of her sweat made me recall a trip to the north in a freighter, how the water condensed on the cool yellow metal above my bunk. Kim began to sob.

I don't know why I felt guilty. "I'm sorry."

"That's alright, I understand." She took off her glasses and wiped them with a busyness meant to distract me from the flushed blood behind her skin. I pulled my hands back.

She shook her head, and put her glasses on again. My fingers had left six red imprints on each of her knees.

Six nightmarish fingers. It was strange that I seldom noticed them anymore.

I was born with six fingers on each hand, and the children of the Kwok family often teased me when I was attending university, but they hadn't recently: maturity brings a little discretion. And like me, they'd grown used to the extra appendages.

She buttoned up her robe, shy now, and smiled demurely, turning to leave the room. I followed behind.

Outside, her parents stood in the hallway. The father, a short man with thick and square glasses, gave me a questioning look. I shook my head. Then he turned to her and she also shook her head before running down the hallway, releasing a sob as she slammed the door to her bedroom.

I noticed the hallway mirror. My face. I was Chinese. The shock wanted to tear me out of the dream.

Open up. Shut it down. Let me out.

No, the dream said. You cannot escape. Now that you have inherited a history and a desire, you will live with it. The dream said I was a successful young man, that my grandfather came over from Hong Kong to work on the railroad at the turn of the century and that I, the third generation, had made good, which is why, in my arrogance, I was so fascinated by the Kwok's inability to become completely westernized. Confused? Yes. But this is a dream. It owns everything a dream owns, complete with exotica and tacky, erotic visions. I was back in the hallway.

Kim's mother, a dumpy and cheerful woman, smiled without restraint. "We must go to the wedding."

It was an hour before Kim could be cajoled out. From the expression on Lee's face, it became apparent he thought her parents cared too much. There are those among us who can only understand authority.

The men were dressed in suits, and the women in fine dresses, but Kim left the house wearing her cutoffs and a T-shirt.

We climbed on our bicycles and pedalled down the hill. I was surprised by Kim's mother as she straddled hers, indelicate, hiking up her skirt and showing the flabby trunks of her legs to everyone. The father sat astride his bike with a rigid air, hurt that we never considered the lush comfort of his new, blue Cadillac.

We went down the hill too fast, and Kim's mother took the corner like a professional, her ornate dress billowing, making her look even fatter — a brocade balloon on wheels.

Then we cycled past the new subdivision where the skeletal ribs of the unfinished houses rose up in a row. The last one had been torched, and its blackened frame made me uneasy.

Down the long stretch between the trees I flowed behind Kim, watching the curve of her buttocks devouring the narrow seat while her legs pumped the pedals, and I began to regret my decision.

At last we arrived at the bank of the river, between the railway tracks and the north fork. Beyond the riprap around the bridge were the mudflats and the wide, sandy beach. In the distance, down the beach on the other side of the tracks where the city ended, another party was assembling — the groom and his family.

While we parked and locked the bicycles, Kim stepped into the change-room under the trestle bridge, followed by her mother and younger sister. Her aunt had been waiting by the door with a bundle perched on her hand. The old woman attempted to enter, but had difficulty wedging the bundle through the door. Once she'd made it, she slammed the door with an irritated, final gesture. The little house under the trestle was barely large enough to hold one person, and there were a lot of crashing noises as the group fidgeted within its confines. An hour of boredom passed before they emerged.

First came the mother, next the younger sister; then the aunt. Last was Kim, decked now in the clothing from the bundle. She resembled a great, eastern queen; her headdress rose almost a foot above her forehead, and was fronted with a gilded crane; her black hair flowed over her shoulders, down the beautiful red and gold dress embroidered with more cranes than it needed. She wore tiny red shoes which made walking difficult, and her hands were joined together, sleeves trailing to the earth.

I wondered if she'd weep on those sleeves before the day passed. The dress's train slid along the ground like a glistening dragon. Her glasses reflected the sun.

The family was pleased. Her father grinned, proud.

"I don't want to get married yet."

The smile on the man's face vanished. He squeezed his hands together. "What would you like, my daughter?"

"I want to catch fish."

"You want to catch fish?"

"I want to catch fish."

Her father looked at Lee.

Lee turned to me. "She wants to catch fish?"

I shrugged my shoulders.

A conference was held among the members of the family while I maintained a discreet distance. Then the cousin left and hurried upriver. He returned in a few minutes, breathless.

He was followed by two miniature gondolas that were at most ten feet long, floating on the river, each piloted by a midget. The navigators were man and wife or brother and sister — they had that kind of closeness, and they were pretty to watch. The woman poled her ornate boat in the lead, and reminded me of a poem from the Tang dynasty. "She was small enough to dance on the palm of your hand."

She beached her craft in the shallows and Kim strode forward, a mischievous wink beckoning me to follow. At first I was too fascinated to move. The gondola's carved seats represented the tongues of demons, the heads winking on the floor of the boat.

Kim stepped in, and I lifted the hem of her dress so it wouldn't get wet. The tiny navigator poled us into the middle of the slow river while the man picked up Kim's father and mother. Lee remained ashore, pacing on the bank and glancing at his watch. Kim's younger brother and sister pouted beside the change-room, guarded by the spinster aunt in her finery.

"There's one!" Kim shouted, pointing to the rocky stretch under the trestle. For the first time I saw her decorated hand, a ring on every finger. The pilot handed a silver fishing rod to Kim. I baited the hook with a worm from the brass jar at my feet, and Kim awkwardly hurled the line upstream, hampered by the voluminous costume.

In the shallows, I saw a purple-bodied fish drifting with the current. It reminded me of a cod, but it had the long, flowing fins of a Siamese Fighting Fish. They rippled dark blue and deep red in the water, trailing a foot behind the fish.

The worm bounced across the bottom, past the creature's head. The fish darted forward, mouth elongated, revealing the clear membrane around the rim of the jaws. It inhaled the worm.

"I've got him!" She laughed, and reeled in line. The fish was jerked into the air and landed with a thump on the bottom of the boat, splashing water over her costume.

Her father beamed, flashing his flawless teeth. He nudged his wife, pointing out the fish as it flopped wildly in the boat near our guide. It was almost as big as the tiny woman.

Kim's mother sat like a stone at the front of her boat.

"She caught a big fish," Kim's father shouted to Lee who had stopped his pacing.

Lee was twenty feet away, and there was no need to shout. "Yes, very good. Is she ready to get married yet?"

Mr. Kwok settled down. He scrutinized his daughter, but I had unhooked the fish and rebaited the line. "There's another one!" I hurled hook and worm behind the boat. This one was bigger and had more blue, resembling an eel with marvellous fins that became purple near the tips.

The fish took the bait and was soon flopping alongside the first. I unhooked its mouth and was spearing another worm when I noticed the bride gazing at the shoreline. "I'm ready to get married now." I held the hook up, the worm writhing before her eyes – silently pleading for her to continue, but she shook her head.

"She's ready to get married now," her father shouted to Lee who had already heard. The boats turned around in the narrow water of the river, and we beached. The bride climbed out first, with me holding her hem too high. I could see her buttocks and black underwear, but I was afraid of the cloth being ruined. Her mother eyed me angrily, and I knew that after today I would no longer be welcome with the family.

Mr. Kwok pulled out a fistful of gold coins and gave them to the midgets. Kim had reached the railway bridge when the distant beat of a drum began.

"Hurry," Lee said to Mr. Kwok, "the groom is impatient. He's starting."

Then I heard a rustling noise and a shape whistled overhead.

"Look, it's the flamingo," Kim's younger sister cried out. The tall bird landed gracefully on the far side of the river by the south fork. The brilliant pink plumage contrasted with the grey sand near the shallows.

It had escaped from the zoo two years ago, and now lived a lonely existence on the delta and in the mudflats, surviving the harsh winters it had never been born to know. Animals can adapt themselves to an unfamiliar world. Yet it seemed lost without a mate, separated from its flock.

"We should release all of the flamingoes," I said. Kim cocked her head at an angle, her headdress tilting towards the sun. She smiled.

Lee took her arm and turned her around as if she were a puppet. The rest of us hurried to catch up as she proceeded under the railway bridge, while her mother gave an annoyed signal to the sister to pick up the hem of the dress I had dropped. It was being soiled as it dragged along the ground. The useless aunt followed behind the procession, trying to appear useful.

"But what about the fish?" Kim's younger brother stood by the bank where the gondolas had beached. The fish lay in the sand, mouths opening and closing, taking a long time to die.

"Cook the purple fish with oil and salt, and I will have it for my wedding feast," Kim said.

"And the blue one?" Lee asked.

"We'll feed the blue one to the dog sharks when they come into the shallows tonight."

I wasn't surprised when she said that. I had often come here with the children to feed the sharks any ratfish I snagged while salmon fishing. We loved to watch those smooth brown torpedoes slide up the shallows of the salty tidal water at the forks.

We used to stand on the bridge, and Kim especially loved the way the sharks' eyes glowed green when they slashed their heads sideways, trying to slice the tough ratfish in half. Often, they rose to the surface and made strange woofing sounds that caused much speculation among us. Were they called dogfish because they barked like dogs in the night?

Mr. Kwok was irritated now. On top of everything else, the idea of throwing good food to the sharks was more than he could bear. "You will not come down to the beach tonight. You will be sleeping with your husband."

"With his cold hands on me?"

"With his hands on you."

Kim, angry, turned to the beach once more. The drumming was insistent in the distance, and we moved forward; her young brother lingered beside the dying fish. In a few minutes, the boy would cry because he didn't know what to do with them.

We passed under the bridge, but the rocky ground around the trestle was difficult for Kim in those tiny red shoes.

Kim's brother wiped away his tears and rushed after us, deserting the ungutted fish. Mr. Kwok was red-faced, yet he said nothing. He wanted to get the wedding over with now.

We crossed the mudflats and reached the sand. It was low tide, the grey expanse of the beach stretched for miles down to the American border. The sun neared the horizon, and strange colours played in the sky.

The groom was dressed in blue, and he let his flowing robe trail on the beach, oblivious to the dirty sand. Behind him walked his family, and behind them a man with a monstrous drum, beating out the slow time as they marched towards us. If we proceeded at the same, awful speed it would take an hour for the two parties to meet.

Even from this distance I could see he had large, ugly teeth. I knew I wouldn't like him. There was something about his forced posture that signalled too much arrogance. He would beat Kim when they were married.

Our wedding party organized itself into a semblance of discipline and stepped forward with the same small steps to the torpid beat of the drum.

"I'm going back," I said. The wedding party stopped. The distant drummer faltered, and then continued the rhythm while I wondered what was going through the minds of the groom's party. Farther up the beach, there was a modest crowd of interested bystanders and relatives seated on the driftwood, watching the show.

"But you can't do that," Lee said.

"I certainly can."

Kim turned around and looked at me. There was a sad expression in her eyes. She nodded once, her face a stone.

"Don't do it, Kim! Come back with me. They can't make you!"

Something rammed against my mouth, and the black world arrived, followed by glittering lights, and I felt my lips swelling as I fell on the sand. Lee had punched me.

He stood above me, fists clenched, waiting to see what I would do.

Warm stuff ran down my chin. It dripped onto the sand, and soaked in. I wanted to whisper "Don't go" to my blood, but it was absorbed by the beach. I let my hand scrabble the sand, and my lip mushroomed. I could see it swelling when I glanced down. At least my teeth were still firm.

There was an apparition moving through the sand, my hand. Six fingers. The blood filled my mouth and I swallowed it. It seemed odd that my blood was warmer than me when it was me. I wished I could take the rest back from the sand and leave this place.

"You're right. You better go," Lee said. "We don't want you . . ." He was going to say something else but stopped.

I climbed to my feet, holding my palm against my mouth.

The blood wouldn't stop flowing. It ran through my fingers. I held out my hand; the lines of blood flowed like open veins down its length. "I can't help it if I've got six fingers."

Kim made a disdainful noise and resumed her slow walk. The family turned away, and I left.

I walked up the flats and under the bridge, by the dead fish with their soiled fins. The gondolas were long gone, and the flamingo as well. The midgets must have poled up the south fork. I took the north fork, and as the river widened, found I had less area to walk on. Greasy, slime-covered stones began to appear in the shrinking bank and they made travel difficult.

When I reached the third bend I discovered the couple. They stood by a fire, in their underwear, their costumes hanging from the branches of an alder. Around the site, stretching from the beached boats to the perimeter of the campfire were scattered pink feathers, bloody at the tips. The headless, plucked flamingo, impaled on a stick, hovered above the flames.

They smiled disarmingly at me, embarrassed by my discovery of them. The man gestured for me to sit by the woman, voluptuous in her underwear, despite her tiny size.

"How much will it cost for her to squat on my lap?" I asked.

When I realized he was considering an answer, I hurled a few coins into the fire, and walked away, making no secret of my disgust.

Beyond their camp the river narrowed, and I leaped from stone to stone on the bank. I slipped, wetting my pantlegs and shoes. Now every step released a mushy sounding squelch. My shoes were ruined, but I didn't stop. As I followed the narrowing creek, I ascended the mountain, towards the glacier at its head.

I came to a bluff, and through the twisted branches of the scrag pines, saw the bay, the ocean, and the archipelago beyond. The sky had turned a threatening orange, and wisps of clouds hung over the water — luminous with the last rays of the sun. Near the western horizon the sky was darkening to a lush purple that reminded me of the second fish's fins.

The wedding parties had almost united, approaching each other at that awful, ominous pace. Despite the distance I could hear the threatening drum beat as both gaudy sides came together. I pressed my tongue against the ragged edge of my lip. The bleeding had stopped. The crowd in the driftwood cheered when the drum beat ended, and the groom lifted his hand to touch Kim's lifted hand.

The voice returned. "Open your eyes," it said. But my eyes were already open, and I didn't want to return.

The dream that was finishing and the dream that I live are the same. I exist in a world I didn't make, one that I cannot justify. The sole thing I can do is refuse it, and remain in the twilight where the lifted hands freeze. Open your eyes. No dream can tell me that. It can make me into a fake Oriental with six fingers and erotic angst, full of the sad conventions of race and family and sex our society promotes. And it can make me hope. It can make me dream a dream beyond the dream, but it cannot make me stop thinking, stop feeling the pain of odd occurrences in an odd world. Open my eyes? Wake up? I am awake. My eyes are open, and I'm going to stay here until the whole stupid, lost, flock of pink flamingoes arrives and survives in the mudflats.

CAN SNOW VULTURES SLEEP
ON ELECTRIC WIRES?

When I arrived on Crystal I was regarded with suspicion by the customs agent. It's not often that driller/blasters come to this isolated and icy planet. He went over my papers several times while the cargo of consumer goods was unloaded. Then he went over them again.

"Not many miners fly in. It's mostly a local crop."

"I'm different. I appreciate the outlander places. You can see from my travel card where I've been." It was fake, but a good fake.

He studied the travel card. "Hot ones, cold ones, jungles and deserts. You relish your weathers."

"There is work here, isn't there? That's what they told me at the Mine Bureau."

"There always is. The boys die regularly in the shafts, but the spacers need their plutonium."

I took the shuttle past the reactors and found the headquarters. Two shifts later I was in the shafts, mapping out my laser holes. I made a few mistakes and broke several mechanicals, but I soon discovered the crews were poorly trained, and I wasn't obvious. The recent month of study served me well. Now all I had to do was pick up enough of the local jargon and habits in order to pass for a Crystalman.

The quarters were cramped, the mechanicals were junk, and the customs agent was correct; the boys died regularly in the shafts. Needless to say, the food was awful. If I'd been an informer I could have gathered enough material on the company to blackmail every manager for life, but that's not my business, and checking out the mine was an aside. I was waiting for the month of no-snow.

The month of no-snow, the month of no spores; it didn't come to South, and I soon discovered this break in the weather caused a genuine difference between the people of the two regions. In the mines they knew little of their distant neighbours, and what they did know was suspicion.

I have a weakness that breaks me down occasionally, a disease that makes me want to give up. I'm a quitter at heart. So I waited until the last days of no-snow before I rigged my blast wrong. When they cleared away the rubble they'd find the mechanicals and a mystery, but this mine didn't care, and they'd file me under terminated. I burned my cards, using my second set when I caught the last shuttle to North. There was no way of tracing me, no way of return until the next month of no-snow, fifteen Terra months away. I had to perform the job now.

I climbed off the snow train, a single-railer, in North and wasn't impressed by the site. The cement domes were seedy, they didn't appear to have a great future. The people walked the streets, their faces empty — oval bags filled with blood. I noticed there weren't many children or older people. There wasn't a hotel either in this frontier town, so I had to move fast. Tomorrow was the end of no-snow, and the weather would return. I had my thermal suit in my kit, but I didn't relish the thought of getting lost in the ice winds.

Tom Sharpe's house wasn't hard to discover. After receiving a suspicious stare from the first couple I asked, a young woman pointed to the outskirts of town and turned away without a word. They don't appreciate strangers in North.

The first spore plants of winter were bursting around me as I passed the last of the cement domes.

The bright, red squabs of the snow vultures scuttled at my feet, beginning to bristle with the feathers they needed to get them through the cold time. I figured the birds must have a fast metabolism to be so immature with the hard weather a day ahead. Then, a few feet from Sharpe's house, I found an unhatched egg. The perfect birds were not so perfect.

His house was the newest in town, and it gave me a pitiful twist in the chest when I saw it. Instead of going with the more practical cement dome, he'd built a wood-frame house, hellish to heat and uneconomical. It reminded me of the slides my grandfather had shown of his father's house in Saskatchewan. I could see I'd be needing a lot of answers from Sharpe, and the answers might be odd from an artist who'd titled his paintings with questions for the last seven years.

A few seconds after I pressed my palm to the view plate, a smooth voice said: "Who?"

I knew he was watching me closely. I gave him my most disarming smile. "Your apprentice."

"I don't have an apprentice."

"You do now."

There was silence. The door slid open and I stepped in. He was sitting at a bone table beside the screen. The house was the craziest assortment of antiques and moderns from every galaxy, the building itself finished with wood and bone and plastic and metal and glass. The stuff must have cost a fortune to ship.

"Sit down."

I sat down.

"What's your name?"

"Jon Kavas."

"What do you want?"

"Can snow vultures sleep on electric wires?"

"Yes," he smiled, surprised. Sharpe was a good-looking man, older than me, perhaps fifty. There seemed no reason why he would desert green fields to retreat to this cold planet, and paint nothing but snow vultures, every painting a question. There was no reason except for an artist's eccentricity and the distant expression that often travelled over his face, giving him a creepy smile.

"What happens when the snow vulture shows its red eye?"

"When they open their eyes, they've sensed that meat is near. They'll break the snow off their shoulders, and fly to the feed." He studied me without emotion.

"Is that a man sleeping with snow vultures?"

"Yes. Why are you giving me the titles of my paintings?"

"I want to know the answers."

He shrugged as if I were a fool; his answers were correct, but my questions were wrong. "Do you want coffee? It's real — Colombian. I have sugar and canned milk."

That didn't surprise me. With what his paintings sold for, he could afford the heavy expense to import anything he wanted. "I never pass on real coffee."

There was a sound behind me, and I half-turned as the woman slipped into the room and took a seat at my side. I nodded. "My name's Jon."

She gave me a tiny smile.

"That's my other half, Ingra." Sharpe rose to prepare the coffee. She was silent. She was also beautiful. Artists don't keep ugly things around them, and from the tone of his voice I could tell she was as much a possession to him as the eccentric furnishings of his house. "She doesn't talk much, so please restrict your questions to me."

When the coffee was ready he set a steaming mug in front of me, as well as one for himself. Ingra sat like a stone between us. "What else do you want?" he asked.

"I want to be your apprentice."

"Why?"

"I looked at your work too much, and now it haunts me. I want to find out what you've got."

He smiled. Those weird eyes scanned me, and I knew I was in trouble. "You from South?"

"I may be the son of a miner from South, but I know how to draw and clean a spray-gun and mix colours." It was true. I'm talented; everything comes to me with an unnatural ease.

"Have you been off planet?"

He was leading me on, sinking me with a big weight. I decided to let him. "No."

Then I understood why he talked and moved so slow. He was drugged. He pulled a tiny can of argon out of the bone drawer and sprayed his finger-tips. You could see the drug slowing him down more, but it couldn't conceal the tension inside the man. "You're an impressive liar," he said.

"No one on Crystal South has seen my paintings. The show at the mine that I've listed on my C.V. is a fake. A private joke. You talk like one from South, move like one, but you're a fake." Then he laughed. "And what's more, you want me to know you're lying." The last words were so trailed out they made me uncomfortable.

I gave him a bit of silence to get lost in. The man was more intelligent and daring than I had been led to believe. One should never talk to artists about other artists. They had me thinking he was a maniacal, pompous idiot, stuffed with postures and poses.

"My past is best kept to myself, because it's not nice. I'm a wanderer, and yes I'm too old to be an apprentice." I paused, sorting myself out. I fly by the seat of my pants and it gets me in trouble a lot. "I saw your paintings in New York. You could go back and be the cultural hero of the age, but you stay here and paint the same thing, each time more beautifully."

"So you're a hungry man, and you've come to feed?"

I shrugged. I was a little annoyed at myself for spending all my time working out a cover in South, and then throwing it away.

"I can accept that." He finished his coffee. "But you can't be my apprentice. I'm up to my ears in unbutchered meat. I'll give you a tour of the house, serve you dinner, let you sleep here for the night, and then you're on your own."

"The train won't be coming around again until the next month of no-snow, more than a Terra year away."

"You've got a thermal suit, haven't you?"

I nodded.

"You can feed off the spores in the air."

I had failed for now, but I had the night to change his mind. I wasn't worried yet.

We walked through the house as if it were a clutter of dreams. Everything was too much. The walls were lined with crazy paintings, stuffed bird-reptiles from Arctura III, glass cases of Cephalonian red dust, intricate rugs from the looms of the spider weavers. There was so much richness I couldn't assimilate a tenth of it; my eyes clicked the details to memory so I could consider it tonight in my room.

We followed a narrow hallway of exotic artificially-lit plants and old stoves. There was a dried arrangement in a blown-glass vase. Instinctively, Sharpe's hand reached out and steadied the expensive vessel. The floor seemed weak here, and the vibrations from his step had set it tilting. "Every time you go by — your room is down there, by the way, and the bathroom at this end of the hall — every time you pass here, you will steady the vase. I don't want it broken."

"Why can't you move it to a safer place?"

"I enjoy it where it is."

I caught it as it started to tip again.

The room was a windowless cube, ten feet by ten feet. The floor was lined with sterilized, straw mats. No insects. When I pressed the sleeper switch the light bed jutted from the wall. I stretched on its luminous cushions, and began cataloguing the details. The most interesting one, of course, was what I had not seen. He didn't show me his studio. Nevertheless, filing the imprints for priority would take me ages. I wondered where and how he got the horn of an endangered Equa. Possession alone was enough to bring a man walled exile on Terra, never mind the smuggling, never mind the several other exotic and forbidden objects I had noticed. And he was watching me as I pretended not to know they were illegal.

It was long into the fifteen-hour night of Crystal before I brushed the lights to sleep-dim and undressed. I kept my watch on and lifted the tamper trigger on my backbag, which I settled within arm's reach. I would have preferred the more primitive arrangement of a real bed with blankets because I could have slept with my hand on the gun. This way, if I was surprised I'd have to yank it out of the compartment. I settled into the warming aura of the sleeper and faded away.

The dream arrived quickly. Green was alone in the hotel room when the fire walked up the side of the building and slipped through the window. She saw it, and leaped out of bed, naked, her milk-full breasts jiggling, but the fire had already traversed the room and cut her off from the door. It was a coiling string of flame, yet alive, an animal, a dog on a scent. She backed into a corner. Then the fire ran up her leg.

She turned around and around like a top, whirling fire before she fell to the floor, her back against the wall. The fire died, and left her charred corpse alone in the room.

When I awoke, I was standing beside the vase and it was falling. I caught it in mid-air, and returned it to the stove-top, dried flowers askew. "Damn." I was naked, sweating, and weaponless. The lights were set to dim. Everyone was asleep.

The sweat cooled on my skin as I walked to the bathroom where I urinated the fear out of my body. Then I decided to attempt some spying.

Apart from their bedroom, there was one other room on this floor that I hadn't been shown. Thinking it might be the studio, I clicked the open button and found myself in a messy workshop. Nothing interesting.

I stuffed the images for priority re-sorting later, in case there was anything I missed. Then I noticed the half-used can of red paint, and I couldn't resist a smile. I found a roller. I mixed the paint. It was high quality, iridescent, what I needed.

There was a rough moment in front of their bedroom door. If they were awake there was every chance I'd be blown away as the door slid open, but I'm a lucky man and Sharpe's argon habit helped, so I touched the button.

The lights were set to sleep-dim, suffusing the room with a ruddy orange. Now I knew why I hadn't been shown the bedroom. The other illegals were teasers. This was a bigger stash than I'd ever heard encountered. A haul like this would make the Terran police ecstatic.

They were sleeping on a real bed, naked, among an assortment of living furs. That bed and those furs were worth a citizen's calendar year intake. He was lying with his back and bare buttocks facing me, one leg straddling her open thighs. She had her hand under his neck. They were far gone into sleep, and I guessed they had sprayed a quantity of argon onto their fingers. Her, I wasn't sure about; she wasn't the type, but she was also under his influence.

I set the can by the door, dipped the small roller in, and began on the near wall. I crossed an engraving, a skinned hide, the top of a Seco Wood dresser — a rare piece, now ruined forever. The red streak had a gaudy artistic quality about it, and I couldn't help chuckling to myself. I ran the roller over the walls, the floor, one piercing slash along the low ceiling and across a rug hung as a screen. On the wall facing the bed, there was an enormous painting of a rhinoceros charging out of a night beach, towards the sleeping couple, and for some reason I couldn't mutilate it. The roller went around the painting. Besides, the rhino already had red eyes. Within twenty strokes I had created the work of a madman.

My attention settled on Sharpe and Ingra. They were beautiful, together on the bed. Despite the difference in ages, a picture of loving domesticity. I knew what I was going to do. Sometimes I've got more nerve than brains.

I dipped the roller and approached the bed, once again breathing a little prayer for the potency of the argon. The living furs eyed me suspiciously, and I ran the roller over the silent eyes of the nearest one. Next, I very gently painted the cheeks of Sharpe's buttocks, and continued across her flat belly, as far as I could reach.

I walked around to the other side of the bed, and started my stroke again. Her eyes were open. I froze.

She cocked her head at an angle, staring like a curious cat. I winked and dabbed her on the nose with the roller, and she smiled as her eyes followed the crazy line of paint that wavered through the dim room. Then she closed up, pretending to sleep. I continued the stroke to the door, where I had begun. Excellent, I thought, admiring my creation. It needed a title and a signature. I stuck my finger in the paint and scribbled "Can Sleeping Lovers Have a Red Conscience?" on the door, signing it with a flourish.

I gloated over my painting. The sleeping lovers with the slash of paint and the red dot were the perfect touch. "What a sweet threesome we shall make," I said softly, and left.

After cleaning the paint off myself in the workshop, I returned to my ten-foot room so absentmindedly that I just caught the glass vase before it hit the floor. This time the dried flowers were even more askew when returned to their perch.

I dressed and took my backbag to the kitchen to wait for the spectacularly long dawn of Crystal North. Once I had the bag settled so the compartment would be accessible from my seat, I perked a pot of the good Colombian and drank coffee for the remainder of the night.

There was no movement in the house until long after dawn. The bedroom door slid open and I heard the patter of feet to the bathroom, followed shortly by another pair of feet. They spent a while cleaning themselves off before returning to the bedroom. There was more silence. I sipped my coffee, undisturbed. I've learned to hold myself quiet, even when my chest is tight with anxiety.

The artist entered the kitchen. He looked bright, more cheerful than yesterday. "That little painting of yours has cost me a hundred thousand credits."

"I can't help myself when the artistic impulse strikes."

Without rising I poured coffee into the mug I had set out for him. I was positioned perfectly — didn't have to rise or move away from my pack and the gun.

He seated himself, studying me with a wry face, appreciating how I had taken over his kitchen. "And I don't suppose you have the money to pay for the damage?"

"Hardly a credit."

"But you wouldn't object to working off the cost as my apprentice?"

"What a brilliant idea."

"I thought you'd enjoy it."

Ingra arrived. She'd been listening in the hallway. I poured her coffee without rising from my seat. She smiled, wordless, and I wondered if she could speak at all. She put her hand on the artist's lap. He ignored her. He was staring at me.

The memory of Ingra's small, naked breasts made me think of Green. Yet, there was no comparison between the slim litheness of her and Green's full figure. "When do we start?"

The door was in the living room. It was an engraved panel made out of wood, with a brass knob attached. I recognized its shape from old family pictures I'd seen, and was lost in thought. Is that what they used in the old days before the first flight out? He grasped the knob, turned it, and the thing swung open on hidden hinges. Very simplistic, but it served its function. I could have kicked myself for not realizing its purpose last night.

We faced a flight of stairs encased with wood-rimmed glass panes — on either side a snow hole, artificially lit, and a few motionless snow vultures.

I ran my fingers along the glass, almost made dizzy by the steep descent of the stairs. "What's the purpose of this?"

"You could call it a combination of eccentricity and energy saving."

We continued down the stairs until we reached a steel door. He tapped the combination and the door slid open. Inside was a large studio that faced a window overlooking the snow basement and the vultures. "I keep these for reference," he said, waving at the window and the stationary birds. "Most of my rough work I do outside." He was trying to impress me with this artist-going-into-the-wilds patter.

"What's there?"

That was a wrong question. He glanced at the tamperlocked door on the other side of the studio — then at me. "You're very curious. That's my meditation place, private, for my eyes only."

"Just asking."

"Don't. I'll do the telling."

"Did you use a real body for the model?"

The painting: three birds devouring the belly of a dead man in the snow. It was gross, and the face was familiar.

"Who are you, and why are you here?"

"I told you my name, and I want to learn. The way to learn is to ask questions."

He studied me for a moment. "Do you think you can clean the jars without any more questions?"

I smiled.

He smiled.

We both knew where we were — a crazy planet miles from the regular routes, one year to go for a trip to the space port. He was a smart man, and if I'd played innocent he would have spiked me within days.

The terrible night came too fast, like every night, and I was alone with my dreams. Green was naked again, so bloody naked and beautiful. She was screaming. The floor crawled, writhed, red and muddy black. Thousands of salamanders slithered about her feet on some kind of mass exodus to a lizard heaven. She spun about, one foot kicking her into a spinning, human top. She circled faster and faster until she burst into flame, her hair a whip of fire. Then she fell against the wall, burning and dead. The salamanders in the blaze — I knew there was a story about this and I tried to remember it, but the files in my head were scrambled.

"Son-of-a-bitch!" It was morning again. I awoke with the gun in my hand. One of these days I'm going to blow myself away on my own tamper trigger. I tucked the gun into the pack, reloaded the tamper, and wondered what was for breakfast.

"It's not that they treated me badly," he said. "They were reasonable, but they didn't care about me because I had no connections. Art is a political business." He was going over the sky with a spray. I knew what was involved, but I didn't believe a man could spend this much time on such a limited space. So far, during the weeks I'd been with him, he had worked on the sky alone. He knew his techniques, every one of them. He had learned a lot in his time. There was nothing from the mixing of egg yolk and pigment for a tempera base to the new solvents of the sprays that he didn't know. This skill was devoted to the image of a dead body being devoured by snow vultures.

"I spent ten years in Los Angeles — the center, the core, the spark of the universe." His voice grew soft. "The height of the finest delineation of life. And they were all shit. The intellectual leaders of our society, they had the morality of night crawlers, didn't care for the paintings, only the painter's manipulative abilities in the art scene. I sucked and I slaved and I ate their garbage and I was a pawn." He had no compunction about admitting his bitterness. He wanted to paint and paint well, and receive the rewards he deserved.

"Couldn't they see your technique?" I asked, cleaning the 10 brush with a delicate, molecule-altered solvent he had developed.

"Technique?" He laughed that quiet laugh. "They didn't give a shit about technique. They wanted images and cults. They wanted connections."

"Is that why you came here?"

"Surely. Now I give them cults. Now I give them an image. And since I'm distant, once I made the first few inroads, the rest of the connections slave and fight to get their letters on the year's first express. I was as good then as I am now except that I'm worse. I've made a routine and a rut, a ritual they can dig their fingernails into and say that's that and therefore this is this. A ready-made myth. Disposable art. I've cheapened myself to make myself great."

Bitter was not the word. I smiled and handed him the brush. He hated my smiles. They drove him crazy; and I would never answer him the same way on the same question. Strangely, he grew softer and quieter when vexed.

He took the brush, and wagged it in front of my nose. "You. You've got the nerve, and you've got the brains. You've also got a little skill. Why don't you quit, and paint?"

"Quit what and paint what?"

"Paint whatever you like. Quit the police. Nobody loves an informer. I can see your anguish."

I gave him disdain. Then I smiled. That was worth a little irritation. "Informers are pigs. And when I'm ready I'll make my art." I smiled again, just to drive him wild.

He returned to his sky, unhappy. "I've often wondered if the words paint and pain derive from the same source."

Ingra was different. I couldn't impress her. She was slow and hard, kept a secret life inside herself. There were no keys, no passes of the hand that opened doors. Often, we'd sit in the kitchen for hours without saying a word, but the relationship developed. I didn't have to say anything.

What I had at first taken for distance, for contempt on Sharpe's part, was that same variety of silent easiness. They worked well together. He was tense and too smart, burning, while she was cool and unthinking; in certain ways, more alive than him or me.

"Why do you paint this, when you're painting less than you can?"

"I'm not painting less than I can, merely more of my best. Do you understand the difference?"

"No."

He laughed. I was beginning to enjoy the man. "I paint because I must paint. I've got a chemical missing, a switch that makes me wrong when I'm not painting."

"You've got the money. Paint what you want to paint. You don't need the adulation."

"Haven't you varnished that panel yet? If you spent less time talking you might get your work done."

"I never claimed skill or speed."

"You never claimed anything."

"That's right."

"Who are you? What do you want?"

"You know my name. I want to learn."

"I wanted to learn once, now I'm tired, jaded. I've read the books, I've bought the objects, I got the woman. I can do anything I want, and it's meaningless."

"Why do you always title your paintings with a question?"

"You asked me that before."

"You never answered."

"I never will."

Frequently, I went for walks in the snow when the tension got too strong. It's a supernatural world, nothing but ice and the bedraggled branches of the crystal trees, the sole plants in this part of the planet, apart from the spores.

The snow made for hard walking, even with my terrain boots. I pushed on because I had no destination. My conclusion was several months away, and I didn't know if I'd make it that far. Besides, I couldn't get away from my memories of Green.

When I saw the three figures on the stump, I realized they were wrong. They were covered with snow, yet the outline of the middle one was disjointed, didn't fit a bird.

"Who are you?" I asked, half expecting a shape-wolf.

The thing shook its head and the snow fell off. "Nickel." He assessed me. "And you've come far into the outland."

I knew who he was. "You were eaten by the snow vultures."

"Is that what he said?"

"What else could he say?"

"First of all, the birds eat dead meat, not live stuff; second, he's a monster."

"He's a great artist. I'm learning from him."

"That doesn't make him less a monster."

"Why are you hiding in the snow?"

"Who said I was hiding? I'm dreaming."

The birds at his side were immobile, but I could feel the energy radiating from them. "Dreaming?"

"They're the real life." He nodded towards the vultures. "They dream about nothing, and they live on everything."

"It must be uncomfortable."

"I've got my thermal suit, and I feed on the winter spores. When the snow gets heavy I shake it off. I'm learning about nothing."

I felt disgusted. "Everybody wants to learn everything about nothing."

"It's been a few months since no-snow. I'm surprised that you've lasted this long." He shook off the remainder of his white coat and stood up, stretching slender legs that had been cramped for a while. "You're not from Crystal, and you're with him. He's going to eat you."

"Eat me?"

"He kills his apprentices. Then he cooks and eats them. Like the birds, he grows bored with living off the spores in winter. But he can afford to buy imported meat; that's what I don't understand."

I stood immobile, recalling the eccentric remark about unbutchered meat that Sharpe made on my first day.

Later, in the evening, I had to deal with it again. When Ingra put the roast on the table, I lost my appetite.

I sent a questioning expression in her direction, but she ignored me. Sharpe happily spread red jelly over his cut. "I don't care what they say," he grumbled, "a man can't live off those bloody spores all winter. He needs meat, and I love my meat."

I cut off a slice, and stuffed it into my mouth. "It must be expensive having this shipped from off world."

"I've got the money, and I enjoy my treats."

He was right, I suppose. The meat went down well when one lived mostly off the air. I finished my plate, and had second helpings, trusting it was pork and not my predecessor.

"There's something excruciating about it."

"The meat?" I asked innocently, finishing the second plate.

He studied me, dubious. "The paintings . . . the paintings . . . ."

"Sorry, I have a one-track mind."

"If you're going to be an artist, you have to learn to think at least a dozen ways at once."

"Sounds painful. It's enough trouble being single-minded."

"Nobody ever said it was nice."

"I though art was great and beautiful and fulfilling and so on."

"It's a stuffed crocodile."

That phrase was familiar, and I pulled the file. "Alfred Jarry, born 1873. He lived in a closet, wore a brace of pistols, and invented the improbable science of pataphysics. A classic artist, he died of malnutrition; his last request was for a toothpick."

"Not many would recognize that line. I'm impressed."

"I know."

When I returned, Nickel was there. A Terran month had passed, and he hadn't moved.

"Are you sure he eats them?"

The head shuddered, a flurry of snow fell, one eye opened. "Is it safe?"

I didn't answer, letting him worry for a bit. He wasn't as calm as the motionless posture suggested. "There is no safety."

He contemplated my remark too long. "He eats them."

"Is that why you're hiding?"

"I told you before; I'm not hiding." The question annoyed him. "When I found Sharpe I thought I wanted to be an artist. I watched him paint those birds for a winter, saw the way he became immobile, a stone, as his hand worked. I cleaned his brushes and primed his panels. He was generous, showed me the techniques, offered his knowledge, but after a while I realized I'd never have the skill he had."

A blast of ice wind swept over us, drowning him out. "... There was another thing, the birds. I wondered what they were thinking. One day I was spraying a gesso ground for a panel, and I got involved with the motion of the gun going back and forth across the wood. I woke up two hours later, the spray gun empty, and Sharpe was angry."

"Did he go for you?"

"No, but there was a weirdness in his eyes. He was sizing me up for steaks."

"Baked apprentice pie?"

"I never wanted to be an artist. I wanted to be immobile, the way he was when he painted the snow vultures. I walked into the snow and haven't been inside since. These birds don't think, they live. It's the thinking that kills me."

"Sharpe did a painting of you not thinking with your snow vultures."

"He did?" There was a moment of fear in his eyes — then wonderment. If Sharpe painted him without his knowledge it meant the artist held no grudge. Nickel wouldn't have been a difficult target perched between the birds. Nickel shrugged. "He's a strange man."

"How do you survive during no-snow?"

"I starve. I hang on until the spores return. That's the worst time, because it's difficult to hold motionless in the warmth. Besides, the young squabs run about everywhere. The only time they move without a reason. They're distracting."

"Don't they eat dirt in no-snow?"

"I can't eat dirt, not the same metabolism." He gazed into the grey clouds. "I don't enjoy dead meat either. I live off the spores, and when there's none . . . I manage."

"What's not thinking like?" I asked, wondering if it resembled my dreams.

"Try it." He shoved the nearest snow vulture roughly. A red eye blinked open; then the bird shuffled sideways, scattering snow. The eye shut again. I climbed onto the snowy perch and settled myself as comfortably as possible, keeping watch on the bird to my right. It was motionless again.

"They'll open their eyes if there's a serious distraction," Nickel said, "and they often fly to another location, maybe three times a season. I think they're looking for a place with more carcass potential. I don't know. But they can survive without meat because of the spores."

"How do I not think?"

He wiggled around, settling himself again, "You just do it."

I shut my eyes and tried not to think about Green. For a while it worked, and I felt peaceful. Then I started to drift. She was in front of a hut, and a volcano was spewing lava. Rivers of it flowed around the hut, shrinking the island of untouched earth "Can't you see I love you!" She pulled the baby from her breast and milk dripped onto the steaming ground. She shook the infant in my direction; then hurled it onto the lava. It disappeared without a sound, a puff of smoke belching from where it sank. "Doesn't that prove it!" she screamed. "Doesn't that prove it!" The lava surged onto her feet and she cried out with horror, with pain too deep to be imaginable. She spun around, smoking, and fell against the hut, her eyes open, tongue dangling, the milk still dribbling from her breast. Then the hut torched.

I opened my eyes. The clearing was quiet. Nickel was covered with a dusting of snow. The vulture pointed straight ahead, silent, not thinking. As I sat next to the bird I could sense its power, and I knew why Nickel had become fascinated with them. Being at its side was the same as sitting next to a god.

The snow crunched noisily beneath my feet as I stood up and walked away. Behind me, the little group remained undisturbed.

Back at the house, Sharpe was out with the elders from the town so I drank coffee in the kitchen, talking to Ingra. I liked her. I used her to forget Green. I had succeeded so well that I desired her more than I should, more than was safe. I'd become convinced that if Sharpe was out of the way, she'd travel with me. She might even go with me and him at the same time, but I wasn't ready to chance that.

Sharpe returned and said we were going to town. I was suspicious, but I climbed into the air car with him. A man has one life to throw away, and he might as well throw it without fear. We drove over the drifts into the little village of cement domes.

At the square we slowed to a halt. Several people approached the car, staring at me, memorizing my face before they wandered off. It made me nervous, but I showed no sign. An armoured vehicle was parked in front of us, and soon I noticed a group of naked people being ushered out of the town hall. The biting cold turned their bare flesh pink as they trod mindlessly into the back of the truck. An older man with a burner kept the weapon trained on them, but that was for show; they were obviously touched with argon. Once they were inside he locked the door, stepped into the truck, and drove away. We followed.

"What's the idea?" I asked Sharpe as he drove behind the large, ugly truck through the deserted streets.

"They're the excess. Either old and feeble or young and delinquent. Troublemakers. The town, you might know, is not under the control of the international force, so this is how we deal with our problems. If the population were to grow it would be too expensive for the locals to import the materials for new domes and so on. Their main income is the fur of the shape-wolves; unreliable during good economic times, let alone bad. Rather than crowding, this is how the town handles its unwanted."

"Why do you bring me here if you think I'm an informer for the police?"

"I never said I thought you were an informer. Are you?"

"Informers are pigs."

We followed the half-buried track of the one-railer until we came to a ravine. The armoured truck stopped and the old man climbed out, burner in hand. He unlocked the back doors and moved away as the naked people stepped from the truck. He waved them on; they gazed vacantly at the mountains.

"Look there." Sharpe pointed. Three snow vultures were perched on the electric wires following the track.

They were eerie, their weight stretching the line almost to ground level. "Amazing muscle control," he said, "to retain immobility on that wire during the ice winds."

"Sleepers on a tightrope."

Suddenly four young men burst from the snow, their bodies flaming red with cold. "They're still alive," Sharpe whispered, astonished. "They're from the first shipment this morning." The drug must have worn off. The guard turned, and levelled the burner. They were cooked, screaming, before they got close. I couldn't etch out the image of one, almost a man — beginning a scraggly beard, rushing across the hill and hollering as if he thought that would scare the guard. I ignored the four smouldering ruins as we drove away. The new victims didn't move.

Sharpe had finished me with the town. Now that I knew their secret they would never let me catch the railer out, especially if they thought I was an informer, which is what Sharpe thought.

But there's no place a man can't escape from, and I wasn't dismayed. While I watched the guard torch the kids I was analyzing the face of the ravine. A few blasts, and enough rocks would fall to slow the train sufficiently for a man in a thermal suit to leap out of the rubble by the tracks and climb aboard. There's no place a smart and lucky man can't escape, and I've had the luck, so far.

That night I left my room a few hours before dawn. They were asleep. I nearly let that bloody vase and its seed pods fall, but I caught it, cursing under my breath, and put it right. Then I descended the glassed stairs to the studio. I was dressed and armed. I had my lock kit with me. For a few minutes I listened, afraid I might be discovered. Then I took out the computer and worked on the combination of the tamper to the inner room. It only needed a couple of clicks because it was a simple outland lock, nothing to worry about when I had chips that could read seventy thousand signals a second.

The door slid open, and there were four bodies inside, dangling on wires. Another was propped against a wall. That was Radja, our informer, his guts pulled out. He was the model for the corpse in the painting. I wanted to kick the pathetic cadaver. "Informers are pigs. Meat for the butcher." The remainder of the victims I didn't recognize. One was a woman, missing an arm. The others were minus a limb or part of a limb. The men had no testicles. "Sweetmeats," I hissed as I examined the grisly bodies. Beyond the door, there was an ill-disguised footstep. I pointed my weapon as he shuffled into the light.

"And delicious," he said, leaning against the entrance, his burner lined up with my gut.

"They say it tastes like pork."

"You should know."

"Should I?"

"Wasn't it lovely with the Endoverian Noodles?"

I smiled. "Actually, it was."

We faced each other, guns pointed, a few yards separating us. A fool might say it was a stalemate. "You're too smart for this business," he said. His eyes flickered in the direction of Radja. "And yet not that smart . . . . You can't escape."

"Police," I flashed my visual card. It was overplayed to say the least, but it distracted him.

"The International? You're not an informer?" He read the glowing syllables in the air. "A captain, licensed to terminate. I'm flattered."

"Don't be. I was passing by Crystal and dropped in to check out the rumours." I've found a little lying never hurt.

"So what are we going to do? If you kill or capture me and try to flee, the townsmen will stop you. They're as guilty as I am. They kill their children and the feeble ones because it's too much bother feeding the wrecks and the surplus. That's evil, isn't it, or is it?"

The pathetic tone of his voice disappointed me. It reminded me of too many men that I'd executed. He was strung out on the argon; the smell of it oozed from the pores of his skin. He was slow and useless, and he knew it. I felt sorry for him. "Why didn't you return when your reputation became solid?"

"I couldn't." He was silent for a moment, sad. "You're a fool if you don't understand."

"You broke yourself for the myth you made."

"That's right!" he screamed, slamming his fist against the wall. The gun slid across the floor, shattered. "Why do you stay with the International when you are what you are!" He pointed accusingly at me, and I wondered if all painters were so melodramatic.

"It's an art," I said.

"Shoot me." He grew quiet, studying the wall, and my respect for him grew. The hammering increased within my chest. I never could be the ice I pretended I was. He leaned against the wall, arms folded. "Free, without me hunting you, on your own in the outland, like Nickel, you have a chance." Then he smirked, as if he understood. "You've been seeing him, haven't you? You've got it figured out."

He was perfectly correct. I pulled the trigger, and the flash glued him to the wall, searing the skin from his face.

The way he fell reminded me of Green. In the studio I picked up the spray compressor and slammed it against the window. The captured snow vultures remained stationary for a moment, until the stench of death invaded their prison, and the red eyes snapped open. I took a last look at the collapsed figure by the door and the hanging bodies beyond him, before I climbed the glass-walled stairs. There was a flutter beneath me. One of the vultures jerked into the air and flew across the basement. It perched on the wooden sill between the broken shards of the window, eyeing the studio and the inner chamber. I banged my hands against the light studs. I was back in the house.

Ingra stood in the kitchen. When she saw me, her mouth twisted. She said nothing.

"Don't be afraid. He's dead. You're free now."

Her terror was obvious. "I'm guilty. I come from the town; the whole village is guilty."

"The village won't be punished. When the International arrives there will be no reprisals, I'll see to that. But none of this will occur again, because Crystal isn't a free world anymore, as of now. We'll make the laws, and enforce them."

"I don't understand. What's the difference between the villagers and Tom?"

I didn't either, so I was stuck without a reply. Revenge, I thought. Revenge for something. "Or me?" I said.

She laughed.

"Come with me, and you'll be free."

She unzipped herself until she stood naked in the center of the room. "Is this what you want?"

"That, and more." This seemed to be the night for gestures.

"Well, you're a fool, because I loved him." She rushed into my arms and embraced me, pressing her breasts against my chest. I holstered the gun, and held her head in my hands, desiring her. Any man would.

"I know."

"You want to put your life between my legs?"

"Don't say that."

She pushed away, and as she moved, she flicked my gun from its holster. It spun across the floor, near the wall. She ran her hand over the lock, and the door slid open while I picked up my gun, as she knew I would. By the time I reached the top of the stairs there was the shattering glass, the sound of her hitting the basement floor with a sickly crunch. I didn't look. I let the red eyes of the snow vultures look for me. I clicked the lock and the door slid shut.

There was nothing to do but collect my pack and get out. When I passed the stove, the vase teetered precariously. I stopped. It swung back and forth as if it had a life of its own, as if it was trying to delay the fall until caught. I didn't catch it. The beautiful glass went over, and splintered on the floor. "Sorry, it was an accident." I strode away from the broken remnants.

It was difficult finding Nickel. The birds had moved, and I scrabbled about the shrouded rocks and spore plant stumps for several earth days before I encountered the group.

I shoved a snow vulture aside, and sat next to him on the boulder. "I want to try not thinking again."

"Is it safe?"

"That depends on your point of view."

"He's dead?"

"He's dead."

"He was a great artist."

"He was."

"You're not an informer. You're police, aren't you?"

I didn't reply. I scuffed the snow off the log, settled myself, and shut my eyes, an act I'm finding harder to do. First, I had to deal with the memories.

The chief inspector met me in the hallway. He said everything was flash-frozen, knowing I'd want to inspect the site in its original condition.

There was my man, pinned against the wall by a dart blast. Nothing in the room had been disturbed. He'd been writing a dispatch when the intruder got him. I didn't waste much time examining the punctured corpse because I'd seen the results of a dart gun before. The last words in the dispatch were strange. "And I should be home Yellow." Yellow was the name of his girl friend; she went missing at the time of the assassination, and the inspector figured the killers had dragged her away for fun and torture.

I thought about the letter on the desk for several minutes. Then I went over the rest of the room. There was nothing obvious, no clues to betray the murderer of one of our best men and a good friend.

It was a simple case of plutonium smuggling, an investigator sent in, a top man who happened to be without assignment at the time, a minor case for him, yet he had died, gruesomely. When I met the officials of the emperor of that supply world, I realized they were slimy. The simple case became complicated.

Yet he had caught on soon. His first report had been one sentence. "Got myself a lead and a girl pregnant." That was him, smug and wild.

I ferreted and I gouged and I bribed. The usual. I confirmed that high people were on the take. All I needed was the hard evidence.

Then I met Green, a free woman with a child at her breast, and I fell into the vacuum, swallowed by the immensity of her gentleness.

I was in bed, waiting for her to finish nursing the child. It clung to her breast, sucking life into its limbs. She pulled it away because she couldn't wait to lie with me. Milk dripped from her as she placed the child in its case. For some reason a poem came into my head. "Then streames ran milke, then streames ran wine, and yellow honey flowede from eche greene tree." She froze, staring at me with horror.

I thought I'd got the line wrong. How crazy the mind is, how stupid I can be. "Or was it, 'and eche greene tree trickled yellow honey'?"

She lifted the cover, and slid in, her warm thigh pressed against mine. I cupped a hand on her breast, my other hand reaching under the bed. "Do you love the rainbow?" I asked, depressed by the stupid, amateurish names.

"Not when it kills me."

"How long have you been an assassin?"

"Does it matter?" she replied.

"No, it doesn't."

"I couldn't kill you."

I looked at her, deep into the grey eyes that led to the center of something beautiful. "No, not when I'm holding the gun."

"I love you." She backed out of the bed, past the child's case, towards the wall where I'd hung my other gun, while I rose like a snake uncoiling from a basket, lifting the burner.

"Don't do it." The blast hit the side of her face, torching her hair. And she spun around crazily. She kept spinning, the unreal nerves of her body turning her until she crashed against the wall and slid to a seated position, facing me, milk leaking from her breast. Three white drops floated on the back of my hand, the hand holding the gun.

"Shit!" My eyes ripped open. The world was tranquil. The snow drifted onto me, drifted as it had since the month of no-snow.

"You're thinking," the smug voice said. I ignored the bundle of snow, resisting the urge to push him over.

I wiggled into a more comfortable position, and closed my eyes. Above me was nothing but clouded sky, and beyond that the million stars, all collecting their planets, each planet holding uncounted people, millions of people living in pain, waiting for someone to save them, someone like me.

TANGANYIKA

After Jim Luster died he went to Tanganyika. He woke up at the wheel of a new car, and the long, black roll of road unravelled into the valley below like a big snake. The landscape was brown, its hills undulating and peppered with stick trees.

He woke up hot and thirsty, his hands on the wheel, his eyes fixed on the nearby trees that were the colour of a deer's hide. The trapped air within the car was suffocating, so he unrolled the window. The heat swept by.

He was tired already.

He noticed the trees on the surrounding hills were twisted — too much wind.

It was an Africa without lions; at least it resembled the Africa he had always dreamed, and Luster was disappointed because there were no lions. If he was going to be dead in Africa, he should have been given lions. But there weren't any animals moving in the valley or the mountains. There wasn't even a bird.

His clothes felt dirty, his mouth dusty, his head full of insect sounds. Yet, he drove on. He wanted to talk, tell himself he was alive, but a squall of crystal-like insect wings drowned out everything, ticking against the windshield and obscuring the route.

He drove for hours down that empty road in the empty valley.

Finally, Luster saw a man gathering hay, and he steered the car onto the dirt shoulder, breaking open a cloud of dust like birds.

The man leaned on a long, wooden rake-thing, waving away the dust from the car with his straw hat as Luster climbed out and slammed the door. The sound of the slamming door echoed in a world that was silent now that the motor was no longer running. It reminded him of when his head hit the rock.

The stranger had dark skin, tanned by years under the sun. A strand of rope held up his baggy trousers. Smiling toothlessly, he resembled a Mexican peasant standing among piles of golden hay.

"Have you died?" the peasant asked, polite, unsure of either the words or perhaps the crazy death they shared in nowhere. He was as solid as stone; big and full of the flesh a man carries in his prime.

"Yes." Luster's ears roared with the sound of the locusts rising from a devoured field. At least something else was alive out there in the empty land. "Where am I?"

"In the valley of Tanganyika."

It sounded logical, and Luster didn't wonder until later if the peasant meant this was a valley in Tanganyika or a valley named Tanganyika. By the time he realized he still didn't know where he was, the man had been left far behind.

Standing lamely in front of him, Luster couldn't think of anything else to say. He wanted to ask the man if he was also dead.

Luster realized the bright hay piled beside the rake wasn't grass. It was the product of huge trees spotted throughout the valley — dead-limbed giants without leaves, burdened by the yellow straw which drifted to the ground at every gust of wind.

"Are you infested?" the peasant asked.

Luster's heart began to pound. His body felt awkward, his thoughts seated above it, as if he were an outsider examining himself. Infested? No, it wasn't disease, unless the disease was too much life. The conclusion was violent and abrupt, but strangely, he didn't regret it. To lie in her arms, his blood leaking onto her, staining the wet stones by the pool, her damp belly cushioning him as the cold seeped from his fingers, up his arms, to the back of his neck. Infested? Is death a disease? Luster looked into the sun. "No." His eyes filled with black spots, so he focused on the peasant, and the spots turned green. The sound of the locusts returned.

The peasant bent to his knees in the straw, searching for something invisible on the ground, ignoring Luster who was still considering infested. There are two kinds of infested. Those who break down, give up, and wait for disease to tag them, and those who fall by chance, get caught by luck and circumstance . . . like him. No, that wasn't a disease. How could he deny the touch of her fingers or that smooth skin on her belly?

The stranger's hand darted forward; he caught something, cupped it in his palm. He stood up and showed it to Luster. It was a silver toad.

"If you're not infested — then you can watch." The man admired and stroked the amphibian his open palm, held it up to the sun and whispered at its head. The toad didn't move. It knew it was in trouble.

He took a small knife from the pocket of his well-used trousers, and with the knife poked out one of the toad's eyes, rolling the tiny ball in his palm as if it were a sacred object. He beckoned for Luster to follow as he walked across the road to a dirt lane while Luster trailed behind like a sick man.

After studying it for a moment, the peasant set the silver toad on the lane and dropped the eye six inches in front of it. The toad sat stupidly in the dirt; then lunged forward and devoured its own eye.

"Let that be a lesson. Never allow anyone to put out your eyes." The peasant shuffled back across the road to his interrupted haying.

Luster couldn't move. The locusts were hungry in the field. It beat at the back of his eyes, that sound like the wind of broken wings, telling him he was going to lose something, and he wanted her arms again, wanted to knead her flesh with his fingers. Alive.

The toad bounced sloppily across the dirt and fell into a pond of clear black water; giant, mossy branches interwove with each other beneath the surface. Green turtles rested on the mud bottom.

One lurched, almost too quick for such a lethargic animal, and its beak engulfed the toad's leg.

Luster turned away, ran to the car, and jumped in, driving off without waving goodbye. He knew he had a long way to go, even if he didn't know where he was going.

And the rock kept rising out of the deep water. Alive. Childhood lovers, they'd come to the same pool and swum naked through the summers for fifteen years, falling more in love each year. The pool. That clear aquamarine water. Cold. The surface rippled around the waterfall. Her naked skin gliding beneath the reflection. It was too beautiful. Why did he jump? Because she had surfaced and cried:

"Come in! Come in!" And he had always jumped. Only this time God had moved the rock.

So he drove down that singing, hellish road for what seemed like eternity. His ears were pounding with locusts. His head was looking for all the memories — those that he loved and those he hated, but mostly those that he loved — the cottonwood trees rising above the river where the steelhead ran, the perfect cup of coffee in the morning, the satisfied leap of joy when the right thing falls into the right place. Her long hair spreading around her underwater. And for the first time Luster realized the insufficiency of life. He was grateful for what he had taken, yet he wanted more. He wanted everything.

She killed him. No, he killed himself. He always had to jump. Take that extra step. More love. More height. There wasn't enough life. His fist split the water and the icy world of the pool engulfed him in silence. Down. Down. The boulder rushed towards him. A black iceberg five feet from where it should have been. And he shuddered at the memory of the contact. His hand knocked aside in slow motion, his forehead striking and bending back. It was a dream, the dark bulk filled his vision, the crack that echoed underwater and his back corkscrewing.

He was lying on the stony bottom of the pool, his eyes open, watching her naked body dive towards him, the bubbles streaming behind her, and he wanted to touch her thighs even though he couldn't move.

When she dragged him onto the shore, crying, holding him, her skin clammy against his, he couldn't tell her that God had transplanted the rock the night before. He couldn't embrace her, say good-bye. But he could see. The blood on the stones, on her. She picked up his bathing suit. She didn't want to leave him naked on the beach. She looked so awkward staring at it, wondering what to do in that pained way he'd learned to love over the years. It didn't matter. He wouldn't be alive by the time she found somebody to take him back to town. He'd just be a body beside a pool in a forest. His eyes filled with blood.

The road veered, and at the curve was a large white house. It was square, lined with small, odd windows, something a cubist painter would design. The walls were made of whitewashed stone.

A young girl, perhaps seventeen years old, stood on the roof, leaning against a stone ledge, waiting for someone. When she saw Luster driving towards the house, she waved.

He stopped the car and got out. Not knowing what else to do, he waved at her. It was then he realized he still didn't know where he was, and worse, he had the vague fear that Tanganyika no longer existed. For a moment he wanted to go back and ask the peasant again.

The dark girl clapped her hands over her head and sprang high into the air.

She started to dance, moving slow, banging her open hands against her body and the stone ledge in a manner that told him she knew of locusts and toads and what they meant on this road.

He could only see the upper half of her body behind the ledge. Soon she was joined by another girl who was smaller but also lovely. They danced and hurrahed and threw themselves into the air.

A young man moved alongside them with a mandolin, playing a song that reminded Luster of the insect wings and hay the colour of gold.

The three sang and laughed and danced while the tears burned rivers down Luster's dusty face as he leaned on the car, one hand resting against the hot metal, one hand held to his mouth.

They shouted for him to join them. He was thirsty and tired, and they were so beautiful he found himself sucked towards the door at the side of the house.

The first girl skipped down the stairs and embraced him at the door. He let his hand rest on her waist, and smiled when she kissed his cheek.

Inside the house there were animal noises, the sound of lions at their kill, and he thought: "At last I'm getting somewhere."

The other girl appeared beside him. She ran her hand over his shoulder as if greeting a lover returned from a long journey. Behind her, the young man strummed his mandolin, half-way down the stairs, pretending he was in a trance. Luster could tell he was a fake, and began wondering about the girls. Luster had done his share of dancing

— the boy didn't have it. And for a sweet moment, he wanted to show him how to dance.

Then the first girl swung open the oak door, and he peered into the belly of the house. There was a party taking place. The darkened interior was filled with people laughing and dancing and talking. Luster could make out no faces.

She smiled and pulled his ear gently. His hand was still around her waist. "Are you infested?" she asked.

And Luster knew that being infested wasn't a disease, no blistering and corruption of the meat. It didn't have anything to do with the body. It was time and chance. It was life. The rock. "Yes." The locusts drummed under his clothes, all around his body. He knew what was going to happen next.

"Do you want to come in?"

He was tired and thirsty. "Yes."

"You must give us your eyes."

He moved backward, dropping his hand from her waist. He'd been warned; the old peasant had told him what was going to happen when he'd been lucky enough to make the wrong answer. "No, I won't give you my eyes."

"But," she pouted, her hands held tight against her chest, "everyone is here; if you take the road you will never find them again."

"Everyone?" That awful lump was in his throat — the knowledge that he was caught on the hook of his dying. The road, he knew it went on forever, lifeless and lonely. The worst kind of death. Inside the house there was no sun. It was shadowy, yet the party was endless.

"Of course." She pointed to the dim interior. The crowd moved aside and he saw his father seated at a long table, drinking and laughing, pounding his glass on the wood. One by one, he saw them: family, friends — drinking and enjoying themselves, but it was dark and he couldn't see if they had eyes.

"You must go in," the mandolin player insisted. Luster didn't know what to do. He looked at the sun, that huge black wave of locusts moving towards the edge of the valley. Then he contemplated the murky room. She was there.

"Come in. Come in!" she shouted from inside the house. She was naked, as beautiful as ever, covered with blood, holding the silly bathing trunks in her hand. And the rock was behind her.